LOKI
ASCENDING

ASA MARIA
BRADLEY

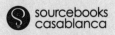
sourcebooks
casablanca

Copyright © 2020 by Asa Maria Bradley
Cover and internal design © 2020 by Sourcebooks
Cover design by Eileen Carey
Cover images © Halay Alex/Shutterstock, FXQuadro/Shutterstock,
Ferrantraite/Getty Images

Published by Sourcebooks Casablanca, an imprint of Sourcebooks
P.O. Box 4410, Naperville, Illinois 60567-4410
(630) 961-3900
sourcebooks.com

Printed and bound in Canada.
MBP 10 9 8 7 6 5 4 3 2 1

CHAPTER 1

SCOTT BRISBANE CURSED THE LATE AFTERNOON SUN that blistered the back of his neck as he concentrated on navigating the narrow trail ahead of him. The path skirted one of the taller peaks in Red Rock Country, Arizona, but the name of the mountain escaped him. The heat had fried his brain, and he was lucky not to tumble down the steep descent on his left. He wiped the sweat from his neck and hissed when he touched the sunburnt skin. He should have put on more sunscreen during the last break. Stopping now would mean getting even farther behind his three companions, and he had enough trouble keeping up with them. Not only were they stronger than any human, their endurance seemed boundless. He'd trained and fought with them for more than a year and rarely seen them out of breath.

He trudged on up the narrow path, and suddenly the hairs on the back of his neck stood at attention. His skin tingled in a way that had nothing to do with overexposure to the sun. Experience had taught him not to analyze the sensation. Instead, he instinctively acted on the flash of an image that popped in his head.

"Rock fall," he shouted, trying to project his voice to his three companions up the trail.

They must have heard, because Pekka, Ulf, and Finn didn't bother to look behind them. They hoisted their heavy packs higher and ran. Their feet pounded the red dirt into a swirl of dust, and Scott coughed as he followed. He stretched his muscles to the limit and sprinted up the path. Two years ago, his body and mind had been so damaged that he'd slipped into a coma. Now, he was in top shape and could outrun and outfight most elite soldiers. But the speed and strength of the men ahead of him were still beyond his. Then again, he wasn't an immortal Viking sent from Valhalla by Odin and Freya, like his companions.

A low overhead rumble jacked up his heart rate, and he quickened his steps. Sand and pebbles rained down, proving his premonition. If he could learn how to control this weird ability, he'd actually feel like an asset to his fellow fighters. The flashes of precognition were after all why Pekka and Ulf had specifically requested that he join them on these desert missions. That and because his sister happened to be married to their king.

A rock the size of a cantaloupe landed in front of him, startling him out of his pity party. He inhaled sharply. A few seconds difference and the rock would have smashed his head.

He picked up his pace, trying to jog in a zigzag pattern, which proved impossible on the narrow path. Hopefully, his luck would hold up. A loud bang behind him made him shudder, but he resisted the urge to glance over his shoulder to see what near-death experience he'd just avoided. Instead, he embraced the adrenaline rush and picked up his pace. His labored breathing grated in his ears, making it impossible to hear how far the others were ahead of him. He lifted his head to get a visual through the red dust.

To his relief, he spotted the rest of the warriors less than fifty meters ahead of him. They'd found an overhang and crowded together underneath, packs by their feet.

When Scott got closer, Ulf caught him by the straps of his backpack and hauled him the last few feet to safety. "Nice work, Brisbane. Your Spidey vibes are really delivering today."

Finn brushed red dust and bits of rock out of his already ginger close-cropped hair. "Yeah, that was a close one." He looked up at Scott, blue eyes twinkling. "If we could hook you up to a compass, maybe you could home in on where the wolverine asswipes are hiding."

They'd been tracking Loki's genetically modified creatures for days but never seemed to be able to catch up with them. The god of chaos was a master of not only hiding himself but also his minions. Their mission was to find the wolverines' camp and figure out what the hell the creatures were doing in the middle of the Arizona desert.

Scott wasn't sure how to respond to the teasing. He still didn't feel completely comfortable discussing his newly discovered ability. Especially with Finn, who belonged to the Taos, New Mexico, band of Viking warriors. Ulf and Pekka had both traveled with him from eastern Washington State and belonged to the group of Norse men and women that his sister ruled with her husband. He had trained and patrolled with them for a couple of years now, but Finn had only been part of their team for a few months.

"It's not that reliable. I get a hunch of something about to happen but never know for sure if it will. And it's not like I can make them appear when I want to." He dug around in his pack for some water—and the sunscreen.

Outside the overhang, sand and grit kept raining down, forming a curtain between them and the spectacular view. They'd been in this red desert for five days straight. It wasn't their first mission in this location, but the formidable rock formations still took Scott's breath away. If only he could get used to the heat. It was August, and daytime temperatures peaked in the midnineties.

"Let us know when you do and we'll see if the compass thing works." Pekka's smile was brief. He stuck a hand in the sand curtain. "Do you think Loki's little fuckers created this rock fall?" Larger rocks joined the grit, and he snapped back his hand so quickly, the strands of his long, dark hair that had escaped his ponytail quivered. "I bet they managed to double back on us once they got to higher ground and are now pelting us with this crap." His brows knitted together.

Pekka's dark eyes looked so much like those of his twin sister, Irja, that Scott had to look away. He couldn't think about her now. He needed to concentrate on the mission.

Besides, it wasn't like Irja was aware of how he felt. To her, he'd been only a patient she helped rehabilitate. And her beloved queen's little brother. He rubbed his chest to ease the ache that always surfaced when he thought about Irja, even though it had been more than a year since he last saw her.

Ulf nudged Scott's shoulder. "Is there any way you can tap into those vibes and see when we can get out of here?"

"It doesn't work that way." His weird tingles came and went sporadically, and sometimes the images didn't even come true. Basically, he had no control whatsoever. Something he was reluctant to admit to these guys since it was the only skill—if you could call it that—he contributed to their little foursome.

"Then how does it work?" Finn asked.

"Sometimes I get an image of something that hasn't happened yet in my mind. Like a weird, brief flash-forward in time." He shrugged. "I don't know when it's going to happen but usually within a few moments." The three Vikings all watched him for a beat. He grew increasingly uncomfortable. "What?"

Finn grinned. "It's like you're our personal Yoda or something." He rubbed his chin, leaving trails in the film of dirt that covered his skin. "Let's get something to eat while we're stuck here." He looked pointedly at Scott's pack.

Scott leaned over and dug through the stuff sacks in his pack. Although each of the warriors carried their own cache of protein bars and jerky, he had the major meal fixings. Ulf had divided up the tents, plus extra weapons and ammo, among the Vikings' three packs and left the food for Scott. At the beginning of their trip, the four packs had probably weighed about the same, but as their mission went on, Scott's pack got lighter and lighter.

It was a surreptitious consideration of him being slower than the others and one he resented but wasn't in a position to refuse. At least he carried his own clothes and sleeping bag. Having to ask for a pair of his own clean boxer briefs from one of the others' packs would have been humiliating.

"Bagels and cheese?" he asked as he pulled out a brown stuff sack. This was the last of the cheese. After this, their options were limited to tortillas slathered in peanut butter and maybe some slices of salami. They burned so many calories each day that what the food tasted like wasn't as important as how efficiently it could replenish their energy.

"Sounds good," Finn said, reaching for the bag. The redheaded Viking would have given that same answer no matter what Scott suggested. Finn was always starving, whether they were on a mission or not. While they'd been staying with the tribe in Taos, Scott couldn't remember not seeing Finn with some kind of food in his hand.

As they munched on their bagels, the size of the rocks falling outside grew smaller and smaller until only grit and sand rained down. Slowly, that stopped as well.

Scott took a long drink of his water bottle. Staying hydrated was an even bigger problem than replenishing calories. Finding water often meant hiking to the bottom of the canyons and off the trail of the wolverines. Loki's creatures stayed at high altitudes most of the time. How they hydrated, Scott had no idea.

Pekka was the first to put his water away and close up his pack. "Let's get moving before their trail goes cold." The dark-haired Viking was their tracker and seemed to be able to pick up the wolverines' trail everywhere, even in the dark. Pekka had been held captive in one of the covert labs where the wolverines were created. Loki had been very clever, using human scientists to create his creatures instead of doing the dirty work himself. That way, technically, his hands were clean. And the fact that he'd asked for creatures that looked like a humanoid wolverine was a big "fuck you" to Odin and Freya's warriors. In Norse mythology, the wolverine was an honored and revered animal.

Pekka didn't talk about his time as a prisoner, but something bad had happened. Ever since it had become clear they were less than a day behind the weird creatures, Pekka's focus on their prey had become even more intense than usual. This was their third mission to the deserts surrounding Sedona, and never before had they been this close to catching the creatures.

Loki's wolverines had started to pop up with such worrisome frequency in the Sedona area that the Taos king, Erik, had created a permanent stronghold of warriors here. Pekka, Ulf, and Scott were there to collaborate since the king had to keep an adequate number of warriors in Taos as well.

They finished closing up their packs and slung them up on their backs. Pekka headed out first, and the others fell in line, with Scott bringing up the rear. The sun was lower in the sky, but the rocks around him radiated the heat they had soaked up during the day. Even after sundown, the stone would keep the air temperature warm for a long while. He adjusted the straps of his pack as he lumbered after the others. The bagels and chunks of cheese they'd eaten hadn't lightened his load one bit. At least his neck was covered in high SPF.

As the hours passed, the distance between him and the warriors grew longer. His pace was just fast enough to keep the Vikings within view. Ulf turned around every so often to check on Scott. Although he appreciated the gesture, it reminded him that he was falling behind. *Curse them and their inhuman pace and stamina.*

Dusk had fallen and night was nearing by the time Scott cleared a ridge and stepped onto a small plateau surrounded by majestic red peaks. In the sky, Venus was about to set, followed closely by Mercury, and the heat had finally abated a few degrees. He joined the others by one of the rock walls. A small spring trickled through the many layers of stone and collected in a pool on the side of the mountain.

Finn had unpacked his water filter and was filling their bottles one by one. He nodded to Scott. "Give me your empties."

Scott slipped off his pack and dug out his empty water containers. He lined them up with the others waiting to be filled and arched his back, trying to work out some of the kinks. After a year of training with the Norse warriors, he'd packed on some muscle, and his stamina had definitely improved, but carrying a pack all day for days on end still took its toll.

"What's for dinner?" Finn asked, eyeing Scott's bag hopefully.

"It's another freeze-dried gourmet experience tonight." He rolled a shoulder. "Would you like a snack to tide you over?" Scott teased. It would take less than half an hour to boil water and rehydrate their meals.

Finn's hopeful expression made him hand the hungry Viking their last bagel together with a pot to fill with water. Finn filled it straight from the spring. Since they would be boiling the water, it didn't need to be filtered. Not that the Vikings had to worry about contamination, but Scott did. Another downside to being human. The Vikings filtered their water because it made it taste better.

Scott dug out their camping stove and got the flame going. He placed the pot Finn handed him on the stove and covered it with a lid. Even though there was no wind, he sheltered the flame with a collapsible, thin metal sheet. Fire could be seen for miles—no need to advertise their position. He took four foil bags of backpacking meals out of his pack and tore off the tops. The group had been on patrol so often that setting up camp was second nature, and everyone did their part of the routine automatically.

Ulf placed their backpacks in a semicircle. "It's going to be in the mid to upper fifties tonight and there's no wind.

Does anyone want to bother with the tents?" His tone had a little bit of a challenge in it. Ulf competed against everything and everyone, most of all himself.

"We'll be okay without tents," Pekka confirmed. He looked at Scott. "Douse that flame as soon as you can. I don't want anything alerting the wolverines to our position." He looked toward the other side of the plateau. "They're close. I can feel it."

"Do you want to push on then?" Finn asked around his last bite of bagel. It took him only three to finish it.

Pekka was quiet for a beat before he answered. "No. It's a new moon tonight. We won't have much light, and I don't want to risk injuries by trekking in the dark."

"We should have brought night vision goggles," Ulf grumbled.

"Next time," Finn said.

Pekka's head shot up. "I don't want a 'next time.' I want to kill those fuckers on this mission." Considering the wolverines had severely injured several of the Norse warriors to the point where they'd have to return to Valhalla to heal, his reaction was understandable, but the vehemence in his voice was unusually strong.

The water started bubbling, the sound startling in the silence that followed Pekka's declaration. Scott snuffed out the stove's flame and removed the pot. He poured equal amounts of water into each open bag of freeze-dried food. At this point, he'd prepared enough of these meals where he didn't have to measure anymore. He stirred each bag with a spoon and then sealed them up to allow the rehydration process to do its thing.

Finn picked up one of the meal bags first. Scott handed

out spoons to everyone and then sighed when he saw Finn massaging his food. The redheaded Viking liked to squeeze the bag while he waited the few minutes it took for the water to be absorbed.

"It's not going to be done any quicker just because your meaty mitts maul the bag," Ulf said.

"But the water is distributed better," Finn shot back with a grin. "I don't want any crunchy parts." He sat down on his pack.

This was an old argument between the two Norse men. Ulf only grunted in reply and reached for his own dinner. Pekka did the same, and both he and Ulf sat down on their packs as well.

Scott opted for a rock. "You should let it steep longer," he said when Finn tore into the food. "Water boils at a lower temperature at higher altitude. The food needs more time to steep and absorb all the water."

"Can't wait any longer." Finn shoveled a spoonful into his mouth. So much for not wanting any crunchy parts.

They ate in silence. Each of the bags was supposed to serve two people, but the massive Norse warriors required one each and usually looked around for more after they'd finished. Scott had already pulled out a stuff sack filled with nuts and dried fruit for them to dig into after the main meal. He watched the men around him as he ate.

At six feet even, Finn was two inches shorter than Scott, but the guy had at least fifty pounds of extra muscle. Ulf stretched two inches taller than Finn but was built leaner, more like a swimmer than the football player physique Finn had. Even though one was a blond and the other a redhead, both Ulf and Finn looked classically

Scandinavian with light eyes and pale skin, although their face and arms were tanned from the time they'd spent in the sun.

Pekka was taller than Ulf by at least an inch. He was all lean, sinewy muscle, built like a runner. Ulf and Finn kept their hair short, but Pekka's black hair hung just past his shoulders when he untied his low ponytail. His eyes were midnight black and seemed to see too much whenever they met Scott's. Pekka was from Finland originally and belonged to the Sami people, a seminomadic tribe inhabiting territories in northern Scandinavia.

Scott hadn't learned those details from Pekka. The guy rarely shared anything personal. It was Irja who had supplied some of the information when Scott asked her questions during their physical therapy sessions. Irja was the medical officer of his sister's tribe of warriors. She was a full-fledged doctor, which was apparently unusual for her position. Many of the tribes had healers, because even though the warriors were immortal, they still broke bones and got wounded. They just healed quicker. But none of the other healers had gone to medical school like Irja.

As if he knew Scott was thinking about his sister, Pekka shot him a dark look from across the stove. Scott took another bite of his dinner as an excuse to break eye contact. He'd long ago figured out there was no use forcing himself not to think about Irja. She was with him all the time and the only thing he could do was put her image out of his mind for a while. As soon as he was idle, like now, she was instantly back in his head. And his heart.

Spending all this time with her twin brother didn't help.

Finn reached for the bag of nuts and dried fruit, poured

a generous helping into his massive hand, and crunched away. "Leave at first light as usual?" he asked while chewing.

Pekka nodded. "Be packed and ready to go." He finished his meal and put the empty bag and spoon on the ground by Finn's dinner remains. Technically, Pekka wasn't their leader. Ulf had started out planning their mission. But as Pekka became more intense, they'd automatically started deferring to what his preferences were. Since he was their tracker, it made sense. He drove the mission, and he drove them. Ulf didn't seem to mind. He reminded Pekka about breaks and told him to hydrate more, but otherwise, he went along with how Pekka wanted to run their days.

By the time Scott had cleared up after their meal and cleaned their spoons, it was fully dark. The men had their sleeping bags out next to their packs, and he dug out his own, together with a thin, self-inflating mat that he unrolled on the ground before spreading the bag on top. Pekka had volunteered to take first watch. He usually did. He claimed he was a night owl, but Scott doubted he slept much at all. It was as if he had too much pent-up energy trapped in his body.

Scott got a fleece jacket out of his pack and put it on. He stretched out on top of his sleeping bag and stared up at the night sky. It was too warm to crawl inside the bag. His clothes would keep him warm enough now that the sweat had dried. Plus this way, he didn't have to take off his shoes. They'd been ambushed in the middle of the night on one of their missions, and he'd had to fight in bare feet on rocky terrain. Not an experience he wanted to repeat.

It was now late enough that both Venus and Mars had set, but Jupiter was still visible as a globe of light just a little bit bigger and brighter than the stars twinkling behind it. Out here in the desert, there was no light pollution, and the Milky Way stretched across the sky in all its glory. The wide band of glowing gaseous clouds looked like someone had taken a brush and messed up the smooth paint of the universe with just one stroke that added swirls of color. Scott stared at the small part of the galaxy visible from earth. As a boy, he'd been fascinated by astronomy and always asked for books on the subject.

His sister, Naya, used to read to him before bedtime. One night, they'd cracked open a brand new book of NASA photographs and seen a picture of the Milky Way galaxy for the first time. Together, they'd traced the Orion Arm of the spiral galaxy and found their "home" solar system. It was the first time he'd realized how far in the outskirts of the Milky Way the solar system that contained Earth resided. He must have been only eight or nine at the time. Just about two years before their parents were killed and their life turned to shit.

The time following that traumatic event was not pleasant. As kids, Naya and Scott had been taken to a rogue research facility that had tried to genetically modify them into superior warriors. Ten years of injections and drills had worked on Naya. She became a super soldier and eventually escaped the facility. The same treatments had fried Scott's nervous system and turned him into a vegetable. Naya returned to save him and succeeded with the help of her now husband and his band of warriors. Scott had been nursed back to health, first in an off-the-grid private medical facility and then by Irja, the warriors' medical officer. The reminder of how much he owed his sister and King Leif left a bad taste in his mouth.

He stood to stretch his legs. A walk around their make-shift camp would work out the soreness. Careful not to disturb the sleeping warriors, he strolled away from his sleeping bag. On the outskirts of their little camp, Pekka's silhouette showed up as a dense shadow against the magnificent backdrop of stars and planets in the dark night sky.

"Can't sleep?" he asked Scott.

Pekka wasn't someone Scott would normally seek out for conversation. One, because the guy hardly ever spoke, and two, because he was Irja's brother and Scott felt like a heel for obsessing about her while Pekka was around. But tonight, he'd speak to anyone just to not have to be alone with his thoughts.

"Need to work out some kinks in my legs," Scott answered. "And I guess I'm feeling a little restless."

One of Pekka's eyebrows arched. "Something on your mind, or is your Spidey sense acting up?"

Scott definitely didn't want to talk about what was on his mind, so he focused inward to see if the nervous feeling he had was related to his weird ability.

"I can't tell," he answered. "The premonitions are basically useless because I can't control them or even figure out how to better use them."

"They've helped us out more than a few times," Pekka offered. "Don't try to force them. Just live with them, and eventually, you'll find harmony with your ability."

"Sounds like you know something about this." Scott sat down on a rock a few feet away from Pekka.

The other man shrugged. "We have more than one *noita* in my family."

"I don't know that word."

Pekka's white teeth flashed briefly. "It's Finnish. Didn't Irja tell you about our weird family when she took you through all that physical therapy? We are all soothsayers, healers, and witches. Irja is a mixture of all three."

Scott sat up straighter. "No, she definitely didn't mention anything about that." Irja had helped Naya figure out how to wake Scott from his coma. Chances were that Pekka was just pulling Scott's leg, but maybe there was some truth to what he said. Irja did have an uncanny instinct when it came to healing people. He kept his voice level. "Which one are you?"

The other man shot him another smile. "Neither. I'm the black sheep of the family—in more ways than one."

"Care to elaborate?"

"Nope."

Scott didn't think he would, but it had been worth a try to find out more about Pekka and Irja's background. "Irja doesn't seem to think you are a black sheep."

"She talked about me during your physical therapy sessions?" Pekka's eyes glittered dangerously.

"No, I just got the impression you two are close."

"That probably has more to do with us both being the odd ones out among all the Scandinavians."

"But you two are Vikings as well, aren't you?" Naya had met the Viking king Leif while working on a way to free Scott from the research facility. She'd actually saved the king's life and in the process triggered an ancient Norse handfasting bond. She had resisted the relationship at first—to the point where she all but vanished and hid from the Vikings—but the king had been persistent in his pursuit and eventually convinced her to marry him. The two were *själsfrändes*—true soul mates—and so in love with each other that it made Scott feel slightly sick around them.

Pekka sighed. "Since we're not Vikings, I have no clue how we ended up in Valhalla in the first place."

From what Scott had pieced together about Norse mythology, Vikings and Valkyries who died an honorable death ended up in Valhalla. What was not mentioned in the books he'd read was that Odin and Freya sent the Norse warriors back to Midgard when Loki's creatures started popping up, threatening the humans.

"But the gods will do what the gods will do, even when they're not my gods. We'll just waste our time trying to figure them out." Pekka threw a pebble a few feet down the trail. "What about you and your sister? You are close?"

Scott sighed. "I guess so." Naya was his older sister and could be a tad too overprotective, which made it hard to earn his place among the warriors. That was one of the main reasons he'd jumped at the chance to go when King Erik had asked for help. That and this awkward obsession he had with Irja.

He purged that thought from his mind as quickly as he could, just in case her brother was a mind reader. He hadn't heard of a Norse warrior who was, but it didn't hurt to be careful.

Pekka wasn't paying him any attention though. He'd turned to look out over the plateau and the continuation of their trail. "What the fuck is that?" He pointed straight out into the darkness.

Scott stood to see a glowing swirl of neon blue and green streaks rising from the ground about two kilometers away.

The back of his neck tingled, and his stomach cramped. "I don't know, but I'm sure it's not anything good."

Pekka widened his stance and held his arms loosely by his sides, battle ready. "Wake the others."

CHAPTER 2

Because the Vikings stumbled as much as he did in the dark, Scott was actually able to keep up with his battle buddies as the men ran as fast as they could across the plateau ridge. The strange neon streaks ahead painted the night sky sinister shades of blue and green. The path rounded a boulder, momentarily hiding the unearthly light show from direct view.

Pekka held up his hand as he stopped. The others paused behind him. He turned to face them. "Proceed with caution and weapons drawn." Unholstering his Glock, he walked ahead at a fast clip.

Scott followed Pekka's lead and pulled his own handgun. Finn and Ulf did the same. The two Vikings were both decent snipers and had Remington rifles slung over their shoulders in addition to their handguns.

As they cleared the shadow of the boulder, Scott had to put up his hand to shield his eyes from the glare. Bright blue and green neon streaks had formed into what looked like a domed cage. Dark, people-shaped shadows moved around inside, but it was hard to separate them from one another in the intense brightness. The back of his neck tingled again, and he held his breath, but no flash of premonition popped into his mind. He raised the gun but kept his finger off the trigger.

"What the fuck are those creatures up to now?" Finn's nostrils flared, a clear sign his berserker—his inner warrior beast—had surfaced and was ready to fight.

The four of them spread out in a wide arc as they approached the illuminated cage. Scott could now make out four wolverines inside the glowing lattice. The animal-human hybrids could almost pass for human if it wasn't for their too-fast movements and the fact that they looked identical to one another. That and their weird eyes.

Instead of irises and pupils, the wolverines' eyes were completely filled with darkness. Just a big, black void of malice. The other little detail that made them not pass for human was that their nails tended to elongate into sharp talons whenever they were about to fight.

The Vikings and Scott approached on silent feet. No doubt Ulf's and Pekka's berserkers were battle ready. Each of the Vikings had one. The berserkers fed on battle fever and, when awoken, gave the Norse warriors superior fighting skills. When they fought together, it was as if they tapped into some kind of invisible connection, communicating with their battle brothers and sisters without words. With their berserkers fully awake, a group of Vikings and Valkyries turned into a well-oiled, fine-tuned, unstoppable fighting unit. It was a majestic thing to behold, and it made Scott feel even more different and on the outside.

Even though he wasn't hooked into the berserker connection, Scott had trained and fought with these warriors enough to instinctively position himself in their fighting formation. The other three always seemed to know where he was and communicated with him through hand gestures.

They were now only two hundred meters away, and the glowing cage towered before them. Several stories high, the dome covered an area of the ground the size of half a basketball court. The wolverines stood in a circle within the dome, their heads bowed. As Scott crept closer, he could see their lips moving, but the humming coming from the glowing dome blocked out any other sounds. He aimed his gun, about to fire on one of the wolverines, but Pekka beat him to it.

The dark-haired man's nine-millimeter bullet zipped through the air and then abruptly stopped and dropped to the ground. A buzzing sound and a short flare announced the hit, but the bullet didn't penetrate the cage's glowing walls. Although the wolverines had been created through some weird science melded with Loki's powers, they were normally vulnerable to regular bullets—as were the Vikings and Valkyries.

Scott fired his own gun with the same result, and then Finn and Ulf squeezed off rounds from their Glocks. The same buzzing flare appeared each time the bullets made contact with the cage and then fell ineffectively to the ground.

The wolverines didn't even flinch. They remained standing in the circle, lips moving as if they were praying.

Ulf's mouth moved as well, but Scott was pretty sure it was a stream of curses dripping from his lips as he brought up his rifle. The Viking looked down the scope and fired. This bullet too caused nothing but a buzz and a flare before dropping to the ground.

The wolverines threw back their heads, still not paying any attention to the men outside the cage. The humming sound of the cage grew louder and the brightness of the light more intense.

Pekka shouted something indiscernible and made the gesture for charging forward.

Scott automatically moved with the other three men as they stormed the cage. He passed through the glowing barrier, but some kind of force ripped the gun from his hand. His ears popped, and he landed on all fours inside the cage. In here, he could hear that the wolverines were actually chanting, not praying. They stopped abruptly as Scott stood. The creatures turned around, and when they saw him, claws popped out of their fingers.

Looking around for where the Vikings had landed, Scott was shocked to see them on the outside of the glowing cage. Ulf and Finn beat their fists against the barrier while Pekka rammed his shoulder into the cage as if he were trying to break down a door. Not a sound of their actions passed to where Scott stood. It was like watching a weird pantomime.

Fuck. He'd never before faced these creatures alone.

Swallowing the lump of panic rising in his throat, he widened his stance as the wolverines slowly fanned out in front of him. He reached for the knife sheathed at the small of his back and gripped it hard. If they attacked, he'd be ready to defend himself. Hopefully, he'd be able to carve a little piece out of at least one of them.

One of the wolverines took a step forward and lifted its head, inhaling sharply several times. "Ah, Mr. Brisbane," it hissed. "What a pleasure to meet you. Where is your lovely sister?"

Great, the creature knew his scent. Just fucking great. Like he was some kind of prey the creature had imprinted on. As if Scott wasn't freaked out enough already.

The creature's lips curled in a malicious snarl. "I'm sure your sister will be more than happy to clear her calendar and come visit us. Especially when she figures out we're keeping you as our special guest." The other wolverines widened their formation.

Scott focused on the one speaking while keeping the others in sight. "Nice neon cave you've built. Thinking of opening a casino way out here in the desert?"

"This is for a much higher purpose than mortals' cheap habit of gambling." The wolverine's freaky empty eyes glittered.

"Like what?" Scott relaxed his shoulders while gripping the knife tighter.

"Our master will come to this dwelling of light," one of the other wolverines blurted out.

"Silence," the first speaker hissed.

What the fuck had they stumbled into? "Master" could only mean Loki, but from what the Vikings had told Scott, the Norse gods were forbidden by the gods' council to visit the human realm. This was supposedly why Loki had created the wolverines. They fought in his place and were a major pain in the ass with all the chaos they created. Loki's sneaky way of working around the no-visiting rule was why Odin and Freya retaliated by sending the Vikings and Valkyries to protect the humans. "So Loki is visiting. When might that be?"

None of the wolverines answered him. Instead, two of them charged, and he had to scramble to get his knife up. The suckers moved with inhuman speed, just a hair's breadth faster than the Vikings.

He managed to slice the arm of one creature with his knife, but the other's claws dug into Scott's shoulder. The pain spread into his arm. Luckily, it wasn't his dominant side.

"We need him alive," the wolverine who had first spoken shouted.

Good to know they shared a common goal.

Scott also really needed himself alive.

The creature he'd managed to cut leaped toward him. Scott instinctively crouched down and grabbed the wolverine's torso as the fucker sailed through the air toward him. Rolling onto his back, Scott volleyed the creature over his head.

The wolverine screamed as it flew through the dome's barrier. The whole structure flickered, and then the creature's wail abruptly cut off and the cage stabilized again with a low hum. Scott jumped to his feet and resisted the urge to turn around to see what had happened to the flung wolverine. Hopefully, the Vikings took care of it. He had enough trouble with the ones inside the cage.

The three remaining creatures fanned out in front of him. Their claws glinted in the blue and green light. The one who seemed to be the leader, the one who had first spoken, snapped his talons together. The other two turned their heads toward him, and after a brief pause, they too tapped their claws together. Scott tuned out the weird chorus of clicks and instead focused on the wolverines' body movements, looking for any small twitch of a muscle that would give away their intent to charge.

The creatures kept clicking their claws and slowly moved toward him. He took a step back and then another. His back was almost touching the glowing lines of the cage. He expected to feel heat from the light, but there was no difference in temperature, just a low vibration that made the hairs on his neck and arms stand up. The wolverines kept advancing.

He considered stepping through the glowing lines, but his pride wouldn't let him retreat. Besides, he already knew they needed him alive. It was really just a matter of how much they'd hurt him when they captured him.

He knew from experience that they could be very creative in their torture methods. After Naya had gotten him out from the super soldier genetics facility, he'd spent almost a year in an exclusive medical clinic. Their doctors had worked with Irja to find a cure for his vegetative state. And once he'd woken up from the coma, he'd been stupid enough to try to leave the clinic on his own. The wolverines had found him and taken him hostage. They'd fed him and given him water but also taunted him while he was tied up and hit him where the bruising wouldn't show. Not something to look forward to. He'd been an idiot to get captured in the first place when he thought he could refuse his sister's help and live a life on his own. Luckily, the badass Valkyrie Astrid had rescued him.

Suddenly, the back of his neck tingled again. Before he consciously recognized the image of two wolverines leaping at him as a premonition, his body had already tucked and rolled to the side. A split second later, he caught identical surprised expressions on the faces of the charging creatures before they sailed straight through the cage wall.

Scott's roll ended close to the remaining wolverine, and as he jumped to his feet, he buried his knife in the side of the creature's neck before slicing across the jugular. Blood sprayed Scott's face and torso. A loud crack sounded through the air. The glowing cage flared brilliantly bright for a short moment and then disappeared altogether. Scott blinked in the sudden darkness, trying to see where the Vikings were.

"Fuck," Ulf shouted.

Scott retrieved and turned on his flashlight. The Viking hunched over on his knees, hands covering his ears. Scott cut the darkness with his beam of light and discovered the other two Norse men in similar positions.

Pekka recovered first. He slowly stood and scowled at Scott. "Why didn't you leave the cage when you noticed we couldn't enter?" He turned on his own flashlight. Ulf did the same.

Scott shrugged to hide his rising anger. Why were they always treating him like he was inferior? Okay, so physically he was, but he'd just fought four freaking wolverines. "I knew they wouldn't kill me." Technically, he didn't know that until they'd told him, but no need to share that part. "If it had been you, would you have retreated?"

Pekka had the decency to pause a moment to consider the question, but then he shook his head. "It doesn't matter what I would have done. You're my responsibility. The king and queen trust me, us"—he gestured toward the other two Vikings—"to get you home safe."

Scott's fists clenched. He took a step toward Pekka. "I don't need a babysitter."

"Seems you do if you go off on half-baked maneuvers on your own," Pekka countered.

Finn stepped between them, holding his hands up, his left palm facing Pekka and the right Scott. "Let's just cool it for a second." He turned to Scott. "Good job on sending the little fuckers through the wall so we could have some fun too."

Scott mumbled a "you're welcome" and then almost fell over as Ulf came up behind him and slapped his back.

"Yeah," Ulf chuckled. "Thanks for letting us in on some of the action and not keeping it all to yourself."

Pekka muttered something under his breath and stalked toward where the wolverines had been chanting in a circle. He aimed his flashlight on the ground. "What the fuck is this?"

Scott followed the other two men to see what Pekka had discovered. A pile of flat, jagged rocks with partial symbols written on them lay by the dark-haired Viking's feet. Pekka crouched and poked a few of them with his finger.

"The inscriptions look like runes," Ulf said. "But I can't tell what they say. There are no whole symbols."

"The wolverines mentioned their 'master' coming to visit because of this cage thing," Scott said. "I assume that means Loki. Do the runes have anything to do with him?"

"Fuck," Pekka said. "None of these fragments are complete enough for us to say. We'll bring them back with us and show the other warriors and King Erik. Maybe someone in his tribe can figure out how to put them back together and interpret them." Pekka looked around. "I need something to carry them in."

Nobody had brought a bag of any kind, and there were too many flat rocks to put in their pockets, even if they divided them between them. In the end, Scott pulled off his T-shirt and handed it to Pekka. "Carry them in this. I have a spare in my pack." No amount of washing was going to get that blood out anyway. He peered at the stone fragments to see if he could recognize the runes. He had read a little about Norse runic symbols. It turned out he was pretty savvy with pattern recognition, maybe because he'd spent so much time studying constellations, but these rock fragments were too small for him to recognize any of the runes.

Pekka put the stone fragments in the garment and tied together the ends into a makeshift carrier bundle.

They investigated the rest of the area but found nothing else. There was no sign of the wolverines making camp or having any kind of food.

"How do these fuckers survive?" Finn asked. "They have to use some kind of sustenance. Right? I mean, we're immortal but still need food and water."

"They live on misery, despair, and dark magic," Ulf quipped as he added the last wolverine body to the pile he'd arranged. As soon as the morning sun hit the dead wolverines, their bodies would disintegrate. In this isolated part of the desert, that would happen way before the dead creatures could freak out any hikers. From earlier missions, they knew that they didn't have to worry about scavenger animals. They avoided wolverine carrion.

Finn kicked one of the legs of the wolverines to straighten it out. "How did you know they wouldn't kill you?" he asked Scott.

"They told me so, plus the scientists Loki hired want to breed Naya and me to make super soldiers."

The red-haired Viking frowned. "But she's your sister."

"Exactly."

"Fuck." Finn's eyebrows shot up. He kicked the wolverine again. "Sick bastards."

Scott silently agreed.

They returned to camp and managed to get a few hours of sleep before the sun rose. Scott's shoulder ached dully, but he was exhausted enough to still be able to sleep.

Before heading back to Sedona in the morning, they checked on the dead wolverines. The bodies had all disintegrated nicely in the bright desert sun. Even their clothes had disappeared. Maybe Ulf was right about them surviving on dark magic.

Scott followed the three Vikings down the trail they'd ascended the day before. Going downhill, it was easier to keep up with the immortal men, although they weren't marching at the relentless pace they'd used when tracking the wolverines.

As the day dragged on, the hiking wore Scott down, even at the more sedate pace. His injured shoulder ached under the backpack strap, and trying to keep most of the weight on the other side made his stride awkward. He tried to cheer himself up by thinking about the shower and clean clothes he had waiting for him in Sedona. And when that lost its temptation, he moved on to motivating himself by thinking about ordering a juicy burger and a cold beer for dinner.

Hopefully, Ulf and Pekka would allow them a full night's sleep in proper beds before ordering them back to their relentless training schedule. He caught Finn licking his lips and smiled. Apparently, he wasn't the only one anticipating good food and drink when they got home.

CHAPTER 3

IRJA VAINIO STEPPED OUT ON THE BALCONY OF THE house that King Erik and his tribe used in Sedona and took several long, deep breaths. The fresh, dry desert air and the spectacular view cleared her sleep-deprived mind, at least for a moment. She marveled at how different it was from eastern Washington where her tribe was located. She'd escaped outside for a few moments of solitude so she could try to re-center. Two days without sleep had seriously depleted her reserves, and she struggled to remain calm and not let the panic she felt inside show. The Norse warriors stationed in Sedona depended on her. Erik had requested Irja fly down to Arizona when his local medical officer wasn't able to figure out what was ailing one of the Valkyries. Irja had a reputation as an unusually skilled healer, but she'd been examining and monitoring the patient for forty-eight hours now and was no closer to finding out what ailed her.

Kari was growing weaker by the minute, and Irja had no idea how to reverse the condition. Her patient had come back from a mission complaining of headaches and blurry vision. Kari's temperature had quickly risen, and she'd slipped into a restless slumber by the time Irja had reached Sedona. She'd now been asleep for the entire time Irja had been in Sedona and her pupils were no longer responding to light. Kari was officially in a coma. The other warriors on patrol with the Valkyrie reported nothing unusual during the mission, so Irja had no clues as to what may have caused the illness. She was clean out of ideas about how to progress the treatment.

Irja took another deep breath and closed her eyes. Before she could stop herself, her senses automatically tuned in to the energy emitted from the landscape around her. Pulsing colors revealed themselves in Irja's mind's eye. The cool blues surrounding the house the warriors lived in showed the elven *förtrollning*, the spells the Valkyries had woven around the perimeter to make it harder for mortals to detect the dwelling. The goddess Freya had gifted them the magic. It didn't make the house invisible, but mortals tended to instinctively avoid areas steeped in the magic. And the spells notified the occupants of the house when someone—mortal or not—strayed too close to its outer limits.

Irja took another breath. Beyond the Norse magic borders that protected the house, shades of red and orange twirled and swooped, undulating like a giant caterpillar across the landscape. This was the native magic of the Arizona desert. It lacked the ordered structure of the Norse spells, and its untamed nature made it powerful and unpredictable. Its energy pulsed around the blue power, prodding and testing it. The act wasn't hostile, more like curious and playful.

As if the native energy noticed Irja tuning in to its presence, the twisting and twirling stopped. She held her breath. The red enveloped the orange and together they became a hot glowing ball. From this bright sphere, tendrils of red energy extended toward Irja, beckoning to her. In her sleep-deprived state, she almost lowered her shielding and freed her senses as if she were about to harness the energy and refill the wells inside her that had been empty for millennia. She'd given up practicing magic when she was a little girl. The power always demanded a sacrifice and usually the price was too steep to pay, as she had painfully learned.

Her berserker stirred and growled. The warning from her inner warrior spirit snapped Irja back into control, and she quickly reinforced her shields against the magic's pull. The effort required more energy than it should and she grimaced.

The quiet swoosh of the door opening had her quickly schooling her features before turning to greet whomever had joined her. "King Erik," she said and bowed her head in formal greeting.

"Please. No need for formality. There are important things we must discuss, and I'd rather you just spoke freely. If I have to follow court protocol, it will take forever."

Irja raised her head to find his cornflower-blue eyes lit with humor, but the strain around the corners showed the king's worry. He was taller than her six-foot frame by about two inches, and she had to tilt her head back a little to meet his gaze. "As you wish." Suddenly, she swayed on her feet and gripped the railing. What had she been thinking, leaving herself so unguarded that the magic could seek her out?

The king reached out and gently grabbed her elbow, steadying her. "Are you okay, Ms. Vainio?"

Irja wiped her forehead and forced a smile. "Please call me Irja. I'm just tired." Hopefully, the king would believe her lie. *Sweet Freya*, she couldn't afford to be that careless. She needed to be extra vigilant here. The sandstone around Sedona was old, much older than the basalt surrounding the Pine Rapids fortress in Washington State. That volcanic rock's magic was easy to shield herself against after living so many years within it. The ancient Sedona red desert's magic was hundreds of millennia older and so very wild and free. It would tempt the most disciplined practitioner with its promise of raw power.

"Irja," the king repeated. "Then you must call me Erik." He released her elbow.

That would probably never happen, but Irja nodded. "I'm afraid I don't have any good news. I still don't know what's wrong with your warrior. My main concern right now is to reduce her fever. I have given her modern drugs as well as herbal remedies, but so far, I haven't seen results. She is still very agitated, so I gave her a mild sedative to make her rest."

"It is a comfort to me and my tribe just to have you here to take care of Kari. Odin willing, she will recover and fight again."

Irja forced a smile on her face, but the truth was that she had no idea how to wake Kari or lower her temperature. In her current state, the high fever might severely damage that Valkyrie's cognitive abilities. The extreme temperature was literally cooking the warrior's brain. It was tempting to open herself up to all the glorious red-hot magic just beyond the walls. To allow that energy to flood her body and channel it into a healing burst of power that could possibly cure the feverish Valkyrie. But Irja knew too well the cost of wielding that magic. The magic burst could just as easily kill Kari. Or someone else.

She had once been young and cocky when it came to her abilities. Now she lived with eternal guilt and the goddesses' punishment of a painful void inside her because she could never again risk to fill it with the energy of magic.

She healed her patients only with traditional and homeopathic medicine. She allowed herself to use what she thought of as her "sight" to diagnose an illness, but that was pure instinct earned from a long career. Her reputation for uncanny healing skills was nothing more than the fact that she'd practiced her profession for a very long time.

Or so you tell yourself.

Irja ignored the little voice at the back of her mind.

The pause in conversation was dragging into awkward territory, and Irja searched her mind for something to say, but she was too tired to get her thoughts to cooperate. Luckily, something distracted the king from scrutinizing her face, and he turned away.

"The warriors I'd sent tracking the wolverines are back from the desert," he said just as the gate in the concrete wall opened. The king lifted a hand to shield his eyes and peered into the courtyard.

Irja mimicked his gesture and discovered her twin brother, Pekka, striding through the opening, closely followed by Ulf and a red-haired Viking she hadn't met before. But it was the man bringing up the rear of the group that drew her attention. Scott's physique had filled out in the year and two months since she'd last seen him. His athletic build spoke more of endurance than brute strength, but his shirt stretched over broad, defined shoulders and a well-muscled torso. Her berserker stirred.

"Excuse me," King Erik said. "I must go ask the warriors about their mission."

"Of course," Irja mumbled. Her gaze lingered on Scott.

As was always the case when she was near him, she couldn't look away. He was her queen's brother and had been her patient at one point. Both were excellent reasons for ignoring the restless feelings he always stirred within her. So she did what she always did when strong emotions threatened to rise—she retreated behind the protective walls she'd long ago learned would shield her from heartache and painted a blank expression on her face. But she still couldn't look away from the dark, curly-haired man walking across the courtyard.

She took a step back to let the shadow of the balcony's overhang hide her. He'd been back to Washington State to visit his sister a few times. Each time, Irja had found an excuse to leave the fortress until he went back to Arizona. She'd been hesitant to come here, knowing she'd probably run into Scott. But her king had asked her to honor Erik's request, so here she was.

As if Scott could feel her watching him, his eyes searched the courtyard, and then he raised his head. When his gaze met hers, his eyes briefly widened in surprise. Of course he hadn't expected her. Why should he? They were nothing to each other, just acquaintances who had once had the working relationship between patient and healer. And yet, Irja couldn't keep down the sharp stab of disappointment piercing her chest when Scott's expression remained remote and bland.

He nodded once before looking away, which meant he missed Irja's limp wave. Scott said something to Pekka, but Irja didn't wait to see if the comment was about her. She slipped inside the house and headed for Kari's bedroom. She should focus on work. Medical research and scientific facts were systematic and safe, unlike the messy world of human interactions and emotions.

An hour later, her brother found her by Kari's bedside. The Valkyrie's fever was still too high. Irja had tried to extend her senses just a little to see beyond the regular medical tests, but she still had no idea how to make Kari wake up.

"How are you, *Sisko*?" Pekka stood on the other side of the bed.

Irja's berserker perked up and almost chirped. Whenever her sibling was near, it turned into a playful child.

Pekka surveyed the bedroom as if he was committing it to memory, and his gaze kept returning to the sleeping Valkyrie in the bed. Kari hadn't spent much effort decorating the room. Except for a painting of a Norwegian fjord, the walls were bare. The furniture was comfortable but minimal.

"I am well, *Veli*." The Finnish word for brother rolled off her tongue automatically, and she embraced the familiar feel of long vowels. She had become used to hearing only the sharper consonants of the Scandinavian languages now that her brother was no longer at the Pine Rapids Viking fortress. Like most Finns, she and Pekka spoke both Swedish and Finnish, plus they spoke the Sami language of their father's people. "How was your mission with the Vikings and the queen's brother?"

Pekka hesitated. "The mission was interesting, and I would like your input on something strange we experienced, but first tell me what ails the Valkyrie." He nodded at Kari.

"I don't know. She came back from a patrol and com-plained of blurry vision and sharp pains in her head. That was before I got here. King Erik's healer traveled here from Taos to treat her but couldn't lower her fever or calm her restlessness. That's when the king reached out to Leif and asked for me to come down here."

"So you're not here to check up on me or Scott then?" A rare smile played on her brother's lips.

"Why would I want to check up on Scott?" Irja regretted her sharp tone as soon as the words slipped out.

Pekka arched an eyebrow. "I figured the queen would have asked you to spy on her little brother for her."

Of course he'd assume that. Naya was very protective of her sibling, and since Irja and the queen were close, it would make sense for Naya to ask Irja to report back on how Scott was doing. "I'm sorry," Irja said. "I haven't slept much in the last two days, and my mind is muddled."

Pekka nodded, but his dark eyes remained watchful. "You need to take as good care of yourself as you do the patient."

"Tell me about your mission." Irja interrupted the rest of the lecture she knew would be coming.

Another arched brow showed Pekka knew she was deflecting. She waited for him to say something, but he let her get away with it. "We found four wolverines that were somehow using stones with carved runes and chanting to build a glowing cage of light."

Irja frowned. That sounded like a magical ritual but not one she recognized. "What color was the cage?"

Pekka laughed harshly. "You know I can't see magic the way you can."

It was an old point of contention between them. Pekka

resented not inheriting the ability to sense and see magic. Most of their mother's family had been able to do so to various degrees. He'd been there when Irja had overreached and had seen the disaster that followed. How could he ever wish for that? But this was a familiar fight and one that had kept her and her brother estranged for a few centuries. They were slowly finding their way back to each other, and she didn't want to jeopardize that by rehashing old conflicts. "You sensed it well enough to see the light the magic created."

He shrugged. "That beast of a structure gave off enough light to power a small township. To me and the Norse men, it looked like just white light, but Scott described it as neon blue and green."

"Scott saw the colors?"

"Yes, it seems even the mortal has better abilities than I. He's developed some other interesting traits as well, but I'll let him describe those himself."

Irja doubted that would happen. Scott and the two other warriors had now been in Sedona for more than a year. During the last month before they left Pine Rapids, the queen's brother had gone out of his way to avoid her. She didn't know what she had done to offend him. Even Naya had remarked on his changed attitude, but not even she knew the cause. Whatever Scott's reasons were, his behavior would likely be the same here. She hid her troubled thoughts from Pekka by asking another question. "What else can you tell me about this cage?"

"The wolverines stood in a circle, chanting words we didn't recognize. The longer they chanted, the stronger the cage glowed. After we destroyed the cage, we found stone fragments where they had been standing. They had runes inscribed on them but are in so many pieces, we can't tell what symbols or words they form."

Irja frowned. This sounded like old rune magic, maybe with Norse spells. But she'd never heard anything about glowing cages. "How did you manage to destroy the cage?"

Pekka grinned. "We killed the wolverines. Actually, Scott was the reason we defeated them. He was the only one who could penetrate the cage walls. Our guns couldn't even shoot through them."

Irja couldn't stop her gasp. "He fought them by himself?"

"He did. And I'm not happy about it. The queen would have my head on a platter if her brother got himself killed while I was responsible for him."

Irja nodded, pretending her concern for Scott was also about upsetting the queen. "I've never seen anything about a magical cage in the Sagas. But then, at the time the ancient texts were written, nobody could predict that we would return to the human realm or that Loki would be creating human-wolverine hybrids. I'll do some research and let you know what I find."

Pekka was watching Kari with a frown. Some emotion flickered in his eyes, but it was gone before Irja could identify it. "Please do." He turned toward her. "And examine the stones as soon as you get a chance."

Her brother turned as if to leave but then reached out toward the sleeping Kari. He dropped his hand before touching her and marched out of the room without looking back.

Irja studied his retreating back. Her brother resented the Scandinavian Vikings and never missed an opportunity to put them in their place. He was good-natured in his ribbing but had formed no close friendships with any of his battle brothers or sisters. He treated them as acquaintances. The lighter-skinned Scandinavians had a long history of discrimination against and outright persecution of the Sami people, so his resentment was understandable. When she first returned to the mortal realm, she had shared his feelings. But after living among the immortal Vikings and Valkyries for a few centuries and finding them loyal and trustworthy, she'd shed most of her prejudices. Although Pekka had also been in Midgard for hundreds of years, her brother had only recently joined the Norse warriors at Pine Rapids. It made sense he still held on to some hostility, which was why his reaction to Kari was so interesting.

Irja fetched a cold washcloth and bathed the fever sweat off the Valkyrie's face while she wondered what the blond woman meant to her brother. Knowing Pekka, she'd never find out, but maybe Kari would tell her when she woke up.

If she woke up.

Irja closed her eyes and let her fingertips rest gently on Kari's temples. She took a deep breath and centered herself. Opening up her senses, she tried to "see" the source of Kari's pain. Usually, she'd get a feel for a kind of "hot spot" in a patient's body where the pain originated. But with Kari, she couldn't see anything; she was somehow blocked.

Irja returned the washcloth to the bowl of ice water she'd put on top of the chest of drawers and reached for her laptop. She needed to research Kari's disease further. If she couldn't diagnose the underlying cause, at least she could try every remedy that had shown results with similar symptoms. But she was running out of time. If she couldn't control the fever spikes, the Valkyrie's cognitive abilities could be severely compromised.

CHAPTER 4

THE ROOM THAT FUNCTIONED AS KING ERIK'S OFFICE had originally been designed as a huge family room. A solid wood desk sat in front of glass doors that led out to the back garden, thereby transforming it into the king's office. Through the glass doors, Scott studied the desert-style landscape architecture of drought tolerant plants. Cacti and grasses sprang up amid rocks and gravel of the same red sandstone he had hiked through enough times to permanently stain his boots. The hematite—the iron oxide—in the soil had permeated the rubber and leather of what used to be his beige tactical boots so they were now an uneven rust color instead.

In the center of the room, four oversized couches surrounded a massive square coffee table. Finn sat next to Scott, while Pekka and Ulf had claimed the opposite couch. Erik had a whole couch for himself. Maybe nobody was comfortable sitting next to the king. Although Erik was fairly easygoing, he was still a king and in charge of their small band of warriors. Maybe a commander could never really be friends with his unit. That didn't seem to be the case with King Leif though. His second-in-command was also his best friend.

The warriors had taken the time to shower and change clothes before this meeting with the king. Ulf had also raided the kitchen and brought a bucket of cold IPAs that now sat in the middle of the table. Everyone but Pekka had an open bottle in their hand. The dark-haired warrior seemed preoccupied. He stared out the window while one leg bounced up and down in a nervous rhythm. He'd only offered a few short sentences as the others had told the king about what had happened with the wolverines in the desert.

Scott was having trouble concentrating. His thoughts kept veering back to seeing Irja on the balcony. Why was she here? He wanted to track her down to see how she was, but things always turned sideways and complicated when he tried to speak with her. He couldn't control his emotions around her. The temptation to touch her was too great. So what should be a straightforward conversation always turned into something awkward, heavy with tension.

As much as he wanted to be more to her than just another warrior, he had no right to expect anything beyond that. She would never see him as anything but her former patient and her queen's little brother. And she deserved the very best. She was surrounded by immortal warriors in prime condition. He couldn't compete.

"Did the creatures say anything about when this 'master' was coming?" the king asked, interrupting Scott's depressing thoughts and jarring him back into the present.

Scott shook his head. "No. I don't think they actually meant to reveal any information about that. The wolverine that blurted it out was told to shut up by the one who seemed to be their leader."

The king sighed. "This 'master' can't be anyone but Loki, but would he be foolish enough to challenge the gods' council by showing up in Midgard?"

"Maybe he thinks he can wreak enough havoc to slip back to Asgard undetected," Finn suggested.

Scott silently congratulated himself for taking the time to study up on Norse mythology and being able to follow the conversation. He'd learned Midgard was where the humans lived and Asgard was where the gods and goddesses hung out. It was weird talking about deities as if they were real people, but considering how freaky the wolverines were and now this glowing cage business, having gods communicating directly with their worshippers seemed like a minor point in all the craziness that was his new life.

"I don't see how," Ulf interjected. "Odin and Freya would know the moment he stepped into the mortal dwelling. Wouldn't they?" He turned toward the king. "If Loki is trying to instigate Ragnarök, he would have to start a shitload of trouble, and I don't see how the gods would not notice that. It seems like trying to start the end of the world would kind of be a big deal."

Erik shrugged. "Who knows what the gods' priorities are. Odin speaks to me only in dreams and always through cryptic riddles. Besides, he hasn't visited for a long time. There is unrest in the gods' council, I think we are very far down on their to-do list." He leaned forward and put his empty beer bottle on the table. "It would have been useful to keep one of the wolverines alive so we could interrogate it."

"Sorry." Finn grimaced. "We couldn't hear the conversation Scott had with the creatures. If we'd known, we'd have captured at least one of them."

"I'm not sure what bothers me most," the king said. "The fact that these fuckers are preparing for Loki to come to Midgard or the fact that they can build magical structures that keep my warriors out." He looked at Scott. "The immortal ones, that is. You are as much one of my warriors as the others. And more valuable than we thought, it seems."

Scott shrugged, which made him wince when his injured shoulder twinged. "I was just trying to stay alive." He wasn't sure if he should be offended about the king's last comment but settled on the positive. At least he could now contribute more to the mission than just hauling around enough food to keep Finn satisfied.

Erik studied him for a moment. "*Nej*. If you'd just tried to stay alive, you'd have left the cage as soon as you noticed the others were barred from entering." He smiled. "You showed true warrior courage by staying inside to fight."

Scott squirmed in his seat at the undeserved praise. "I kind of knew they wouldn't kill me. They've been hunting my sister and me for a while and want to capture us both alive."

Erik scratched his chin. "Leif has told me about the wolverines' interest in you and his *själsfrände*, but I thought Queen Naya destroyed the lab in which she and you were raised. Why are the wolverines still so interested in the two of you?"

Ulf cut in. "The queen destroyed one of the rogue labs, but there is a big network of them."

"Somehow, they think we're the link to create a successful super soldier program. Our father was one of their original creations, the only soldier who survived the experiment." Scott took an extralong sip of his beer to hide his discomfort over the memories that flooded his mind.

He and Naya had never known why they had to move so often while growing up. Now they knew it was because their dad had been hiding from the scientists who thought of him as nothing more than a science experiment. "Going on an adventure" Dad had called it whenever they packed up all their belongings and left in the middle of the night. But one night, the scientists had caught up with the family. They executed their mom and dad right in front of Naya. She had hidden Scott under the stairs, but the sound of the gunshots and Naya's screams had reached his ears no matter how much he'd tried to cover them with his small hands. He'd been eleven years old at the time and Naya only a year older.

Erik turned to face Ulf again. "Any luck following the money trail to see who's behind these labs? Loki must have a human representative somehow to handle the finances."

Ulf grunted. "Astrid, one of our Valkyries, and her *själsfrände*, Luke, are still tracing the money but have not found who the main financier is." Luke and Astrid had met while Luke was working undercover investigating the rogue science labs for the FBI.

Erik nodded and then looked to Pekka. "I understand the queen rescued you from the lab she destroyed. Do you have any additional knowledge about these labs? Is there any link between Loki working with these scientists and their experiments on Scott and his sister? Did the trickster god engineer the meeting of your king and Queen Naya?"

Pekka seemed not to have heard the king. He kept staring out the window, deep in thought, until Ulf nudged him with his foot. "Huh?" Pekka blinked and focused on Ulf, who leaned his head toward King Erik.

"Are we boring you?" The king's tone was sharp.

Pekka straightened on the couch. "My apologies, King Erik." He inclined his head slightly. "I went to see what progress my sister had made with Kari's illness. I was distracted by thoughts of what could have made the Valkyrie so sick."

"I too am very worried about Kari," the king admitted.

"She is a valiant fighter and a key member of my warrior team. My medical officer could not determine what ails her. Your sister comes highly recommended, so I have high hopes."

"My sister is the most skilled healer I know," Pekka said.

Erik nodded. "She has reached out to other healers to see if they have encountered anything similar to Kari's symptoms. They have not and have no idea how to help us. I'm afraid your sister's skills are what we must put our faith in now."

Ulf quickly returned to the king's question about the experiments to Pekka. "We have not been able to find a connection," he said. "As far as we can tell, it is nothing but a coincidence that Naya had a connection with the lab and became King Leif's *själsfrände*."

Erik sighed. "I'm afraid I have too much experience with the gods manipulating the faith of mortals to believe in coincidences."

"My sister has no connections with the wolverines. She is honorable and pledged herself to the king only because she fell in love with him." Scott's hands fisted.

"I didn't say she was manipulated by Loki," Erik said with a wry smile. "It could just as easily be Freya or Odin putting her in Leif's path. The gods always have an agenda, and it does us no good to try to figure it out or change it."

Ulf and Finn both nodded in agreement, but Scott opened his mouth to protest again.

The king held up a hand to interrupt him. "Whatever the gods' reasons, the outcome is that Leif and Naya met and restored our faith in the *själsfrände* bond."

To find your *själsfrände*—your true love—was a rare

occurrence among the Vikings. The Pine Rapids tribe now had two such bonds: Leif and Naya as well as Astrid and Luke. And both of them were between an immortal warrior and a mortal human. This had given the other Viking tribes around the world hope that they too could find their soul mates with a mortal partner.

Not that they needed any encouragement to go out and have sex with humans. It was one of their favorite activities for calming their berserker. Or at least that was what Ulf and Finn claimed when they headed for the local bars and clubs to pick up women. Astrid had also indulged in a busy night-life before she met Luke. Scott didn't want to think about what methods Irja used to calm her inner warrior.

Finn cleared his throat. "Could we get back to what our next step should be in terms of how to stop the wolverines from building another glowing portal for Loki?"

"I'm going to increase patrols in the desert," Erik answered. "I may have to reach out to some of the other tribes for more warriors."

"We should also investigate the stone fragments we found. Maybe we can puzzle out the runes inscribed on them," Pekka said.

Erik nodded. "Yes. Rune magic can be nasty. We need to know if that is what the wolverines are practicing. And if so, what kind."

"I've asked my sister to take a look at them," Pekka added. "She has experience with magic."

"Is she a practitioner?" Erik asked, eyebrows raised. "I have not met an immortal warrior magic wielder before. Although Freya practices *Seidr*, and has taught some of those spells to Odin, I'm not comfortable with bewitching and shapeshifting. Those are the corrupt skills of Loki and therefore suspicious."

Pekka paused a brief moment before answering. "You are like most of the Norse then. I mean no disrespect, but among my people, magic is common. Power runs in our bloodline."

Erik turned to Scott. "Since you were in the cage with the wolverines, you had the close-up view, so to speak, of what these bastards were up to. I want you to work with Irja to decode the rune fragments. We have laid them out in one of the spare bedrooms that nobody is using."

Scott shook his head. "I have only some rudimentary skills, and only with one of the alphabets."

The king waved his hand in dismissal. "I have heard you are good with patterns. I'm sure you will figure it out with the help of Irja. Plus, considering how long ago it was since any of us studied runes, your knowledge is probably the most current." He stood and walked toward his desk. "I'm going to ask the other kings for extra manpower right away. See you at the evening meal."

And with that, they were dismissed. Ulf collected the empty beer bottles and grabbed the bucket before heading out the door. The others followed, leaving Scott on his own to contemplate how he was going to survive working closely with Irja.

Irja stared at the flint fragments that her brother and the other warriors had brought back from the desert. She'd checked them for any foreign substances but had found nothing other than regular desert dirt. She'd been moving them into different patterns for the better part of an hour but still had no clue what runes they spelled out. She rubbed her forehead. Exhaustion was setting in, and she would need a few hours of sleep soon unless she wanted to end up in the sickbed herself. She'd thought examining the stones would be a distraction from worrying about Kari, but instead, being away from her patient just stressed her out more.

One of the other warriors had offered to sit with Kari for a few hours while Irja grabbed a shower and a quick nap. On orders of the king, she was not allowed to return to her patient until after the evening meal and then only for a short visit. The orders had also said for her to take the night off completely unless Kari's condition rapidly deteriorated. If that happened, someone would come and find Irja. She suspected her brother was behind the kingly directive.

The nap had been a failed experiment. Her mind wouldn't quiet down enough to allow any rest. Instead, she'd gone to this small spare bedroom to examine the rune fragments brought back from the desert. And she was no use here either. She'd failed Kari and King Erik by not finding a cure for the Valkyrie. And she would fail the king in the task of solving the rune puzzle as well.

Maybe she'd become too prideful of her healing skills, and now the goddesses were punishing her. She'd been trained by Freya as a Valkyrie during her time in Valhalla. When Freya discovered Irja's skills and interest in medicine, the goddess had also asked Eir—the goddess of healing and mercy—to help with the lessons.

Once Irja returned to Midgard, the human realm, she had practiced as a healer for a few centuries. When modern science improved the applications of medicine and pharmacology, she had enrolled in medical school. Even in the early years—before she incorporated western medicine into her healing repertoire—she had not lost many of her patients. Healing was what she excelled at. It was why she was valuable to her warrior brothers and sisters.

She had never fit in with others. She made people uncomfortable, and they considered her stoic and strange. She had forged a close friendship with Astrid and Naya, but even that was founded on her role as a medical officer. It was really all she had. It was who she was.

It was how she served her king and queen.

If she failed them now, she would lose her purpose. Her place among the warriors.

Irja turned one of the stone fragments, but the new position did not reveal a new pattern. Her head throbbed with an emerging headache, and she massaged her temples. The rune pieces faintly glowed of magic, but it was…wrong. It felt perverse somehow.

She closed her eyes to get a better read on the power trace. The colors she saw in her mind's eye were twisted versions of Norse magic. Instead of the cool, comforting blues and greens of the Baltic Sea, the runes glowed sickly lime green and harsh electric blue. She tried to center herself deeper, but the throbbing in her head intensified. Her berserker growled a low warning, and she dropped the connection with the runes and opened her eyes. It took a moment before she'd calmed her inner warrior. It had been restless ever since Irja had arrived in Sedona, and the lack of sleep made her control even more tenuous.

A quiet knock announced someone at the door across

the room and it opened with a hushed whisper as Scott stepped through. Irja allowed herself a brief moment of pleasure at the sight of him but averted her gaze when he looked at her. Her berserker stirred. It was alert but calm. Irja hoped it would stay that way. She had very little energy reserves left, and keeping herself together as well as controlling her inner warrior was just too much to ask at this point.

"Are you unwell?" Scott frowned as he stepped toward her, a beer bottle dangling from his fingers.

Great, she didn't just feel crappy, she obviously looked it too.

"I haven't had much sleep," she answered. "Kari is getting worse, and I am no closer to finding out what ails her." To her horror, she felt moisture gathering in her eyes, and she blinked rapidly to clear it. The last thing she needed was to completely lose it in front of the queen's brother.

"I'm sorry to hear that." He raised his free hand as if to touch her but dropped it before it moved more than an inch. "I don't know her very well, but she is a fantastic fighter. She was also very kind to us—Ulf, Pekka, and I—when we first arrived."

Irja nodded. She didn't trust using words in case she'd start crying or blurt out all the questions tumbling over in her mind. How had he been since he left Washington State? Why had he avoided her before he left? What had she done to offend him? She couldn't help her attraction to the queen's brother. It was more than just her berserker being—how did the modern English put it?—horny. There was something in Scott's calm demeanor, his stoic nature, and his will to keep fighting against odds that drew her to him. He'd been on death's door, his body so weak he'd not been able to walk but a few steps before exhaustion claimed him. She'd watched him force his muscles and nerves to cooperate again. And that was just the physical. He'd also overcome the emotional abuse he and his sister had experienced while they were prisoners in the rogue labs.

She rubbed her forehead again, but she couldn't tell him how much she admired him or that she wanted to know why he kept his distance. It would show how attached she was, and whenever she cared about people, they usually ended up hurt in the process. Especially if she let her powers loose. Maybe she should just go with why he was here in this room.

As if he'd read her mind, Scott answered that last question. "King Erik wants me to take a look at the rune fragments. He thinks I may have an advantage since I was inside the cage with the wolverines." He poked one of the stone pieces. "I don't think there's any chance of that though. These just look like small rocks with scratches to me. I am a little familiar with the Younger Futhark runes, but at first glance, these are nothing like those symbols."

Irja's blood ran cold when she thought of the danger he'd put himself in. "Naya won't be happy when she hears you fought the wolverines on your own."

Annoyance flashed in Scott's midnight-blue eyes. "Then maybe you shouldn't tell her."

"I won't have to. It will be in the report Ulf or Pekka will send to King Leif." She kept her tone bland to hide how much his lashing-out hurt.

"I'm sorry," Scott said. "I'm just cranky and tired." He rubbed the back of his head and then grimaced as he dropped his arm back down.

"You're hurt."

"It's nothing. One of the wolverines scratched my shoulder."

Irja walked around the table that separated them. She lifted her hands but then paused. "May I?" she asked.

Scott studied her for a moment and then nodded.

She stretched out his T-shirt collar to peek underneath. He was only a few inches taller than her, so she could easily peer at his shoulder this way. Scott's breath hitched, and she immediately dropped his shirt and stepped back. "I'm sorry. I didn't mean to aggravate the injury."

"You didn't," he mumbled. "It's just sensitive."

"We need to take a closer look at your wound. And you should take an antidote just in case the wolverines laced their claws with poison again." She turned to retrieve the medical bag she'd brought from her own bedroom.

About two years ago, one of the younger Vikings had almost died when the wolverines tainted their weapons and claws with poison. Only a blood transfusion using the queen's genetically enhanced blood had saved the warrior. Although the evil creatures didn't seem to use poison anymore, Irja now had an antidote and she didn't want to take any chances with her queen's brother.

"It's fine. I cleaned it in the shower, and it's not bleeding anymore." Scott shrugged and then winced again.

Irja snapped her bag open. "Indulge me." She pulled out one of the chairs by the small table that held the rune fragments and gestured for him to sit.

He sighed loudly but did as bid. Irja retrieved an alcohol swab for the shot. The soap and water from Scott's shower should have cleaned the wound well enough. She quickly averted her thoughts from the image of him standing naked under cascading water as he soaped up his body, but not before her berserker hummed low. Through her mental connection, she ordered the inner warrior to settle down. All she got back was a disappointed grumbling.

She was almost done pulling the antidote from the vial into the syringe when the swish of fabric caressing skin made her look up.

Freya's mercy. He'd taken off his shirt.

She had seen and touched his body many times while he'd been her patient. And she'd been drawn to his sleek physique then, but this was something completely different. His shoulders had somehow become broader. And the expanse of sun-kissed skin covering an expanse of well-defined muscles was too much for her sleep-deprived brain to process. She stared at the narrow strip of hair that started below his belly button and disappeared into his jeans, the syringe and vial in her hands forgotten.

Her berserker growled and paced in tight circles.

"Are you okay?"

Scott's words brought Irja out of her stupor, but she had to breathe deeply before she could center herself enough to calm the inner beast.

"Yeah, fine. Just tired." She tried for a smile, but judging by the worried look he threw her, it probably looked more like a grimace.

"You should rest before the evening meal."

"I'll try." She finally managed to finish prepping the syringe and placed it on the table.

Scott reached for her hands, clamping them between his. "Irja, you have to take care of yourself. You are of no use to anyone if you drive yourself to exhaustion."

She couldn't meet his gaze. The heat from his hands touching hers distracted her to the point where she held her breath. She slowly pulled away from his grip and inhaled deeply. "You sound like my brother." She tried for another smile.

"Pekka is not wrong."

His dark eyes studied her, but she still couldn't meet his gaze. He would see too much, and right now she was too raw to hold up her emotional walls.

"Let's take a look at your shoulder." She winced at the false perkiness of her tone but quickly stepped to the side so she could look closer at the back of his deltoid. As she leaned closer, she had to stop herself from deeply inhaling. He smelled of the soap he'd used in the shower, clean and citrusy. And underneath that, there was a unique male scent that made her think of open desert skies and dry winds.

This was ridiculous. He'd been her patient for almost a year back in Washington State. She'd never felt the need to sniff him before. She mentally shook herself back into reality and reason. Her inner warrior disagreed. It wanted to linger on Scott's delicious smell and growled its disappointment when Irja forced it to stop scenting the air. Lusting after the queen's brother was not proper. Even if he had not been her patient, Irja knew she was not a worthy partner to him. The beast resisted, but at least it calmed down and stopped pacing.

Irja swabbed his bicep with the alcohol pad and gave him the shot of antidote. It had been tested on the immortal warriors and on Luke, who was a regular mortal. She had faith that if Scott had been in contact with the wolverine's poison, this would spare him any symptoms.

Scott's jaw clenched as the needle went in. "I don't think I'll ever be a fan of injections," he said in a low voice.

"I'm sorry. I wasn't thinking." Irja fumbled as she put the medical supplies in a plastic bag and dropped them into a trash can. She shook her head. "That was so insensitive."

"You weren't insensitive. I get that you're doing this to take care of me." His dark eyes were intense. "It's not the same."

He didn't have to tell her what he was thinking. While captive in the lab, Scott and Naya had endured shot after shot of toxic chemical cocktails that would supposedly make them into super soldiers. Irja should have known better than to just jab a needle in him without warning.

"Let me just have another look at the shoulder," she said when the pause in conversation became loaded with too much tension.

Scott hissed when she prodded the injury. "I guess it's a little more serious than I let on."

Irja studied the puncture wounds. They had stopped bleeding and looked clean. "I don't think the claws hit anything vital. It looks like muscle damage only." She placed her fingers on the injury and closed her eyes briefly. Although she never used powers to heal anymore, her sensitivity to magic allowed her to detect what she thought of as "troubles." If a wound was infected or if an injury extended to vital organs, she could sense the body's distress and pinpoint the underlying cause quicker. Scott's injury didn't give off any troubled vibes. "These should heal fine on their own." She withdrew her fingers and had to once again clamp down on her connection with the berserker as it hissed its disapproval when the skin-to-skin contact ended.

She'd never had these types of control issues with her inner warrior before. She really needed to get some sleep before the evening meal.

Scott stood, and Irja stumbled as she took a step back to get away from all that delicious bare skin.

Scott grabbed her elbow, and to her horror, she swayed toward him. She had to put a hand on his chest to steady herself and avoid smacking her nose into his collarbone. Heat traveled from where her palm touched his skin and up her arm. The air between them crackled with electricity. Her nipples tightened into hard peaks. Heat pooled low in her abdomen and then moved even further south. The berserker threw back its head and howled in approval.

There was no external sound, but under her palm, Irja felt an echo of that growl vibrating deep in Scott's chest.

She looked up to find him staring at her, shocked.

"What the fuck just happened?"

She had no idea. "I need sleep," she whispered, her voice cracking. She had to get away from him before she completely lost her mind.

She quickly gathered up her medical bag and fled the room. Scott called her name, but she ignored it.

If she had to drug herself into slumber, she'd do it. Anything to regain control and composure. Bad things happened to people whenever she lost control, especially if she cared about them.

CHAPTER 5

MIDWAY THROUGH THE EVENING MEAL, SCOTT GAVE UP watching for Irja. His belly was full of food, but he had no idea what he'd eaten. He'd been too busy watching the entryway out of the corner of his eye so he could catch a glimpse of the dark-haired Valkyrie when she came to eat and hopefully ask her what the hell had happened. When she'd put her hand on his chest, he'd felt a vibration deep within, an echo of something primitive and wild inside his own body. Scott rubbed his rib cage and shook his head.

"What was wrong with it?" Finn suddenly said. The red-haired Viking sat in the chair next to Scott and watched him with a frown. "What didn't you like about the salmon?"

Somehow, he had completely missed whatever Finn had said, but apparently it had been about fish, so that must be what Scott had devoured for dinner without tasting a single bite. "No, it was good."

"Then why are you shaking your head?"

"I was thinking of something else."

Finn's eyebrows shot up as if missing his scintillating conversation about salmon was the craziest thing he'd ever heard. The guy truly loved food. If he wasn't eating it, he was talking about it. Actually, when he was eating it, he usually talked about it too.

Ulf snickered from Scott's other side. "Not everyone is as obsessed with food as you." Scott threw him a grateful look but shouldn't have bothered, because the blond giant smirked. Nothing good ever came after one of Ulf's smirks. "You can stop looking for her. She's gone into town with Pekka. They're having dinner together."

Scott froze. Had he been that obvious? How long had Ulf known about his fascination with Irja? More important, how much did he know? And how would it come back to bite Scott? He thought he'd been careful about his attraction to Irja. If it got back to Naya or Irja herself, Scott would have to leave the warriors altogether. The embarrassment of his sister pitying him when the inevitable rejection happened would be too much. Irja was not only beautiful and smart, her healing talent was sought after. She'd never lower herself to be with a regular mortal.

"Looking for who?" Finn asked while loading a huge mouthful of potatoes into his mouth.

"Nobody," Scott shot out quickly.

Ulf just smirked again.

Finn shrugged and focused on his plate. "I think maybe they cured the fish before they baked it." He stabbed a piece of salmon with his fork and held it up in front of his face, gazing longingly at it. "It's both moist and flavorful." He put the fork in his mouth and closed his eyes and chewed.

Ulf barked out a laugh. "May you one day find a woman who loves you as much as you love food."

"Only one?" Finn grinned. "I'm a big man. I may need more than one to satisfy my appetites."

"How about one who's insatiable in bed and an amazing cook?"

"That's the winning combination," Finn agreed.

Scott wanted them to stop their banter so he could pepper Ulf with questions. Why had Irja and Pekka gone into town? Did the siblings skipping the communal meal have anything to do with the freaky thing that had happened in the bedroom?

The big dining room was not the best place for this conversation though. Not unless he wanted everyone to discover how he felt about Irja. King Erik and two of his Taos warriors were deep in conversation on the other side of the large oval oak table. Vimer and Haskel were both tall, broad-shouldered, blond mountains of muscles—just your average immortal Norse warrior—but they had unusual eyes. Instead of the usual blue, Vimer's were green as jade and Haskel's chocolate brown. The three men looked preoccupied, but he didn't know if their immortal Viking superpowers translated into extraordinarily keen hearing as well. He should ask Ulf and Pekka at some point, but knowing them, they would say no if they did have super hearing and yes if they didn't. In other words, he'd still not be any wiser.

"How is Kari?" he asked Ulf instead. Maybe the change of topic would throw him off.

The half smirk playing at the corner of Ulf's mouth said it didn't, but then the warrior's expression turned serious. "She's not improving. Everyone's worried."

Scott didn't know the Taos-based Valkyrie very well, but she'd trained with them, and she'd fought valiantly during one of their run-ins with the wolverines. Either way, she was a fellow warrior, and therefore they all worried about her.

"I'm sure Irja can find a cure," Finn said. "Her reputation as a healer is legendary. I just wish we knew what made Kari sick." The fact that nobody knew what ailed her had them all on edge. They could not eliminate a threat if they didn't know what it was.

Scott worried about Irja as well. She was under a lot of pressure to make Kari better, and it was taking a toll on her. Maybe her exhaustion and worry caused what had happened between them earlier. He frowned. He needed to make sure she took care of herself as well as her patient.

Finn misinterpreted the frown. "Don't worry. Kari will get better."

"Irja is the best. Our queen's brother here is proof of that." Ulf nodded at King Erik and the other two warriors as they stood and left the room. Scott and Finn echoed the gesture.

The Finnish Valkyrie knew more about medicine than the most famous doctors from the most prestigious research institutions. After Naya saved him from the lab, she'd checked him in at an exclusive private clinic. He'd been hiding in plain sight among famous actors and wealthy socialites under the care of the best doctors money could buy, but none of them had been able to cure him. It wasn't until Irja started working on his case that he showed any kind of improvement.

"If there is a cure, Irja will find it." He pushed around the potatoes left on the plate. "She healed me, and I was considered a lost cause."

"Are you going to eat those?" Finn asked.

Scott didn't bother to look at the red-haired Viking as he slid the plate over to him.

Ulf growled. "We need to stop sitting around gossiping and"—he gave Finn a poignant look—"eating our feelings."

"Hey," Finn said, but Ulf held up a hand and interrupted him.

"We need to get the wolverine crap and the worry about Kari out of our heads for a while. Even if it's just for one night. Let's go out. I feel like dancing and drinking."

"And wenching," Finn added, all smiles now. He'd apparently forgiven Ulf for the slight about eating his feelings now that the blond Viking was listing his other favorite activities.

"That's a given." Ulf smirked.

"I'm not sure," Scott said. "It's been a long day."

"True warriors fight all day and wench all night." Finn's grin stretched almost all the way across his face.

"Then from what the wenches tell me, you're not a true warrior, since you rarely last more than a few minutes." Ulf ducked as Finn's fork sailed toward his head.

"I'll have you know, I only sleep with the type of women who won't sleep with the likes of you," Finn interjected. "So you've heard nothing."

Ulf only laughed in reply.

Scott couldn't help but join in the laughter. As much as he felt like an outsider at times, the camaraderie among the warriors was what he most enjoyed about the unit he fought with. Hopefully, Ulf would keep his mouth shut about Scott's fascination with Irja, and he wouldn't have to disappear from his sister's life again.

The beat of the dance music reverberated through Irja's body as she lost herself to the rhythm of the song. She and Pekka had dined at an authentic Mexican restaurant before heading to the club to feed their berserkers. Their inner warrior spirits became restless and hard to control if they weren't satiated with emotional energy. A warrior with a restless berserker risked succumbing to permanent battle fever. The berserker would be in control instead of the human, and the Viking or Valkyrie became a danger to everyone, since they no longer could tell the difference between friend and foe.

In the old days, the days before any of them had been sent to Valhalla, the berserkers were kept happy when they absorbed the energy rising above big battles. As the warriors' swords and shields clashed, the increased battle fever fed their inner beasts. But modern warfare rarely called for big warrior-to-warrior battles, so the Vikings had had to find a substitute. Sex was one way to keep the berserker happy, and that was how Irja had first fed her berserker when Freya sent her back to Midgard. But unemotional hookups had become tedious, no matter how well her partner performed in bed.

She raised her arms above her head and swayed her body to the music. Pekka was somewhere in the throng of people as well. She'd lost track of him as people entered the dance floor as the night went on. Their writhing bodies created a delicious blend of human physical energy and pent-up sexual frustration. The dark club with flashing strobe lights encouraged kissing and touching, and quite a few of the people indulged even though they were technically in public.

Irja tilted her head back and let her berserker absorb the energy. This was her favorite way of *feberandas*—fever breathing—and it pleased her berserker too. The worry about Kari was still there but had moved to the back of her mind. She allowed her berserker spirit to swell and take up more space in her consciousness. The beast purred like a cat—a very big, predatory cat—as it lapped up wave after wave of human emotions. It obviously had needed to be fed. Her hungry berserker and her lack of sleep must be why she'd reacted so strongly to Scott earlier in the day. She'd been on the verge of ripping his clothes off and straddling him. She couldn't remember ever reacting so strongly to anyone. Just thinking about it made her blush. She was always in control of her emotions. Always.

She had to be in order to not endanger those around her.

A mortal male glided up to her and put his hands on her hips. Irja sidestepped him and continued dancing alone. He was handsome, but she wasn't tempted. She'd been in Midgard for close to two centuries now and had enjoyed lovers during that time. But after a few of them had wanted something more serious than just sex, she avoided casual hookups. Now she rarely sought a sexual partner, because modern technology had made it possible to have amazing orgasms without the complications of a one-night stand. Although, that unfortunately did not satisfy her inner warrior, but that's what the dancing was for. Now that her berserker was satisfied, this weird attraction she had to her queen's brother would become a lot easier to control. The temptation of acting on her emotions would go away. It had to.

The male who had touched her sidled up to her again. He put an arm around her waist and leaned in. "You're so freaking hot," he all but yelled in her ear.

Irja sighed. Why would anyone think blurting out an unoriginal line like that would be attractive? "Thank you but not interested," she replied.

"I bet I can make you interested." He bent down as if he was going to yell in her ear again.

Goddess's Curse. Did the jerk just lick her neck? Irja's

berserker growled, but she clamped down on the emotional connection she had with the beast and ordered it to lie low. "You shouldn't have done that," she told the man as she grabbed the hand now sliding down toward her butt and pulled his wrist around and over so that it bent at an unnatural angle. "Women don't like to have to say no more than once."

The guy grimaced as he tried to get out of her grip. "What's your problem?"

She bent his wrist farther back. "No problem here. You, however, seem to have quite a few issues." She was careful not to snap his bones, no matter how tempting it was. Her berserker growled its disapproval. The beast had never really gotten on board with the Hippocratic oath, preferring to shatter bodies rather than heal them.

The guy whimpered but maintained his macho bravado. "I didn't want to fuck you anyway."

"That was never an option." Irja let him go and pushed him away from her.

He stumbled, earning himself a few pissed-off looks from the dancers he jostled. He turned toward Irja, but whatever he saw on her face made him swallow the words he was about to say. Cradling his wrist, he disappeared into the crowd of dancers.

Pekka chose that moment to appear next to her. "If you keep scaring off your partners, you'll have nobody to dance with." He smiled and took her hand, twirling her around before executing a perfect dip. Her berserker let out a yip when it recognized Pekka's inner warrior and squirmed like a playful puppy.

Irja laughed when he smoothly led her into a classic

foxtrot, keeping perfect rhythm with the upbeat music blasting through the speakers. "When did you learn ballroom dancing?"

Pekka pushed her out for another twirl and then held her close again as they glided across the dance floor. "I didn't just wander around aimlessly among the mortals these past few hundred years. I picked up a new skill or two as well." His grin made him devastatingly handsome. Too bad he so rarely smiled.

"I like this new skill of yours. It must be a tremendous asset when interacting with the mortal women."

"A true gentleman warrior never kisses and tells."

Irja laughed, enjoying this new playful side of her brother. When they were children, he'd always been the more serious one. The planner and voice of reason to her impulsive and reckless personality. After the disaster that killed her mother, she'd changed her ways and become more like Pekka. But she still wished her brother would relax and allow himself some pleasure and joy. "Is Kari one of the people you've kissed but won't tell about?" She regretted her words as soon as they left her lips, because her brother's face shut down. The joy that had been there seconds ago disappeared so quickly, she thought she may have imagined it in the first place. "I'm sorry," she stuttered. "I didn't mean—"

"You don't have to apologize, *Sisko*. I do care for the Valkyrie, something I must remember to hide better." He gave her a rueful grin. "But there has been no kissing." He maneuvered them off the dance floor and toward one of the bars. "I have expressed interest, but she has made it clear that she is not interested in a dark, moody Sami like me."

Irja had so many questions but kept them to herself. "Any woman would be lucky to have you."

Pekka arched an eyebrow but didn't say anything as he, with his hand on her lower back, guided her toward the bartender.

Irja opted for a lighthearted tone. "If they don't appreciate your mad skills on the dance floor, then they don't deserve you no matter how moody you can be." She turned toward him with a smile. "The Sami part, however, should be recognized as a bonus. Among all these boring fair-haired Scandinavians, you stand out as a handsome dark devil."

Pekka stared at her for a moment before throwing his head back in full-blown laughter. The people next to them turned at his mirth. "Are you drunk, *Sisko*?" he said once he'd contained the laughter.

"Not in the least," Irja said. "I meant every word."

"Well, let's try to get some alcohol in you then. I can't wait to hear what comes out of your mouth once you're inebriated."

It was Irja's turn to laugh. "*Veli*, you know I've always been able to outdrink you."

Pekka just shook his head at the lie. She was a notorious lightweight when it came to alcohol. One or two glasses of mead and she was more than a little tipsy. "I know you don't want to put that to the test," Pekka said. "Neither would I, because I don't much look forward to carrying you out of this bar when it's time to go home." He waited for the bartender to notice them and then placed their drink orders. Irja opted for a light beer while Pekka chose an Arizona-brewed IPA.

They sipped in silence for a while, and Irja watched the

people around them. The people in the club were laughing and dancing, oblivious to all the evil preying on the world. Loki's plan to start Ragnarök—the final battle of the Norse gods and the end of the world—would wipe out the entire human population in a massive flood. Or so the ancient texts said.

She tipped her bottle back again. Or maybe they were aware of how fleeting and short their lives were. Maybe squeezing every ounce of joy out of life was the way to make it really count.

Irja checked her bottle. Yep, half of it was gone. No wonder she was having deep philosophical thoughts. That was what happened when she drank alcohol. She looked over at her brother and found him smirking at her as if he could tell what she was thinking.

"Enjoying your beer?" he asked.

"Very much." She took a defiant sip and turned toward him. "There's something I've been meaning to ask you."

"Does it have anything to do with my love life? Because we're done talking about that." Pekka looked at something over her shoulder, and a flash of a grin appeared briefly on his lips before he focused his gaze on her again.

"Not about your love life," Irja said. "About your berserker."

"What about it?"

"Does it do anything weird when you are around me?"

Pekka mumbled something that sounded like a curse under his breath and looked away from her.

She waited for a moment, but when it appeared he wasn't going to answer, she nudged his elbow. "Well?" Her berserker became more alert, as if it too was waiting for an answer. But instead of focusing on Pekka, it seemed intent on something behind Irja. She was about to turn around to see what it found so interesting, but then her brother said something she couldn't hear. "What was that?" she asked.

Pekka cleared his throat. "I said it prances. It frolics around like it wants to play."

"Mine does too," she said.

"Let's not share that with anyone though." Pekka smiled. "It will hurt my warrior image if anyone finds out my sister makes my berserker behave like an idiot."

Irja was about to answer when all of a sudden her inner beast went on full alert and growled deep in its throat. A threat was near.

Pekka had also gone on full alert and once again looked behind her. He nodded at whomever he saw there before scanning their surroundings. Irja turned around to see whom he'd silently communicated with, but there wasn't anyone there that she recognized, nor did anyone seem to pay attention to them. She turned back and continued to try to pinpoint where the threat was coming from. Her berserker's growl was the same one it let out whenever a wolverine was close by. But surely the creatures wouldn't come into a crowded dance club. They could pass for human, but only if nobody looked too closely. Loki's minions had always hid in the shadows before, targeting mortal populations that were on the fringes of society. That way, they wouldn't attract attention. If law enforcement or the media started reporting on the creatures, the Norse gods' council would no longer be able to ignore Loki's rule breaking, and he'd be thrown out of Asgard for sure.

Her brother leaned in. "Let's split up," he said.

Irja nodded and opened the mental connection with her berserker more fully as she headed in the opposite direction from where her brother skirted the dance floor. Her inner warrior sampled the energies in the club, looking for the otherworldly signature that would be tainted by Loki's magic. As she tuned in to the beast inside her more fully, it connected her to her brother's berserker, and she could tell where in the club Pekka was. To her surprise, two more berserker signatures showed up on the map in her mind's eye. One of them she recognized as having Ulf's unique imprint, but the other she had not encountered before. She guessed it must be Finn's.

It didn't surprise her that the two warriors had ended up in the club. Pekka had told her that many of the bars in town had dance floors, but this was the only proper nightclub, and it had the biggest dance floor. The more people dancing, the more energy to feed the berserkers.

A faint fourth berserker signature flickered on the web connecting her to her brother, Ulf, and Finn, but it disappeared before she could home in on who it might be. Maybe one of King Erik's other warriors was out patrolling the streets of Sedona.

Irja scanned the crowd as she weaved her way through. Her berserker still insisted there was a threat and grew frustrated when it couldn't detect where the danger was coming from. The throng of people made Irja's progress slow. Fighting a wolverine in this crowd would make it impossible not to hurt the mortals.

She'd traversed the circular dance floor by one hundred and eighty degrees when she caught a too-fast-to-be-mortal movement out of the corner of her eye. She cautiously turned and scanned the crowd before her. Toward the back by the wall, she thought she caught another flash of other-worldly speed. The berserker growled and urged her to pursue the movement.

Irja pushed her way through the people as quickly as she could without violently shoving them out of the way. When she got to the wall, she discovered a set of stairs that led up to a closed door. A small brass sign on the dark wood door declared it to be the VIP room. She shoved the door open and stepped through.

CHAPTER 6

A TALL, MUSCULAR MAN DRESSED IN A TAILOR-FITTED black suit held up a hand as Irja stepped through the door. The berserker growled, intent on its prey, which was somewhere in this room, but Irja commanded it to calm down. The man gave her a once-over and said something into a microphone in his lapel before giving her a nod of approval. Apparently being female and in good shape gave you access to the VIP room.

The space was a huge balcony overlooking the dance floor. Small round tables surrounded a smaller dance area, and the room was illuminated by short lamps that cast a soft glow on each table. Women in short dresses that were probably supposed to look like a tuxedo weaved between the tables with trays of drinks. A bar was tucked discreetly into a corner.

Only a few of the tables were occupied, the couples caught up in themselves and not noticing Irja as she strode through the room toward a table in the back where a lone wolverine sat. It stared right at Irja with creepy eyes filled with a matte darkness that absorbed the light.

The creature grinned and beckoned for her to come closer. At least it had sheathed its claws. Irja looked around the room and mapped the position of each of the humans. Should she make them leave, or should she leave things alone until she knew what the creature's intentions were? The smirk on the wolverine's face showed he knew he was at an advantage here. She cared about the mortals in the room.

He definitely didn't.

In the end, it came down to the oath Irja had taken to do no harm. Telling the people to leave might incite panic, so she decided to leave things alone for now. She approached the table with the wolverine and positioned herself such that she was shielding the nearby tables from the creature. Odin and Freya had tasked Irja and her fellow warriors with protecting humanity. And protect them she would. If Loki wanted to play games, then she would indulge him as long as no mortals were in jeopardy.

The wolverine extended its claws and then quickly sheathed them, as if it was showing off just because it could. It was obviously as narcissistic as its master and maker. Loki's move to create his minions in human laboratories was genius. The Norse gods' council was preoccupied by infighting and political upheaval. The lifespan of the mortals meant very little to the gods when they were locked in a power struggle for what passed as millennia in the human realm. Loki had found a nice loophole in the rule that forbade the gods from taking their fighting to the human realm. Technically, Loki wasn't entering Midgard. Neither were his minions, since he created them in the human labs.

"What do you want?" Irja had to dig deep to not show her disgust at being so close to the creature and not killing it. Her berserker paced and pushed against the mental restraints Irja used to keep it from taking control of her body. It roared its disapproval.

"My master, Loki, wants your queen's brother, but he also wants to communicate with you, fair Finnish Valkyrie.

Prophecy has foretold that you will be a key player in the drama my master has planned for the mortal humans and those of you who call yourselves their protectors."

"Let's not talk in riddles," Irja said. "Just say straight out whatever you came here to say. And then we can go outside to a nice unpopulated area so I can kill you." She kept her tone even and friendly.

The wolverine's Adam's apple bobbed as it swallowed, but then it rallied and shot her a fake smile. "My master has a message for you, Valkyrie. It would be in your best interest to listen."

"Tell him to send me an email," Irja countered. "I don't have time for this crap." She moved as if to stand up.

The wolverine's freaky hand shot out and grabbed her wrist. "This won't take long," it hissed. "And as long as you sit down and listen, I won't damage any of the humans in this room. You care too much for these fragile stupid mortals who are but a bleep on the timeline of my master's reign."

"Loki is master of nothing and has no reign whatsoever. Anyone who thinks otherwise is delusional," Irja answered.

"Listen to me, you foul Valkyrie. If you don't listen and show my master the respect he deserves, he won't spare you, no matter how pivotal you are to his plan."

She was so done with this. "I don't care what Loki thinks of me."

The wolverine grinned. "Your confidence is one of the things my master most admires about you."

Irja tried to hide her shudder. "Either give me this freaking message or let's go out back so I can shut you up."

"Today is not the day we meet in battle," the wolverine

countered. "My master's message is simple. He wished to tell you that when the time is right, he'll meet you in the cave."

"What does that mean?" Irja asked. "What cave? And why would I ever want to meet with him?"

The VIP door slammed into the wall as Ulf and Pekka burst through, closely followed by Finn and Scott. The bouncer tried to stop them but stepped back when he better assessed the size of the men.

"That is my cue to leave," the wolverine said before leaping over the tables and vaulting over the balcony railing.

Irja ran to the edge of the balcony, only to catch a glimpse of the creature as it scurried through the mass of people below and slunk out the back.

Pekka and Scott collided with the railing at the same time, as if they'd raced across the room. They leaned over and swore when the wolverine disappeared from view. "What the fuck do we do now?" Pekka said.

Scott stepped around Irja's brother and cupped her elbow in his hand. "Are you okay?" he asked. "What were you and that creature talking about?"

"He delivered a cryptic message," Irja explained. "I have no idea what it means."

Pekka swayed on his feet, and beads of sweat had broken out on his forehead. "You should have called for one of us to protect you," he said.

"Protect me from what?" Irja wanted to know. Did her brother think she couldn't protect herself from one lone wolverine?

"These creatures keep evolving," Pekka said. "Every time we encounter them, they have some new skill, some new weapon, and some new nastiness that can be used for whatever game it is these fuckers are playing."

"Still," Irja insisted. "I can take care of myself as well as any other warrior."

Ulf and Finn became quiet and seemed to urgently need to be on the other side of the room. Scott studied her with a curious expression on his face. For whatever reason, his scrutiny really pissed her off. He was always doing that. Watching her without ever really engaging. Not that she wanted him to engage—that would be too complicated— but still, she wanted…shit, she had no idea what she wanted.

She rubbed her temples, trying to ease the threatening headache. Her berserker was still hyped up and did not want to settle down. It was going to be a challenge to calm her inner warrior. Scott's proximity was not helping.

Pekka wiped the sweat from his forehead and gripped the railing. "It's not about that," he said. "It's all about keep-ing you safe."

"More like keeping me in the 1950s or even the 1050s," Irja countered. "Let's find these creatures and kill them. Forget trying to figure out their agenda, just neutralize the threat. The warriors need to all come together, male and female, and defeat them once and for all." Plus a big brawl would satisfy her berserker.

Scott squeezed her arm gently. "It's not about your gender," he said. "You are the best doctor any of the Norse tribes has ever had. Losing you would be devastating."

Pekka nodded, swaying on his feet. "That," he mumbled and then crashed to the floor.

Irja rushed to his side, putting her fingers to his neck. His pulse was erratic and weak—just like Kari's had been when Irja first arrived in Sedona. "Help me." She looked up at Scott. "Please, help me." She couldn't lose Pekka again. She wouldn't survive it.

Scott paced in King Erik's office. His thoughts were a jumbled mess. When Pekka had collapsed in the club, Irja had turned white as a sheet, and for as long as he lived he would remember her looking up at him, her beautiful dark eyes filled with despair, pleading with him to help her. And he would forever remember how fucking useless he had felt over not being able to do anything more than scoop up her brother and carry him to the car.

"What the fuck is happening?" Erik's fist hit his desk. "What connects Pekka and Kari?"

Ulf, who was sitting on one of the couches, briefly met Scott's eyes. The same despair and anger that Scott felt were mirrored in the blond Viking's gaze. "I don't know yet," he said between clenched teeth. "But I won't rest until I find out." He nodded at Scott and strode out of the room.

Irja had determined whatever ailed her brother was the same disease that had attacked Kari. Pekka's body was racked with fever tremors, and his heart rate was weak and irregular. The healer had taken the same samples that she'd done with Kari and administered all the same drugs, all while it looked like she herself would collapse any minute.

Ulf had tried to talk her into resting, but she'd looked at him with such rage that both he and Scott had fled the sick room. Which made Scott feel even more like a heel.

He turned and paced the length of the room again.

"For the first time in a very long while, I'm not sure what to do next." Despair strained King Erik's voice. "I've never failed my warriors the way I've failed these two."

Shit, if an immortal king who'd walked the earth for centuries didn't know what to do, there wasn't much comfort Scott could give him. "We'll find whatever it is that caused their illness," he offered feebly. "Ulf is one of the best information miners I've seen. Only my sister is better, and she's working on the problem too. If the answer is out on the Net, they'll find it."

"And what if the answer isn't on the Internet? What if this is some sort of ancient curse that has no cure?" Erik asked. "Irja is the best healer anyone has known for millennia, and even she can't find a cure. I can't even imagine what losing her brother will do to her."

It would break her, Scott thought. "Give her time," he said out loud. "It took her months to find a cure for me, and I was considered beyond all hope at the time."

The king nodded. "I'm sorry for giving in to hopelessness. The gods must have a plan for getting us out of this disaster. They don't always lead us where we want to go, but they show the way to where we need to be."

Scott wished he had Erik's faith. In his experience, if there were any deities out there who listened to prayers from mortals and immortals, they were awfully slow at responding. When Naya and he were first imprisoned in the training camp, he'd prayed often for someone to save them until he figured out nobody was listening. "What can I do to help while we wait for answers?" He needed something to do. What he most wanted to do was to comfort Irja, but that was an impossible task at the moment, so he needed something to occupy his mind and time or he would drive himself crazy.

Erik sighed. "You are right. There are still other things we must deal with." He looked out the window. "We still have the wolverine pests to defeat. And we still don't know how the fuck they built that cage of light. I have warriors scouting the desert, just in case the creatures decide on trying for another portal. Some of the other kings are sending me men so I can step up patrols."

"Do you want me to join the ones who are out now?" Scott didn't really want to. He didn't know those men. They would treat him with respect because of his status as Naya's brother, but being dropped into a group of immortal warriors without training with them first might lead to disaster.

"I think you are needed here." Erik studied him for a moment. "Are you feeling okay? There is something different about you."

"I'm fine," Scott said. "Different how?"

"I can't really describe it, but it's like my berserker is suddenly aware of you in a way it hasn't been before."

Oh great. Now an inner warrior spirit had problems with him as well. "I'm not sure what to say. I feel just like before." Except for this restlessness he couldn't shake and the desperate anger he couldn't purge.

"Hmm," the king said and then shook his head. "Well, in any case, we still need someone to figure out the stones with the carved runes."

"I'm probably not the best person for that," Scott interjected. "I've only briefly studied the Younger Futhark alphabet."

"You better get familiar with the others too then." Erik

turned to the laptop on his desk. "I'll print out the one you know and the other two best known alphabets, the Anglo-Saxon Futhorc and the Elder Futhark. That should get you started."

"Exactly how many rune alphabets are there?" Scott asked.

The king smiled briefly. "You'll figure it out. If these don't fit the patterns, the Internet has all the other examples for you to reference."

From what he remembered of the stones, the partial patterns were little more than scratches on fragments. With a myriad of alphabet possibilities, he didn't think he had a good chance of finding any matches.

Armed with printouts of the rune alphabets, Scott first stopped by the room where the sick warriors lay. Kari's bedroom was too small for two beds, and Irja wanted to have access to both her patients at the same time, so they now occupied a larger bedroom. He wanted to check on them and Irja before trying to solve the impossible puzzle of the runes. He knocked lightly on the door, then slowly opened it.

The lights in the room were dimmed, and there was a slight scent of herbs. Both Kari and Pekka lay motionless in two separate beds, but while the Valkyrie seemed to breathe peacefully, Pekka's breaths came in bursts with long pauses in between. Irja sat by her brother's bed, holding his hand, her head bowed as if in prayer.

Scott approached as silently as he could. He put his

hand on Irja's shoulder and she startled, looking up at him with panic in her eyes.

"I'm sorry," he blurted out, withdrawing his hand. "I didn't mean to scare you."

"It's okay," Irja mumbled and then cleared her throat. "I was concentrating on something, but I can't make it work."

"Make what work? Is there anything I can do to help?" He rubbed his chest. The ache that had been there ever since they got back from the club throbbed harder.

"No." Irja hesitated. "I shouldn't be doing this anyway. It's just that I'm blocked."

"You'll think of something," Scott said, feeling as useless as ever.

Irja stood. "Is there something you wanted?" She stumbled.

Scott reached out to steady her by the elbow. "When was the last time you ate?" He felt the same weird connection he had before, something wild and primitive responding to his touching Irja. To not creep her out, he forced his face to remain neutral but kept his hand on her elbow.

She closed her eyes. "When Pekka and I went out to dinner."

"That was hours ago, and your body has been flooded with adrenaline more than once since then." He steered her toward the door. Her skin felt clammy and cold. She really needed to get some nourishment inside her. "Irja, go to the kitchen and get something to eat."

"No. I have to figure out how to regulate Pekka's breathing."

"You'll be no good to him or Kari if you collapse." He guided her more firmly toward the exit. "Go get something to eat. I will stay with your patients, and if anything changes—good or bad—I promise to come and get you right away."

As they reached the door, Irja looked back at the beds and hesitated. "I can't. I—" She swallowed loudly. "You don't understand how much he means to me."

He shook his head in reply. If anyone knew how much a sibling who always had your back was worth, it was him. "I do know how much he means to you. And I understand how hard it is for you to leave him. I would feel the same way about Naya."

She shot him a startled look and then rubbed her forehead. "I didn't mean to imply that you aren't close. It's just that…he's the only person who truly understands where I come from, what I've—"

"What you've been through?" Scott interrupted. "He's the only one who's shared what it was like growing up under crappy circumstances?" He didn't know the details of her upbringing, but any fool could see that there had been issues.

Irja nodded, a tired, sad smile on her face. "Yes, that is exactly it."

He wanted to take her in his arms and hug her until all her sadness disappeared. However, she wouldn't be happy again until Pekka was well—until both her patients were well. "You have to maintain your strength," Scott insisted, opening the door. "I will make the king order you to eat if you don't." Irja shot him an irritated look, and he blanched inwardly but kept the expression off his face, hoping for a stoic and firm look. "Go."

She looked over her shoulder one more time before slipping out the door. "I will be back in a few minutes."

"Make it at least thirty minutes, or I'll get the king on your case." He was a jerk for blackmailing her, but she looked as if she could faint at any minute. Moisture beaded her upper lip and forehead. "And then spend another thirty minutes taking a hot, invigorating shower."

"Are you saying I stink?" She shot him an incredulous look.

"I'm saying you should take care of yourself with nourishment and a refreshing shower. You smell lovely, as always."

Irja's face turned red, and she mumbled something under her breath before quickly disappearing down the hall.

Scott turned toward Pekka and Kari. *Don't die on me*, he thought. *I like you both too much to lose you, but also she would never forgive me if you died while I was here and she was not.*

As if he was responding to Scott's desperate thoughts, Pekka let out an extra hoarse breath.

CHAPTER 7

IRJA RELEASED A BIG SIGH OF RELIEF WHEN PEKKA'S breathing finally evened out as dawn arrived. She'd slept in fits in the chair by his bedside, ready with oxygen and a small portable breathing machine, but thankfully he hadn't needed it. Kari's condition remained unchanged, which gave Irja a tiny measure of hope for her patients. They were still in a coma, and she needed to figure out how to wake them up.

She leaned over and touched her brother's hand. When she'd first started treating Kari, she'd tried to connect to the Valkyrie's berserker but couldn't establish a link. She'd thought it had been because of a combination of the two belonging to separate warrior tribes and Kari being weak and sick. Now she wasn't so sure, because she couldn't reach Pekka's inner warrior either.

Irja closed her eyes and breathed in deeply before exhaling and then repeating for a few more breaths. She centered herself and opened the connection with her own berserker. Her beast became alert, immediately probing for their link to open more widely. It was always this constant struggle with the inner warrior. Although the Vikings and Valkyries talked about the berserkers as if they were separate entities, the truth was that they were very much part of themselves. Their inner warriors were the primitive, battle-hungry side of Odin and Freya's soldiers. Connecting with their berserker spirit made the Norse warriors close to indestructible when they fought. The heightened senses the beasts provided enabled them to predict their enemy's next move almost before their opponent thought it. It also flooded their bodies with such vast quantities of adrenaline that they felt no pain and could fight for hours and hours without tiring.

She clamped down on the link she'd established with her berserker, making sure she was in control of their connection. Having such a ravenous beast inside her came at a cost. The berserker operated on instinct and emotions. It didn't have time for thought or analysis. It just acted.

Irja slowly allowed the beast to take over more of her senses. She probed for the connection she usually had with her brother's berserker when she and Pekka were near each other. Her own inner warrior growled and then whimpered. Irja felt the sounds deep inside her. She opened their connection a little further, but the beast shied away and hid in the shadows of her mind.

Freya's mercy, what had scared it?

She'd never before felt her berserker frightened of anyone or anything. The experience chilled her.

A soft knock echoed through the room, and the door opened. King Erik stepped in. "Am I disturbing you?"

Irja waved him in. "I'm trying to connect with my brother's berserker, but it's as if it has disappeared." Her voice broke on the last word.

The king pulled up a chair. "I'm always connected with all my warriors on some level. It's like there's a web in my mind's eye connecting us all." He closed his eyes. "Right now, I can see most of my warriors, you included." He opened his eyes again. "But I can't detect Kari or Pekka."

He shot her a worried look. "My own inner warrior doesn't like it. It's worried and"—he closed his eyes again, his brow furrowed—"frightened." He opened his eyes.

Irja nodded. "Mine is too when I try to connect with Pekka. I don't know why it is scared. Because it can't sense Pekka's berserker or because of something else?"

"I can't tell you the reason. Just that my warrior spirit is angry about this. It is a leader as much as I am. I'm always connected to my soldiers. They are my responsibility."

"That is how King Leif connects with his warriors too. How long have you been conscious of Kari's absence in your awareness?"

"I can't tell for sure, but probably since she became unconscious." He rubbed the back of his head. "I made a note to mention it to you, but then I got distracted by the wolverines and the runes. I should have said something earlier, but I thought it was just because she was unconscious."

"Don't feel bad," Irja said. "Knowing Kari's berserker was somehow dormant would not have changed how I treated her. Nor do I think it would have helped me in terms of figuring out what to do next." She sighed. "I actually have no idea how to proceed." Normally, she would never have admitted that, but she was out of all options and could no longer pretend she didn't need help. She'd failed Kari, she'd failed King Erik and thereby her own king and queen, and now she would fail her own brother too. To her shame, she could feel her eyes well up.

"Healer." Erik took her hand. "Do not despair. Together, we will figure something out. And maybe our inquiries to the other tribes will bear fruit."

Irja wasn't so sure it was wise to get her hopes up. None

of the other tribes she had reached out to had ever heard about anything like Kari's symptoms, but she nodded. "Freya and Eir will guide us."

The king nodded. "The gods will lead us to where we are meant to be. Also, Ulf and Queen Naya are working hard to find a connection between Kari and Pekka to see what could have made them both sick."

"Have they ever been out on patrol together?"

"That is the puzzling thing. They have not. Except for when they saw each other here in the mansion, they have not interacted very much." He put his hand on top of the sheet where Kari's shin was. "Ulf tried to chat her up, but she put him in his place. Maybe that is why she didn't interact with the Washington State warriors very much. She's always felt strongly about being treated as a warrior first and a woman second."

Irja could relate but was also offended on her brother's behalf. "Pekka wouldn't have treated her with anything but courtesy and respect." Her tone was sharper than she intended.

"Of course not, but he may have flirted with her a little."

"My brother does not flirt."

Erik regarded her with something close to pity. "Of course he doesn't flirt with you, but he's probably a different man when he's away from his sister."

Irja thought of learning about Pekka's ballroom dancing ability and turned away when she felt her cheeks heat up. Obviously, her brother didn't share every detail of his life with her. And they were still catching up on the century they hadn't been speaking to each other. She swallowed the lump forming in her throat. She'd just found him again.

She couldn't lose him now. She trailed her fingers on the bed next to her brother's leg. "I just meant he would have respected her wishes and treated her like a warrior."

"Of course. I meant no disrespect toward your brother. He's an honorable man and a fine warrior. But Kari still avoided him. I thought it was because she didn't want to go to the trouble of having to prove herself, the way she had to prove herself to my men when she first joined our unit." He shrugged. "I would like to say everyone has to prove themselves when they are new to a battle tribe, but the reality is that women have to work harder at it."

Irja could definitely relate to that, but in her brother's case, it probably had more to do with Pekka having told Kari that he liked her. That, however, was not her story to share. "You speak the truth." In the Pine Rapids tribe, there was one other Valkyrie in addition to her and Naya. Even if the queen had been born a mortal, she had always had the fierce spirit of a shield maiden and was definitely a Valkyrie now after mating with the king and forming the *själsfrände* bond. Astrid, their other warrior sister, had better battle skills than most of the male warriors, and yet she still had to remind the men every now and then when they forgot about her prowess and got a little too arrogant. "I am sorry if my tone was sharp. I meant no disrespect."

"None taken, Healer." Erik turned toward Kari again and watched her for a beat. "I need to return to my duties, but I am glad that my warrior is in your care."

Irja was still uncomfortable with how much faith the king placed in her, but she nodded as she stood to show the king respect and then kept her head low in the traditional bow as Erik left the room. She returned to the chair that she'd pulled close to the beds in order to keep vigil over her patients. They both looked as if they were asleep, their breathing deep and even. She tried to take some comfort in that they were no longer agitated, but as a healer, her need to know how to solve their ailment was so strong, and not having any idea of how to proceed was not only frustrating but scary. She'd never before been this lost when it came to treating illness. Either she knew what to do for someone who was sick or injured, or she knew there was nothing she could do.

Her eyes prickled with tears, but she blinked them away. Even if nobody could see her, she would not give in to despair. She would just have to figure out what to do next. She would not give up until she saved her brother and Kari. Losing Pekka was not an option.

Resolute, she reached for her laptop to continue her research, but her cell phone vibrated in her pocket. She pulled out the device and checked the display. It was the queen.

"How is he?" Naya asked when Irja connected the call. Just like the queen to get right to it. She was as impatient as she was a loyal friend. Just hearing her friend's voice brought prickles to Irja's eyes again.

"He's calm now," she told her queen. "As is Kari, but I don't know if their sleep is making them better or if they are just slipping deeper into a coma where I won't be able to reach them."

"Hold on," Naya said. "Astrid is playing prompter behind me, so I may as well put you on speaker." The three women's bond was as close as any sisters'.

"What's happening?" Astrid asked. "Is Pekka alright?"

Irja filled them in on the progression of Pekka's condition

and how she could no longer sense his berserker and that King Erik couldn't connect with Kari's either.

"That is very worrisome," Astrid said.

"I agree," Naya interjected. "I'm especially concerned about Irja's berserker acting as if it is afraid."

"Maybe we should try to connect with Pekka's inner warrior from here," Astrid suggested. "He's part of our tribe, and maybe the three of us can wake up his berserker."

"Let's try it," Naya said.

Irja felt a tiny seed of hope take root. Maybe this would work. "Okay," she said. "I'm connecting with my berserker now and will try to reach Pekka's again." As his queen, Naya should be able to connect with her brother since his berserker was hers to command.

"We're with you," Astrid said. "Should we also ask Ulf to join us?"

"I think we should keep it just us three," Naya said. "With three Valkyries—especially if they are as close as we are—we should be able to channel a lot of Freya's power. Hopefully, the goddess of love will help us connect with her warrior."

Irja opened her mind to her inner warrior and ordered it to connect with Pekka's. Her berserker balked and growled its displeasure. A faint outside pressure pricked at Irja's awareness. The berserker perked up and demanded Irja give over more control. She slowly funneled energy into their bond, opening the connection a little bit wider. The berserker rumbled its approval, and the faint pressure pushed a little harder. The berserker paced for a moment or two and then settled down.

Irja became aware of Naya's and Astrid's inner beasts,

but their presence was very faint due to the geographical distance between her and Washington State. She tuned in to Pekka, willing her berserker to focus on her brother's inner spirit, but the beast resisted. She pushed harder, and it growled again. Astrid's and Naya's inner warriors appeared in Irja's mind next to her berserker as very faint outlines. The three beasts appeared focused, but Irja could still not sense her brother's inner warrior. She opened her connection a little more with the berserker, urging it into action, but there was nothing to focus that action on.

"What the fuck?" Astrid said through the phone speaker. "I have no awareness of Pekka at all. Maybe we're too far away, but I can sense you, Irja. You're faint, but you're definitely there."

"It's the same for me," Naya said. "I'm definitely connected with Irja. I can even see a faint trace of Ulf, but there's nothing where Pekka's berserker used to be in our warrior tribe web." As the queen, she served as a focus of the web that connected all the tribe's berserkers and should have access to all the warriors who swore loyalty and duty to her.

All of a sudden, a sharp pain pierced Irja's mind. She cried out and heard the other two women shout as well.

"Crap," Naya said. "That hurt."

"There's no way that's normal," Astrid said after a few moments. "That was something fighting us. Something or someone severed the connection we tried to forge with Pekka's berserker."

Chills ran down Irja's back. "You think something has invaded his mind?"

"I don't know," Astrid said. "I just know that was an attack."

Irja's throat tightened. She had no idea how to deal with an entity that could break the connection the berserkers had with each other.

"What are your plans for treatment?" Naya asked.

That was the whole problem. She had no plans, no suggestions, no clues. The healer had no idea how to heal. "I don't know," Irja admitted. "I've never seen anything like this, and I can find no information online, in the Sagas, or in any of the healer journals I have. At this point, I'm all out of ideas. If you have any suggestions, they would be most welcome."

There was a long pause before Naya spoke again. "Come home," she said softly. "You have your medical equipment here. The lab calms you and always enables you to do your best work."

"Yeah," Astrid agreed. "The lab is where your mojo is the strongest. Bring Pekka and Kari here and get going with your test tubes and centrifuge thingy." Astrid had always been more interested in weapons and battle than science. The fact that she actually knew the word *centrifuge* was impressive. "And," Astrid continued, "if we get our battle brother back here, we can better protect him from whatever is holding his mind hostage." Back to the shield maiden's comfort zone: fighting.

Warmth spread through Irja's chest when she thought of her state-of-the-art lab. Astrid was right. It was where she felt the most comfortable, the most capable, and the most confident. "You may be right. But I'm not sure how to transport them back to Pine Rapids."

"You let us worry about the logistics," Naya said. "Just tell us when you're ready to leave, and we'll get you here."

This time, it was impossible to hold back the tears, but they were of gratitude instead of despair. "I want to try one more thing before I make the arrangements. Maybe if I gather the Taos tribe, they can somehow connect with Kari's inner warrior."

"That's a great idea," Astrid said. "Let them know what happened to us, and maybe they'll be able to push through the resistance that severed our connection since they are in close proximity and will be prepared for the attack."

"Keep us posted," Naya said. "And let us know if there's anything we can do to help from here."

They said their goodbyes, and after another lingering look at her two patients, Irja went to find King Erik so that he could gather his warriors and get them ready for psychological warfare.

Scott watched five warriors gathered around Kari's still shape. They'd moved the Valkyrie into Erik's office. Finn had told Scott that back in Taos, they had a sacred space behind the Viking fortress, but something like that had not been established here in Sedona yet. So far, the lodgings were treated as temporary, and as soon as the wolverine threat was eliminated, the warriors would return to Taos. In Pine Rapids, there was also a sacred place behind the fortress that the Vikings used for ceremonies and celebrations.

Ulf stood with Vimer by one of Kari's sides and opposite Haskel. Erik had the vigil by the Valkyrie's head and Finn by her feet. Even though Ulf wasn't technically part of the Taos tribe, he'd patrolled with them often enough, and his inner warrior had connected with theirs during several battles. Scott would remain on the outside of their configuration since he didn't have a berserker. This gave him plenty of opportunities to watch Irja. She paced around the room, beautiful as always, but her face was pale and drawn, lines marring her forehead. Although she no longer avoided him, she still seemed a little uneasy.

And now he felt like a major dick for worrying about the state of their relationship—ha, as if what they had could be called that—when he should be thinking about Kari and focusing on how to get her better. Which was obviously what had Irja so stressed out.

The warriors tightened their formation around Kari. Irja had explained how she, Naya, and Astrid had failed to connect with Pekka's berserker. Irja couldn't explain what exactly had happened but said Astrid was certain it was some sort of attack.

They were all watching Erik, and with a nod, all the men closed their eyes, inhaling deeply. In a great whoosh, they exhaled as one, and a deep hum reverberated through the room. Scott couldn't tell who made the sound. It seemed to come from all the warriors, and yet all of them seemed to be silent.

Irja too had closed her eyes and stood by the window, her hands gathered together in front of her. Her eyes moved rapidly behind her eyelids.

The humming grew louder, and the hairs on Scott's arms stood up as if the air was charged. He rubbed his forearms, wishing he could be of more use. When Irja swayed back and forth, he stepped quietly to her side. Her body shuddered, but he was afraid to touch her in case it would startle her out of whatever trance she was in and interrupt the male warriors' connection.

All of a sudden, Finn cried out, followed by Erik bellowing. En masse, the Vikings clasped hands, the sounds of their palms meeting echoing through the room.

Irja whimpered and crumpled to the floor.

Scott reached for her, enfolding her in his arms. A powerful shock of electricity crackled from her body to his. Irja's eyes flew open, and she looked as startled as he felt. She tried to push away from him. He held her by her upper arms until she'd straightened her legs, the strange current between them still sizzling where his hands touched her. When she was steady enough to stand on her own, he reluctantly let go. "You okay?" he asked.

She nodded, wiping her forehead. "Yes. There was a force...or something. I don't know." She peered around him at the Vikings. "Are they okay?"

Scott turned around. He'd been so focused on Irja, he'd almost forgotten about the warriors. The men's biceps and forearms bulged as they gripped each other's hands. He automatically winced, imagining how hard they must be squeezing. The low humming still floated through the room but was offset by staccato grunts from the Norsemen. "Can you tell what's going on?" he asked Irja.

"I think they are in battle, but I don't know what they're fighting. I could only observe from afar and didn't get a clear impression of what attacked them when they tried to connect with Kari. Then someone—something—pushed me out, and that's when you caught me." She rubbed her arms where his hands had touched her.

"Did I hurt you?" That was one hell of a jolt.

"No, I just..." She rubbed her arms again. "What was that?" She frowned.

"I have no idea." It had felt like a hundred amps of current passed through his body when he'd held her. Technically, that was enough to electrocute a person, but in matters of Irja, his scientific brain didn't serve him well at all.

She tentatively reached out and touched his forearm with her fingertip. The sizzle was not as sharp as before, but it was still there. He covered her finger with his hand, keeping their skin-to-skin connection, and a deep growl rumbled through his chest.

Nope, no logical explanation at all when he was around her. He was so fucked.

CHAPTER 8

IRJA'S EYES GREW ROUND AS SHE GAZED INTO HIS. "AND what was *that*?" She started to retrieve her finger.

"I was kind of hoping you would know." He captured her whole hand in his, transferring the crackle of sparks from his arm to between their palms.

She blushed and then paled. "We need to figure this out, but I can't deal with it right now."

"The last thing I want to do is cause you problems." From the onset, he'd been nothing but an aggravation for her. First, she had to cure him, then she had to rehabilitate him, and now it seemed like she felt she had to avoid him because of this strange current that appeared whenever they touched. He wanted to be someone she could lean on instead of someone she considered a burden or a duty.

"I didn't say you caused this, just that I can't concentrate on it right now." She pulled on her hand again, and this time, he released it. "Pekka and Kari are my priorities."

As crazy as it was and as shitty as it made him feel, he was jealous of the patients for claiming her attention. "Of course they are." He took a step back and winced inwardly when her shoulders relaxed as he gave her space. Shit, he seriously needed to check himself. Stressing out the woman you loved was not okay.

Wait, what?

When did he decide he loved her? He knew he couldn't

stop thinking of her—whether she was there or not—but love was a strong word.

He tried it on again. Did he love Irja?

It felt right. It calmed him and somehow anchored him in the midst of the chaos of this fucked up world.

Irja had turned her attention to the Vikings surrounding Kari. Their grunts had stopped, but their bodies shuddered. Their neck and torso muscles strained as if they were being electrocuted. Finn looked like he was about to pop a vein in his forehead, his face bright red. And Erik's jaw was clenched so hard, it was a wonder his teeth hadn't cracked. Their eyes were still closed, and the humming still rumbled through the room.

Ulf cried out, and then his body shook as if it had absorbed a blow.

Irja took a step toward him but stopped when Scott reached out to halt her. She shot him a glance, and he dropped his hands.

Right, no touching until she could deal with the weird electrical shocks.

A strong wind swept through the room, despite all the doors and windows being closed. Vimer's and Haskel's hair whipped around their heads, and the sheet that covered Kari took to the air like a demented, oversized butterfly. Irja chased after it.

Ulf's body convulsed as if he was being hit by invisible blow after blow. Scott took a step toward him when Erik yelled something in Swedish and Finn shouted back. Ulf sagged, a grimace on his face, and then both Vimer and Haskel dropped to the floor like dead weight, dragging the rest of the Norsemen with them.

Scott rushed to Ulf's side as Irja hurried to Erik. She put her fingers on his neck. "He has a strong pulse." With quiet, professional efficiency, she checked the other men while Scott tried to locate Ulf's pulse. "They're all okay. Just passed out."

Scott finally managed to find Ulf's pulse. It was strong and steady. "It looked like Ulf took a beating," he managed to say. "Should we check him for internal damage?"

Irja crouched down by Ulf. Her hand stroked his body. Scott looked away, determined not to do the crazy jealous thing and imagine what it would feel like for her to stroke him like that. "I can't see or feel any bruising," she said, "but that doesn't mean there aren't internal injuries." She took out a little light and shone it in his eyes. "He's reacting to the light stimulus, so he's just passed out, like the others. You'll have to watch him when he's back on his feet again."

Scott frowned. "Why won't you watch him?"

Irja looked up at him while she checked Ulf's pulse. "Because I'm taking Pekka and Kari back to Pine Rapids. I need to be in my lab if I'm going to figure out what's ailing them. It's obviously a lot more than a physical ailment."

"Should Ulf and these warriors go with you too?"

She shook her head. "If they don't regain consciousness, I'll come back for them, but right now I want to concentrate on…" she had to stop and swallow, "…my brother and Kari. I'm running out of time with them."

———————————

Irja leaned back in the opulent leather seat of the private jet Naya had chartered for their trip back to Washington

State. The queen had spared no expense, and the airplane came with two pilots and two cabin crew members. In the back of the jet, there was a bedroom with a king bed where unconscious Pekka and Kari rested side by side. Once he woke up, she would remember to tell her brother that he'd been in bed with the woman he had a crush on. She smiled at the thought. It felt brittle, but she stubbornly kept her lips stretched. She refused to think about Pekka and Kari not waking up.

The smile must have turned into more of a grimace, because one of the cabin crew—a slender man in his twenties—gave her a peculiar look. Irja relaxed her face and sank lower into the seat. Her whole body felt bruised and battered, as if she'd received the blows that had vibrated through Ulf's body.

She shook herself mentally when thoughts of Ulf led to her thinking about the weird disturbance she'd felt when Scott had touched her. It had felt like she'd hit a strong electric fence. And for an instant, it was if he had a berserker inside him. An inner warrior in which her beast was suddenly very interested. Her berserker had perked up and actually purred like a large predatory cat in heat.

When a Viking or Valkyrie met their *själsfrände*, their soul mate, they formed a mating bond between their berserkers. But mortals didn't have berserkers, so her inner warrior showing interest didn't make any sense. When Naya bonded with King Leif, she had somehow developed an inner warrior spirit. And mortal Luke now had an inner warrior after bonding with Valkyrie Astrid. But there was no way she and Scott could have that kind of connection. First of all, they were not in love. She didn't do love, just like she didn't do any other strong emotions. It was too hard to lock down the magic and the berserker if she allowed feelings to rule her body.

And second, the bond always formed during an act of intimacy, and she had not had sex with Scott.

Images of what that would be like flooded her brain. She forced them from her mind and instead reviewed what Erik and the other warriors had told her once they woke up. They'd all had the same experience, even if Ulf's had turned into a more violent one. Each of the warriors could sense the others in the web they tapped into while in battle mode, but when they searched for Kari's berserker, they'd met resistance. They'd all pushed against it, but the harder they tried to overcome whatever it was that repelled them, the stronger the force pushed back.

When Erik ordered them into battle formation and they rammed the invisible barrier, Ulf had disappeared from their connection, but they could hear his screams as something pummeled him with blow after blow. And then the wall had turned into a raging fire, which was when Vimer and Haskel had lost their footing and a fierce wind filled with ash and debris had severed their connection with their berserkers. Shortly after, Finn and Erik had succumbed to the same thing.

As hesitant as she was to use the word *magic*, this was obviously not a regular illness that Kari and Pekka were battling. She swallowed hard. She would find a solution. Her research lab had equipment that would enable her to find a cure. It had to.

She'd abandoned magic when she was a teenager and instead relied on other remedies to cure her patients. Once she discovered science, she'd put all her effort into bending the laws of nature and mathematics to do as she ordered them.

The cabin crew guy offered to make her a drink, but she declined. Although alcohol would help her relax, she preferred to keep a clear head. It would be early morning by the time they touched down, and she wanted to get started on her research as soon as possible. Some rest now would help her focus once she got into the lab. She forced her body to relax and tried to shut her mind off.

Sleeping was always hard for her and even more so when she was stressed. Back in the 1980s, she'd gone to medical school and then done her residency. She'd trained herself then to function on very little rest.

This flight would give a few hours respite since there was nothing she could do while they were in transit. A press of a button on the side of the seat lowered the back while pushing the bottom cushion forward to the point where Irja was almost completely supine. One of the ever-attentive cabin crew members came over with a lightweight blanket, and she snuggled down.

She thought she'd only been asleep for a few minutes when a strange sound woke her. It sounded as if someone was tapping on the plane's window. Disoriented, she opened her eyes only to discover that she was no longer on the plane. Instead, she'd somehow ended up in a forest of extremely tall pine trees. But these were not the trees that grew around Pine Rapids. It was the forest of her home in Finland and it formed a rich canopy that, together with a gray swirling fog, blocked out the sunlight. The sound she thought was tapping on the window was actually moisture dripping from the branches of the trees.

The ground was covered in fallen pine needles, and her steps were soundless as she walked along a path that led through the trees. Other than the dripping, it was eerily quiet. Not a single bird call or rustle of a squirrel could be heard. The air was completely still, as if nature was holding its breath.

"Hello, Ms. Vainio." The greeting started out as a soft whisper by her ear but then the phrase repeated over and over again, echoing louder and louder through the forest even though there was no one but Irja on the path. She shivered and pulled the blanket draped across her shoulders tighter around her. Wait a minute. That was the blanket from the airplane. *Freya's crazy wagon-pulling cats. What is going on?*

She'd say she was dreaming, except she was much more aware of her body, and pinching her arm definitely hurt.

A man appeared in front of her on the path. "I am delighted you could join me, Ms. Vainio. Or may I call you Irja?"

"Who are you?"

Tilting his head, he smirked at her. "You know who I am."

She studied him. Tall with broad shoulders, he had short, auburn hair. He was handsome, but there was something sinister in his hazel eyes and in his smile. He wore black jeans and a charcoal button-down shirt, covered with a wool suit jacket. All of it looked expensive, tailored to his frame. She definitely didn't recognize him. "I've never met you."

"Perhaps not, but that does not mean that we don't know each other." He smiled again, and this time his pupils elongated until she was looking into the eyes of a goat.

"Loki," she whispered as a chill traveled down her spine.

"At your service." The trickster god made a sweeping bow.

Irja took a step back. "What do you want?"

"Now, now, don't be scared. I'm not going to hurt you." He paused for a beat. "Today."

Irja retreated another step.

Loki laughed, his strange eyes glittering. "Look at you, scared because of all the bad stories you've heard about me."

"And because of the evil creatures you send to kill me and my friends."

He swept a hand through the air, dismissing her words. "They're not evil. They're simply misunderstood beings with very simple minds."

Misunderstood, Thor's thundering ass. She had scars on her body from wolverine claws and had treated more than a few broken bones, knife cuts, and bullet wounds that were caused by the rodent-like creatures. She shifted her feet into battle-ready stance.

Not that she would have much of a chance in a fight with a half god, but she would strive to get in a few good blows before he killed her. She loosened her shoulders and let her arms hang relaxed by her sides.

Loki studied her, doing that irritating head tilt again. "Now, now, Irja. You disappoint me. Why must you be so hostile?"

"I don't remember giving you permission to use my first name." When you were scared out of your mind, it helped to show false bravado. Something she'd learned from Naya.

That earned her another creepy smile. "I like your spunk." His gaze traveled up and down her body in an obvious sexual appraisal.

She shivered in disgust. "What do you want?" she shot back. "Why did you bring me here?"

Loki made a point of looking around the forest. "Don't you like this place? I made an effort to match the fauna of your childhood forest." The trees shifted, and all of a sudden, they stood in a little meadow with a fox's burrow in the middle.

Irja tried to suppress the shudder that traveled the length of her body. This was the place where, as a child, she had unintentionally killed her father. She had ruined her family and earned her mother's hatred. Bad memories haunted this place. "I like my new home better."

"I bet you do." Loki's face turned serious. "But it's really a waste of a location for you since you refuse to tap into all the lovely magic in the basalt rock around your new home. Why won't you take advantage of all that wonderful power?"

"I don't do magic." How did he know so much about where the Vikings and Valkyries lived? It felt both creepy and threatening to imagine Loki spying on them. To her knowledge, even though they were Freya's and Odin's soldiers, the deities did not keep them under constant surveillance. Leif was sometimes contacted by Odin, and Astrid and Naya had both spoken to Freya. Those instances had definitely been in dreams, so maybe she was dreaming now.

He tsked. "You don't do magic *anymore*, but as a child, you were a prodigy with such great potential." He tilted his head back, inhaling deeply. "And it is still there. All that lovely ability going to waste."

Fully creeped out now, Irja took several steps back. "What I do with my curse is none of your business. I heal using science and modern technology, not magic."

"Curse?" He laughed again. "You humans are so tedious and ungrateful. *Jänta*, your ability is not a curse. It's a gift from the gods, and you disrespect us when you don't use it."

"Last I heard, you were only a half god," Irja shot back, regretting her quip as soon as she'd said it. Dammit, she really needed to stop channeling Naya's attitude.

Loki's face turned dark, and the fog grew dense around them. The trees seemed to loom lower and closer. "I don't think you are in a position to be particular about parentage. Your mother was definitely no prize." He straightened his spine, his whole body growing larger and his eyes glowing. "We can't pick who gave birth to us, but we can definitely choose what we do with the gifts they pass down." He took a step forward, and she felt truly threatened. "You've had your abilities long enough, and if you do not use them, I am happy to offer an alternative. Why don't you let me siphon the power from you?" His voice echoed through the forest again.

She turned and started running up the path, her feet beating a dull rhythm against the pine needle–covered surface. Angering a god—or a half god—was never a wise choice. She didn't get very far before Loki appeared in front of her again, and she skidded to a stop to keep from slamming into him. Even though she'd only run a short distance, she was gasping for breath.

Loki smiled his creepy smile again, and this time it was tainted with triumph. "I think you've understood my message."

Irja nodded as she slowly eased backward.

"You asked me earlier what I want from you, and it is very simple. I want your cooperation."

"Cooperation?"

He took a few steps toward her and leaned down low, his face right in front of hers. "Let me use you as a vessel to pull magic from this plane, from Midgard."

Irja leaned back so far, she thought her spine would snap. "I would never help you steal anything from Midgard. I'd kill myself first."

Loki's eyes glittered with barely concealed anger. "That could be arranged, but don't you want to try to save your brother and his Valkyrie friend first?" He slowly straightened, his eyes glowing with triumph.

Cold fear flooded Irja's body. "What have you done to them?"

He focused his eyes on a point somewhere behind her, and his face took on a slightly bored expression. "Nothing that can't be undone as soon as you decide to help me."

Her mind was racing, and she couldn't focus enough to hold on to one thought. She needed information. She needed clues that would help her break this hold Loki had over her brother and Kari. "What exactly would this help look like?"

Loki's smile turned feral. "You would work with my wolverines to funnel enough magic into a portal that would allow me to come visit for a spell." He laughed, an evil, cackling sound that grated on Irja's nerves. "See what I did there? Magic? Spell? Oh, I am such a delight. I do crack myself up sometimes."

Irja wished he'd stumble and crack his head. Then again, opening the half god's head might not be a good move. Who knew what kind of evil would be let loose? She tried to concentrate again. She would not seriously consider the bargain, but she also needed to get out of this weird vision alive so she could help Pekka and Kari. "I need to think about it."

The trickster half god studied her, a satisfied smirk playing in the corner of his lips. "You have forty-eight hours until we meet again." He turned abruptly and walked away from her but then stopped and looked over his shoulder at her. "And Ms. Vainio, your answer better be yes, or I'll crush the minds of your brother and his friend like wrinkled apples in a cider press."

Irja watched him disappear into the fog. As soon as he was no longer visible, she was pulled backward and then sat up, startled and hyperventilating, in the seat on the plane.

CHAPTER 9

Scott worked hard to copy Ulf and Finn as they strode soundlessly through the desert eighteen miles northwest of Sedona. Due to an alert from Ulf's computer algorithm that monitored social media groups and chat rooms for certain keywords, they were on the lookout for mysterious neon lights in the night sky. A person in a chat room reported seeing a glow close to the Palatki Heritage Site where the ancient Sinagua people's rock dwellings were built out of red sandstone.

In order to not scare off the wolverines—if they were there—Ulf had parked the SUV far from the visitor center parking lot, and they hiked in across the desert. Since it was nighttime, the temperature had dropped, but there was no bright moon, and the stars were covered by clouds. The darkness seemed impregnable, and it was hard not to trip on the small brush and rocks that littered the desert floor.

The Vikings had taken the time to strap broadswords to their backs. Scott approved of their choice of weapon considering bullets had been useless against the last glowing cage. He also wished he'd taken the time to learn swordplay so he didn't have to make do with the dinky knife he had strapped to his lower back. It had been efficient last time though, so maybe he'd get lucky again.

The rock formation that sheltered the Palatki rock pueblos loomed up ahead as a denser blackness against the stygian sky. So far, they had not seen any neon glow. As they got closer, Scott listened for the low vibration he'd experienced when they discovered the first light cage. The desert, however, was eerily quiet, which was also a bad sign. Usually, there was rustling from smaller critters scrambling around in the more pleasant temperatures of the night. The desert should be more alive now than during the day.

The silence weighed heavy, as if something malevolent helped gravity push the air toward the ground.

Ulf held up a closed fist, and both Finn and Scott stopped in their tracks.

"Listen," the blond Viking whispered.

Scott strained his hearing, but he could hear nothing but the oppressive silence that made the hairs on his neck stand up.

"Whoa," Finn exhaled quietly. "That sounds like the same chanting."

So that answered Scott's earlier question about whether or not the Vikings had keener hearing than regular mortals. And he figured it all out without having to ask. Yay for him. "I can't hear it," he murmured.

"It's very low," Ulf said as if he wanted to make Scott feel better.

"It's from over there," Finn said and started walking again.

Ulf and Scott fell in line behind the ginger Viking. Like on the previous mission when they'd encountered the wolverines chanting a glowing cage into existence, Ulf seemed more than comfortable letting someone else in front even though he was technically the patrol leader. It contradicted some of the things Scott had heard about the guy in Washington State, where Ulf had a reputation for being a bit of an arrogant prick. Apparently, he had nursed a major crush on Astrid and had been a total douche about her dating mortal Luke. The Viking had been put in his place, however, when Astrid beat the crap out of him in a hand-to-hand combat sparring session.

They were now almost at the base of the cliffs, and Scott's ears finally picked up a low sound of voices. It did indeed sound similar to the chanting they'd heard when the wolverines had created the glowing cage, but there were still no neon lights in the darkness. Maybe this was some other kind of ritual.

The sound came from their left, and Finn led them slightly off the path in that direction until they reached the cliffs, where they positioned themselves with their backs against the sandstone.. The rocks were still warm from the sun. Scott had seen the rock dwelling in the daylight and knew there were pictographs and petroglyphs on the walls depicting ancient hunts of animals that looked vaguely like wild pigs and deer.

"My berserker does not like this," Finn whispered.

Ulf sighed. "Mine either."

Since Scott could not check with anyone but himself, he kept quiet even though he agreed with both of the berserkers.

When Finn started moving, still with his back pressed against the rock, Ulf indicated that he wanted Scott to follow. "You are our key to penetrating the cage walls," the blond Viking whispered. "Finn and I will distract them while you sneak inside and fling the bastards outside to us."

"I don't think there is a cage this time. There are no lights."

"Then we'll all get to hack them to pieces," Ulf said. His white teeth glimmered in the dark.

Scott caught up with Finn, and as they skirted the cliff, the chanting grew louder.

Finn stopped again and closed his eyes.

"Do you understand the words?" Scott whispered. He had studied old runes and could even say a Swedish word or two. This, however, did not sound like anything he'd heard before.

Finn shook his head. "It's not any language I've ever heard."

"It doesn't sound like any of the Scandinavian languages, not even Old Norse," Ulf agreed.

Finn headed onward, and Scott and Ulf followed. They rounded the cliff wall and entered a small ravine. At the end of the crevice, dark shapes moved around. The chanting was definitely coming from them. There was no light cage anywhere, but the shapes seemed to be standing in some kind of formation with their heads bowed. It was hard to see exactly what was going on since the ravine became darker the deeper in they walked.

"How many?" Scott asked no one in particular.

"Three," Finn said as Ulf chimed in with, "One each."

The two Vikings grinned at each other like little kids in a candy store who'd just found out their favorite treat was on half-price special.

"What's the plan?" Finn asked Ulf once the idiots stopped flashing their teeth.

"Let's go on three," Ulf shot back. "Seems like a good number tonight."

"One," Finn counted, and Ulf took off before he got to two. "No fair," the redhead shouted as he followed his bloodthirsty colleague.

Scott sighed and ran after the two Vikings. They both had their swords out, ready to swing. Since there was no bullet-stopping cage this time, Scott opted for his Glock. He knew Ulf and Finn had also brought guns, but apparently they'd penciled in "swordfight" on tonight's battle calendar and were reluctant to change their plans.

The ravine was too narrow for the three of them to line up shoulder to shoulder, so Scott hung back, ready to back up the Norsemen.

Finn swung his sword, a battle bellow erupting from his throat. Ulf answered with a shout of his own, and to Scott's surprise, he himself cried out as if he were running ashore, ready to pillage.

A growl then rumbled from somewhere deep in his chest and up through his throat as pain exploded behind his eyes. He stumbled and sank to one knee.

Both Finn and Ulf stopped in their tracks and turned around to watch him, their eyes big and round.

"What the fuck?" Ulf said.

The pain in his head slowly subsided, and Scott tried to catch his breath. He looked up. "Behind you," he wheezed as the wolverines attacked, their claws already elongated.

The Vikings whirled around, swords ready. Finn grunted as one of the creatures ducked underneath his sword and swiped at his torso. Ulf ran his sword through the chest of another wolverine, quickly withdrew it with such force that the body bounced on the ground, and then hacked at the creature's neck so ferociously blood streaked up the cliff wall and also splattered the Viking's chest.

Scott finally caught his breath and readied his gun to shoot, but the melee in front of him was too hectic for him to get a good aim and he didn't want to shoot one of the

Norsemen. They'd survive a bullet wound—probably—but he didn't want to take the risk.

He concentrated on the fight.

Finn had cut both of the arms off the wolverine that had clawed him, and it crumpled to the ground as he rammed his sword upward and into its neck.

The third wolverine watched from deep in the crevice, hovering as if it was protecting something. It locked its weird, dark gaze on Scott and seemed to be taking his measure. Those creepy eyes gave him the willies every time.

The creature looked right and left as if measuring the distance between Ulf and Finn. The two Vikings were still happily hacking away at their slain opponents. Scott's muscles tensed as the wolverine bent down, swiped something from the ground, and then leaped toward him.

Without having to think about it, Scott took a long, steadying breath and lined up his sight. A deep rumble vibrated in his chest as he calmly pressed the trigger. As if in slow motion, he watched as the bullet entered the center of the creature's forehead and exited the back of the head in a projectile stream of fleshy chunks and blood. Scott moaned low and then sank to the ground as his mind checked out and blackness claimed him.

He came to lying on the hard ground next to the SUV with Ulf slapping his cheeks. His head rocked from side to side from the blows while glimpses of the Viking's face flittered back and forth in front of his eyes.

"What the fuck? Stop." He tried to shout, but it came out more like a croak. "What's wrong with you?"

"What's wrong with me?" Ulf asked. "I'm not the one who took a one-in-a-million shot and then fainted like an *oskuld* on her wedding day."

"I didn't faint," Scott muttered, rubbing his forehead. The blinding pain he'd felt in his head had subsided, but a dull ache still throbbed in the back of his mind.

"Yeah, right," Ulf said, still on one knee on the ground and leaning over him.

Finn's head popped into Scott's field of vision. "You okay now?" he asked.

Scott stared at the two Vikings' faces peering down at him. They both looked like demented axe murderers. Their pupils were huge from adrenaline overload, and the blood splatters that streaked their faces looked like a bizarre version of war paint. Finn had a fleshy chunk of something hanging off one earlobe. Bile rose in Scott's throat, and he forced himself not to think about what wolverine part was currently serving as Finn's earring. "I'm fine," he said and started to push off the ground so he could sit up.

White, blinding light pierced his vision, and the sharp pain stabbed his brain again. He sank back down.

"Sure you are," Finn said. "But we'll just give you a little boost into the car."

A car door opened, and hands hoisted him into the air. He was airborne for a split second, and then his butt hit the back seat, followed by his shoulders. Someone shoved his legs in, and his boots banged down on the rubber mat on the floor. Lying half on and half off the seat, he managed to push himself a little bit further up, but lifting his feet up on the seat was too much of an effort.

The car door closed, and then the two front ones opened and closed. There was some rustling as the bloody Norsemen situated themselves in the front. The engine cranked and then started with a familiar low rumble.

"Good fight," Finn said.

Scott hoped the meaty chunk had fallen off Finn's ear before he got in the car, because he had a feeling he'd be on car-cleaning duty to make up for passing out. He also had a feeling he would be the butt of several jokes in the near future.

"Invigorating," Ulf agreed.

"Did you find it enjoyable, Scott?" Finn asked.

"Sure," Scott muttered.

"Yeah, what was it like to enter battle with a berserker inside you for the first time?" Ulf asked, his voice curiously flat.

Scott's eyes flew open. "What do you mean?" He lifted his torso off the seat, but when his vision blurred, he quickly lay down again before he hurled. Between the chunk that might still hang from Finn's ear and the blood soaking the Vikings' clothing, there were enough disgusting biohazards in the car already.

"Your berserker," Finn said. "Your inner warrior." He turned toward the back seat and tapped his chest as if that would make things clearer.

"I don't have an inner anything," Scott said, keeping his eyes open but swallowing deeply when bile again rose in his throat.

"You do now." Ulf didn't turn around, but his left hand tapped the steering wheel a few times as the right one gripped it tightly.

"How do you know?"

Finn's red eyebrows flew upward until they met his hairline. "You didn't feel it?"

He'd felt something, but he wasn't a Viking. And he wasn't immortal. That couldn't have been a berserker. "I don't know. I just got dizzy all of a sudden." He carefully pushed himself into a sitting position.

Ulf's eyes met his in the rearview mirror. "It's disorienting the first time the berserker tries to take control over your body."

"I'm not one of you. I can't have a berserker."

Ulf's eyes gazed into Scott's for a few beats. "You've always been one of us, even though you keep on telling us you're not. It's a bit insulting actually." He flashed a grin.

"Yeah, are we not good enough for you?" Finn asked, also revealing gleaming white teeth.

Scott shook his head but stopped midmotion when his stomach heaved. "I just mean I'm a mortal. We don't have berserkers. Why do you think I do?" Secretly, he enjoyed the warmth that had spread through his chest when Ulf said he'd always been one of them. He quickly looked down to hide his face in case he'd blushed.

Finn turned to look at Ulf, who just shrugged. "Well," the redheaded Viking said, twisting in his seat so that he faced Scott more fully again, "you answered Ulf's battle cry."

"That was just a shout," Scott said.

Finn looked at him for a moment and then smirked. "You're not known for shouting during battle."

Scott opened his mouth to answer, but Finn held up a hand and interrupted him before he had a chance to utter a word. "It's not just that. Both Ulf and I could feel the presence of your berserker while we were fighting."

Now Scott's lips closed and opened repeatedly. He felt like a guppy. "How?" he finally managed to squeak out.

"It's hard to describe," Ulf said calmly, facing the windshield. "It's like your awareness expands and you always know the number of fighters around you."

"And you automatically know who's against you and who's with you," Finn filled in. "We felt your berserker as a solid presence behind us. In other words, we knew you had our backs and could focus solely on the opponents currently engaged with us."

"But you've known I had your backs in other battles before," Scott insisted.

"True," Ulf agreed. "But that's because we've trained and fought with you. In those instances, we trusted you to back us up because we all stuck to the formation we'd trained for."

"This time, we like *knew* knew," Finn said as if that made it at all clearer.

Ulf glanced at the other Viking briefly. "What he means is that this time, we didn't have to use any parts of our brains to analyze where you might be at any given moment. We just instinctively knew where you were and what you were doing."

He hadn't known the Norsemen used any parts of their brains during battle. Sure, they were always working in a cohesive formation according to what they'd trained for, but usually, it seemed like the Viking warriors pushed through by brawn more than careful analysis. More than a little overwhelmed by the discussion, Scott rubbed his forehead and sank back into the seat. "I don't know how to handle this."

Finn shrugged. "What's to handle? You've got an inner warrior to help you out in battle."

Ulf shot Scott an amused look in the rearview mirror.

"Don't worry. We'll teach you how to keep control of your body and how to *feberandas* properly."

Finn turned to Ulf. "This is the third human in your tribe who develops a berserker. I guess we should all get used to it by now. Maybe set up some sort of training camp." They both laughed heartily, getting even more on Scott's nerves.

"And contrary to what you may have heard, you don't have to actually fight or screw. You can open your senses and funnel power to your berserker wherever strong human emotions are present." Ulf shot Scott another look. "Irja, for example, likes to go clubbing when her berserker is hungry. The emotional frenzy that builds up on the dance floor is perfect for *feberandas*. The drawback, of course, is that you get all the buildup without the actual penetration."

He did not want to hear Irja's name in the same sentence as penetration, but at least this answered his earlier worrisome question about how she fed her inner warrior.

He ignored Ulf's smirk and instead looked out the side window and tried to change the topic. "What was it that the wolverine I shot picked up from the ground?"

"More stones with engraved runes," Ulf answered, patting the pocket on his thigh. "They're broken but not as badly as the ones we found before."

"Maybe they didn't get as far as resurrecting the cage this time," Finn said. "But that doesn't explain the lights the guy in the chat room reported."

"Or they failed to complete the cage and had to start over," Ulf offered. "Who the fuck cares anyway? We stopped the bastards, and now we have a better chance of reading what's on these rocks."

"True." Finn agreed. He turned toward Scott again. "So have you decided which way you're going to *feberandas*?"

So much for changing the topic. "I don't think we need to worry about how I'm going to feed my inner warrior," he said. "I am very certain I don't have one."

The car was quiet for just a moment, and then both Ulf and Finn threw their heads back and bellowed out loud.

To his horror, Scott automatically mimicked the gesture and the sound.

CHAPTER 10

IRJA LOOKED UP FROM HER MICROSCOPE, RUBBED HER tired eyes, and then peered through the eyepiece again. She tried to ignore the ticktock in her mind as the deadline Loki had given her loomed closer. It was hard to figure out the time zone for dreams, so she wasn't exactly sure *when* her meeting with the trickster half god had taken place. But she did know she'd spent a full day in the lab since they'd arrived at the fortress outside Pine Rapids, and she was no closer to finding a cure.

There was a knock on the door, and then Naya entered the lab, carrying a tray. "I bet you forgot to eat again," the queen said.

Irja thought for a moment. Had she eaten anything? "I'm not hungry." So she must have had something. Right?

Naya placed the tray on the counter next to the microscope.

Irja quickly shoved it farther away so it wouldn't contaminate her samples. "You can't put food here. It's a clean area."

The queen sighed and rolled her eyes, but she took the tray away and put it on a side table by the door. "What would you tell a patient who behaved the way you are right now?"

"To please continue with their work. And then I would leave them alone," Irja said.

"Nice try." Naya hopped up on one of the tall stools next to the counter where Irja was working. The queen was six inches shorter than Irja's six feet, and although they both had dark hair, the queen's was very different from Irja's regular black color. Naya wore hers chin-length, and it was the color of raven wings, the blue highlights making her midnight-blue eyes the most arresting feature in her elfin face. Especially now, when they sparkled with mirth.

Irja rubbed her forehead. "I'm sorry. I'm extra cranky today."

"Because you haven't eaten," the queen insisted.

Because she had twenty-four hours or less before Loki would find her and kill her. But she couldn't tell Naya that, so instead, she offered a limp smile. "I'll have a bite later."

"Sure you will." The queen didn't sound very convinced. "What are you working on, and can I help?"

"I'm looking over blood and tissue samples." *Again*, she added silently. She'd been over the samples so many times, looking for anything abnormal. And when she couldn't find that, she'd looked for any common pathology between Pekka and Kari, but that didn't exist either.

"Is there anything I can do? Any way I can help?" Naya fingered a clean, empty petri dish on the counter.

Irja's focus narrowed in on the queen's fingers. Was that a small tremor?

She covered Naya's hand with her own under the pretext of removing the petri dish from her grip. Yes, there was definitely some shakiness. "Are you feeling okay?"

Naya shrugged. "I've been a little tired lately, but there's a lot to worry about, so I don't think that's anything unusual."

A chill ran down Irja's spine. The queen had only been sick one time in her whole life, and that was when the wolverines had poisoned her. She knew this because Naya had told her when she'd showed up at the Viking fortress for the very first time, feverish and weak. The queen was so full of chemical enhancements and nanoparticles after her time in the super soldier program that her pathology was completely different from regular mortal humans. And that was before she'd bonded with the king. After that, she'd become a whole new specimen whose blood was a unique concoction. They'd even used the queen's blood to save one of the Vikings who had also been poisoned by the wolverines and then to synthesize an antidote to the wolverines' poison.

She turned to search for her medical bag. "I'd like to take a look just to make sure you're okay."

"That's not necessary." Naya hopped down from the stool. "I'll just make sure I get to bed a little earlier tonight so I can catch up on sleep."

Irja held out an arm, blocking the queen's escape. "Naya, you're never sick. I want to make sure everything is okay. At least let me take a blood sample and run some tests."

The queen rolled her eyes. "A little tiredness doesn't necessarily mean anything is wrong. Just because Leif acts like I have the plague whenever I say I need some rest doesn't mean you have to overreact too."

"You've been tired for a while?" Irja took a thermometer out of her bag and slipped a protective covering on it.

"No," Naya protested vehemently. "I just meant hypothetically."

Irja hid a smile. It was true the king's reactions were a little extreme when it came to his *själsfrände*'s safety, but you couldn't really blame him. He'd almost lost her once, and besides, Naya's well-being was essential to Leif's berserker. If something happened to the queen, the beast would go...

well, berserk, and the king would lose control and fall into permanent battle fever. He'd become a danger to himself and his people.

"Humor me, will you?" she said to the queen. "That way, if the king gives you a hard time, you can say I've already examined you and all tests came back clear."

Naya threw her a suspicious look. "I guess you have a point."

Irja stuck the thermometer in the queen's mouth before she had a chance to protest. The queen glowered at her until the instrument beeped that it was finished. Irja checked the reading and exhaled a breath of relief. "Normal," she said.

"Well, there you have it." Naya scooted forward on the stool, ready to leave again.

"Hold on. Let's just cover all our bases. You know, to make sure Leif doesn't get worked up."

"Fine." Shoulders slumped, the queen settled on the stool.

Irja went through the general physical examination routine and checked blood pressure, heartbeat, lungs, ears, and eyes. She found nothing that would explain unusual tiredness.

Naya gave her a triumphant "I told you so" for each result.

"Last thing," Irja said and prepared a vial to collect blood.

"Look," Naya said as Irja inserted the needle and the little clear tube filled with deep red liquid. "I know how worried you are about Pekka and Kari. Concentrate on them now, and forget about my minor complaint."

"It won't take me long to just run some tests on this." Irja held up the vial.

"But it will distract you when you should focus on your brother and the Valkyrie from the Taos tribe."

"Fine." Irja marked the tube with the queen's name and put it in one of the floor-to-ceiling refrigerators that lined the lab's walls. "But if the king asks again about your health, you'll tell me immediately so I can run the blood tests."

"Sure," Naya said, avoiding her eyes.

"Promise." Irja tried to make her voice as stern as possible.

Naya hit her arm playfully. "I will. I promise." She walked to the door and opened it. "I will tell you if Leif makes a fuss if you promise to eat the food I brought you," she threw over her shoulder.

"Fine," Irja shouted back and turned back to the microscope. She looked through the eyepiece but then hesitated.

With a sigh, she turned toward the tray of food. A promise was a promise. She wasn't looking forward to eating whatever the queen had brought since it would be cold by now. Lifting the cover, she found a sandwich and chips next to a note that said, "I figured it would take me a while to make you eat, so I brought you some cold stuff." Smiling, Irja took a big bite of the sandwich. It was turkey and Swiss, her favorite.

Scott was in the small bedroom trying to match pieces of stone fragments so he could read their engraved runes and compare them to the symbols on the printouts King Erik had given him. The new pieces were promising, but they still required a lot of trial and error in order to make coherent symbols.

It would have helped if they had a unique shape or different breakage lines, but each of the new fragments had the exact same geometry as the others and had broken in exactly the same rectangular shape, which made it close to impossible to match the pieces.

So far, he'd managed to match two of the stones to symbols in the Elder Futhark rune alphabet, but it might have been complete luck, and maybe the pieces he'd put next to each other actually belonged with completely different pieces.

There were just too many unknowns in his life at the moment. He had no idea what was going on with Irja and the strange attraction between them. He could possibly, or possibly not, have a beastie lurking inside him whose sole purpose seemed to be to take control over his body unless he fed it human emotional energy. And now these tiny fucking pieces of stone fragments were besting him. His life was way out of whack, and he was so fucking tired of not ever being in control or having a clue as to what might happen next.

Ulf entered the room. "Any luck?"

"No idea."

The Viking came closer and peered down at the table. He poked the pieces Scott had matched with his finger. "Well, these look promising."

"I think they may match two letters in the Elder Futhark, but they are not the exact same shape."

"Even engraved letters are unique by whichever scribe wrote them. Think of it as distinct handwritings. You'll have to be happy with a close match. Don't shoot for an exact one." Ulf looked at the printouts of the alphabets that Scott had laid out on the table.

"Do you read these?" Scott asked.

Ulf shook his head. "Some of it, but I'm more fluent in the Younger Futhark runes." He rubbed the top of his head. "I mean, give me some time and I can decipher the symbols, but I wouldn't be able to translate just off the top of my head."

Scott looked at the two whole runes he'd patched together after hours of work. "Well, if I got it right, then this one is thurisaz." He pointed at one of the runes that looked kind of like a triangular capital *D*. "Which supposedly symbolizes change or maybe cleansing fire." He rubbed tired eyes. "Each freaking letter has so many meanings. How are you supposed to know which interpretation to use?"

"It's all in the context," Ulf said. "You'll figure out what they all mean once you have the full set. That's why archeologists don't interpret a rune stone until they've pieced together most of the slab."

"Wonderful," Scott grumbled. He pointed at the second match. "And this one is ansuz." This rune looked like a capital *F*, but the horizontal lines sloped downward at a forty-five degree angle. "It also has a ton of meanings, including a revealing message or truth."

Ulf studied the rocks. "Each rune can also symbolize a god. Ansuz stands for Odin, and thurisaz stands for Thor."

"Wonderful." Scott threw up his hands. "This will take forever since every single freaking letter can mean more than a dozen things. What kind of alphabet is that? Why didn't they just invent more letters?"

Ulf grinned. "Like I said, it's all in the context once you have them all pieced together."

Scott threw him a disgruntled look. "You are absolutely no help."

"You need a break. Come and help me search Kari's room."

"Why?" Scott asked, wondering why the Valkyrie was all of a sudden under suspicion. "What did she do?"

"Nothing," Ulf said, already striding toward the door. "I'm trying to figure out what she and Pekka have in common. I'm searching the room he stayed in next."

Scott looked down at the rocks that littered the table. He didn't think he could stomach another minute of staring at the pieces. "Sure," he said and followed the Viking out the door.

They only had to walk down the hallway a few doors to reach the Valkyrie's room. He wasn't sure what he had expected of her room, but the starkness of Kari's little abode surprised him.

Ulf studied the small room. "Well, it shouldn't take us long to look through this." There were basically four things to search through: a twin bed, a nightstand, a closet, and a chest of drawers.

"Do we need to look for things she may have hidden?" Scott asked, eyeing the vent in the ceiling. "Do I need to get a screwdriver?"

Ulf looked up at him and then turned his head to follow his line of vision. "Nah, that's the kind of shit Astrid or Naya would pull. The two of them are the most secretive people I know. We're just looking for what Kari and Pekka may have had in common. Something that connects them to the same place or maybe even eating the same food." He scratched his chin. "Shit, I don't really know what we're looking for. I just want to find something."

Scott shared that sentiment. "I'll do the closet." He walked over and opened the folding doors. Shirts and jeans hung in a neat row with a few cardigans and a couple of dresses mixed in. Two pairs of combat boots, a pair of sneakers, and a pair of dressy sandals were lined up on the floor of the closet. He felt a little pervy going through a woman's clothes without her permission. Oh crap. Would they have to dig through her underwear? He side-eyed the dresser. He'd leave that one to Ulf.

"So," the Viking drawled. "Want to talk about whatever is going on between you and Irja?"

"Nope." Scott stuck his head as far into the closet as he could. He worked on looking as busy as possible while patting down Kari's clothes.

"Want to discuss what it's like living with a berserker inner warrior?"

"Nope," Scott shouted without turning around. Talking was way overrated. He much preferred his normal way of dealing with problems: ignoring them until they went away. All men were familiar with this method. Why wasn't Ulf using it?

Unfortunately, it didn't take very long to search through Kari's clothes, and eventually Scott had to come out of the closet, so to speak, and face the Viking in the room.

Ulf was searching the nightstand.

Dammit, that meant he'd have to pilfer through Kari's stuff in the dresser. He liked women's underwear as much as the next guy, but it just felt wrong going through the Valkyrie's private things without her knowing about it. He opened the top drawer. Phew, nothing but socks and T-shirts.

"Hey," Ulf said, and Scott turned around to find the Viking studying him with a serious face. "We really should talk about Irja."

"We really shouldn't," Scott countered. Had the Viking crushed on Irja just like he'd apparently had a thing for Astrid? Was that why he insisted on bringing her up all the time? A stab of jealousy hit Scott's chest, and then a wave of rage flooded his senses. "Why do you keep bringing her up? Stay the fuck away from her," he grunted.

Ulf smirked. "And that is what it's like to have a berserker inside you when you think someone is edging in on your girl."

Fuck. They were back to the other topic he didn't want to discuss. He closed his eyes and took a few deep breaths. The violent anger that had risen so quickly slowly subsided. Scott did not have a temper. If anything, his sister complained he was too laid-back and let people take advantage of him. But Naya had such a short fuse that her opinion wasn't exactly objective. "Why do you have this keen need to talk about everything? Did you go through counseling training or something?"

Ulf smiled. "Believe me, I like ignoring problems as much as the next guy. But this is important. How much do you know about Irja's background?" He sat down on the bed.

Scott closed the drawer he'd been searching—nothing but clean shirts and socks in it—and leaned against the dresser. "Just what she's told me. She grew up among the Sami people in Finland, and she's been back in Midgard for a few centuries. Why? What is it you think I need to know?" He'd done quite a bit of research on the nomadic Sami people who lived way up north in Norway, Sweden, and Finland. Everyone thought of them as reindeer herders, but throughout history, they had been so much more. During the Viking age, they'd been known as the best ship builders, and many of the ships that sailed across the sea on marauding trips had been built by Irja's people.

"It's not so much what I think you need to know as what I need you to do."

The heat of anger rose in Scott again, and he crossed his arms over his chest. "What *you* need *me* to do?"

Ulf held up his hands, palms out. "Hey, calm down. I'm not infringing on your turf here." He shook his head. "Odin's ravens, I had forgotten what it was like when the berserker was newly awakened. Add to that the possible beginning of a *själsfrände* bond, and you are well and truly irritable today, aren't you?"

"What the fuck are you talking about? What *själsfrände* bond?"

Ulf shot him a look full of pity. "Here's the thing. It's obvious—at least to me—that you have strong feelings for Irja."

Scott opened his mouth to tell Ulf it was none of his business, but the Viking held up a hand.

"Just hear me out. The only two cases we know of a mortal acquiring a berserker are Queen Naya and Astrid's Luke. Both of them ended up with inner warriors a short while after they became bonded with their *själsfrände*, their soul mates."

Scott's knees gave out, and he slid down to the floor, his back against the dresser. He hadn't thought about the fact that Luke and Naya both had berserkers. Oh holy shit, emphasis on the holy, both Christian and Norse. Could it be that he actually did have an inner warrior? Something wasn't right. The passing out. The extreme emotions. The howling, for fuck's sake.

But *själsfrände*?

That was even more messed up. His sister hadn't exactly shared the intimate details of how she'd activated the bond with King Leif, but she had made it clear intimacy was definitely involved. He shuddered. Thinking about his sister having sex was not a pleasant notion. He switched to think about Irja instead. There had been intimacy, that weird attraction between them that made his skin sizzle whenever she touched him. And there had been that strange rumbling inside his chest when she'd taken care of his injured shoulder.

Oh fuck. Had that moment been when the berserker first showed up?

He rubbed the back of his neck and peered up at Ulf. "I haven't even kissed her."

Ulf quirked an eyebrow. "Shit, battle brother, there must be some potent pheromones between the two of you if you've triggered a *själsfrände* bond without any true physical contact." He leaned forward, elbows on knees. "You need to be careful with Irja. As strong as she is, she's also fragile. She's always been a bit of an outsider because she's half Sami. She's definitely my battle sister and one of the Norse warriors, but there has always been prejudice against the Sami, and some of the older warriors in the tribe have made it clear they think less of her."

Scott's blood heated again at the thought of someone treating Irja unfairly. "Who?" he barked. His heart ached at the thought of Irja having to deal with any discrimination.

The Viking grinned at him. "I fully approve of your berserker, but you don't have to concern yourself about that now. It has been dealt with. What you have to worry about is completing the bond."

Scott frowned. "What else is there to do?"

Ulf barked out a laugh. "Well, you might actually enjoy this part. You have to bed her properly."

Scott's face flushed red to the top of his hairline, both from anger and embarrassment. He was not going to indulge in some kind of warrior locker room talk with Ulf. "That is definitely none of your business." He started to stand up, but Ulf leaned forward farther and pushed him back down. Shit, the guy was strong.

"Calm down." Ulf was all business now, his voice serious. "I'm not trying to engage you in some kinky dirty talk here. In order to complete the bond, you and Irja have to actually sleep with each other. And you have to complete the bond—there are no other options."

"Why?"

"Because if you don't complete the bond, Irja's berserker will go into permanent battle fury. She'll be a danger to all of us. She'll be recalled to Valhalla."

He'd lose her forever. The thought chilled him to the core. "This is something I should discuss with Irja."

"Of course, but if you have any questions, you can ask me. I wish I could say what happens to you if the bond doesn't complete, but the truth is we don't know if a mortal would also be claimed by Odin. You may just…you know, die."

Scott shot him a look. "I'm not asking you about how to bed Irja."

"About the bond, you idiot." Ulf grinned. "But if you need pointers on that other matter, I could be of assistance there as well."

"Not a chance," Scott said. "Plus, we don't actually know the bond has been triggered. The berserker may just be some sort of weird thing happening because I have spent so much time with all of you."

"Like inner warrior by osmosis?" Ulf arched a brow.

"Sure," Scott said, getting a little excited. "That could be it."

Ulf ran a hand down his jaw. "Yeah, not very likely. There is, however, a sure way to check."

"How?"

"If you've triggered the bond, a serpent's tail will appear on the back of Irja's hand. It will be faint at first but then fill in and twist up her arm until it connects with the head she already has on her bicep."

All the Vikings had a snake head tattooed on their non-dominant arm. Or as they called it, the arm other than their sword arm. Even his sister had a tattoo now that had appeared after she and Leif had been handfasted—engaged.

"Okay, got it." He'd make sure to check out Irja's hands when he next saw her.

"One more thing." Ulf got in his face. "If you hurt her in any way, I will mess you up. Badly."

Scott nodded. That was fair. Not that he would hurt Irja or that he would take an ass-kicking without fighting back, but he understood Ulf's position. He felt the same way when Naya met Leif. Actually, he felt the same way should *anyone* hurt Irja or Naya. "Shall we finish searching the room?"

"Yeah." Ulf turned back to the nightstand.

Scott's neck tingled, and an image of Ulf collapsing flashed through his mind. "Stop," he shouted.

The Viking froze.

Scott walked over to where Ulf was standing. He slowly opened the drawer in the nightstand. The two of them stared down at the stone fragments laying inside. Scott had just spent the better part of the day trying to piece together bits of rock just like these. "I thing we've found what connects Pekka and Kari and what made them both sick."

Ulf swallowed loudly. "Oh fuck," he said. "I can't tell you how glad I am for your Spidey sense, but I'm afraid that this time, it's too late."

Scott silently agreed. It wasn't just Pekka and Kari who had touched the stones.

So had he and Ulf.

And so had Irja.

CHAPTER 11

IRJA RESTED HER HEAD BESIDE HER BROTHER'S STILL body. She rubbed her arms for warmth and winced at how clammy her skin was. From how achy her body was, she knew she was running a slight fever. She needed sleep but couldn't calm her mind enough to get any rest. After rerunning all the tests on the samples from Kari and Pekka and still not finding anything, her frustration was edging into panic. Today was Loki's deadline, and she wasn't sure how to approach her own impending doom. Should she spend her last hours continuing her work for Pekka and Kari, even though she had no clue what to do next, or should she try to get as far away from the fortress as possible so Loki couldn't hurt any of the other warriors?

Lifting her head, she peered at her brother's face. His features were relaxed, his breathing even. She reached for his hand. In contrast to hers, his skin was dry and warm, perfectly normal. *Everything* about him was perfectly normal except for the fact that he just wouldn't wake up. She stroked his face with her free hand. They'd been estranged for a century because she wouldn't use her magic to save a girl he'd been in love with. A promise to her dying mother—a mother who had despised…no…hated her—caused her to lose her twin brother. They'd found each other again thanks to Naya, but Pekka had been back in her life now for only two years. A tear trickled down her cheek. She couldn't lose him again. They hadn't had enough time together.

She gripped his hand more firmly and closed her eyes. Straightening her spine and squaring her shoulders, she centered herself through a few deep breaths. Her mother was dead and buried, but Pekka was here with her. She would break any promise to make sure her brother stayed by her side. Opening up the connection with her berserker, she tried again to connect with Pekka's inner warrior. Her beast growled in protest but tried its best to find her twin's battle spirit. Where Pekka and his berserker had before been warm presences in her consciousness, there was now cold darkness. It was like looking into a void.

Undeterred, Irja planted both feet on the floor and relaxed her shoulders further. She maintained the open connection with the berserker and then tapped into another awareness, one she hadn't fully used since she was a teenager. The berserker growled as she reached with her mind for the basalt that surrounded the Viking fortress. Inside the ancient volcanic rock rested layer upon layer of power that it had absorbed through the ages. She opened herself up completely, expecting cool blue and green strands of energy to meet her. Instead, there was a great empty space between herself and the magic. She couldn't get a grasp on what separated her and the basalt's power. There wasn't a barrier, but when she moved toward the power in her mind's eye, it slipped away. She felt the pulsing throb of the magic, but it was out of reach.

Pulling on her connection with the berserker, she tried to draw the power to her. Her inner warrior snarled and roared but couldn't help her find a way to reach the magic. Irja let go of her brother's hand in case his condition somehow blocked her. Perspiration beaded her forehead. She stood up and raised her arms and palms together in a classic vessel of power pose, but still the energy was beyond her reach.

Defeated, Irja sat again. She slowly closed off the senses that would have opened her up to the magic and then the connection with her berserker, which whimpered, so she soothed it before placing a more restrictive leash in place. When she opened her eyes again, the room looked exactly as it had before. Pekka and Kari lay unnaturally still in their beds, calmly breathing in and out. Irja's own breath was rapid and shallow, each inhale and exhale echoing loudly in her ears. Her heart beat rapidly, and sweat poured down her face and neck. Her muscles quivered as if she'd just run sprints.

She'd lost her magic.

For hundreds of years, she'd fought so hard against her natural abilities and taught herself to resist the temptation of reaching for unlimited powers when she wanted to heal a patient or fight an enemy. And now that she had finally allowed herself to open up to her true nature, the energy eluded her. If there wasn't so much at stake, she might have laughed.

How would she cure her brother now?

While running all the tests, somewhere in the back of her mind, she'd counted on the magic as her last desperate resort if everything else failed. She sank forward and folded her arms on her brother's bed, her head resting on top of her arms. She had failed him completely. When Loki came for her, she'd meet her death as a failed Valkyrie healer who couldn't even cure her own brother, despite at one time being powerful enough to raise the dead.

Irja allowed the tears welling up in her eyes to fall unimpeded. She eventually dozed off and wasn't sure how long she'd been out when the chime of an incoming text on her phone startled her.

It was from Naya, asking her to join her in the king's office.

She went into the en suite bathroom to wash her face. Before she left, she stroked her twin's cheek. "*Veli*, I am so sorry to have failed you." She choked back the tears threatening to spill again and headed out to meet her queen and inform her that all hope was now lost.

Irja was surprised to arrive at the door of the king's office at the same time as Harald, Leif's *stallare* or second-in-command.

His green eyes watched her solemnly, and his red beard was as bushy as ever. "How are you today, Healer?" He gave her a small bow, the informal way of showing respect.

The gesture surprised her. Harald and she got along now, but there had been a time when he'd been very opposed to her being part of the Viking tribe. It had gone as far as the man accusing her of treason. "I am fine, *Stallare*," she said but didn't return the bow, even though technically he was of a higher rank. It wasn't that she held his previous behavior against him. Actually, that was exactly it. She wasn't out for revenge, but she definitely hadn't forgotten his accusations. "Do you know what news the queen wants to share with us?"

Harald shook his head. "I didn't know the queen would be in this meeting. I received a summons from the king." He held the door open for her, and she entered ahead of him.

Leif was sitting at his big oak desk. Behind him were four huge stained-glass windows depicting various scenes from the Sagas, the Icelandic books that were the only written records—except for rune stones—of the tales of Norse men and women from the Viking age. The king had tied back his blond shoulder-length hair, and his ice-blue eyes focused on Irja with their usual intensity. Leif had a way of looking at someone like they were the only one in the room. His gaze could be so cold, you felt as if it would freeze you in place, and it could sizzle—as when he looked at his queen—which made you want to leave the room to escape the heat.

Naya lounged in one of the three visitor chairs in front of the desk. She sprang up when she saw Harald and Irja. "How is your brother?" she asked, hugging Irja tightly. The queen looked a little better than the day before, but Irja still made a mental note to run tests on the blood sample she had collected. If something was wrong with Naya, she needed to let the king and queen know before Loki made it impossible for her to be of any use to the Viking tribe.

"No change." Irja's voice broke, and she cleared her throat.

Naya gave her an extra squeeze before letting go. "Come, sit by me," she said, leading Irja by the hand to the chair next to the one the queen had occupied.

Irja clasped the queen's hand briefly before letting go. Her friend's support made her feel marginally better.

Harald took the remaining seat, and the three of them faced the king expectantly.

He focused on Irja again. "I am sorry about Pekka and Kari. Anything you need to cure them, you just ask. All our resources are available to you."

Irja thought about how all hope was gone now that she

could no longer use magic, but she swallowed the lump rising in her throat. "Thank you, *min kung.*"

Naya reached for Irja's hand again. "My friend, we have news. It is both good and bad." The queen hesitated. "Or maybe just bad, I don't know."

"Just tell me." The situation couldn't really get any worse.

The king leaned forward and placed his hands on the desk. "Ulf and Scott are on their way back here."

Irja's heart did a little leap when he said Scott's name. She forced it to beat regularly again. Now was not the time to be distracted by her infatuation with the queen's brother.

"They think they have figured out what made Pekka and Kari sick," he continued.

Irja sat up straighter. "What is it?" If she could get a sample of the plant, the food, or whatever it was that had made her brother sick, then she could develop an antidote. She was sure of it. "Can they bring me a sample of what poisoned them?"

The king's eyes softened. "They found a fragment of flint with parts of engraved runes in Kari's room. It looks like she had it in her pocket when she was brought back to the Sedona mansion, but it was overlooked in the chaos that erupted when she fell ill."

The stones? "But I tested them," Irja said. "There was no poison on the fragments." Her shoulders slumped. Not poison, but she had felt traces of something else when she studied the stones. Magic. Warped and terribly wrong. "They're not toxic, but they are still dangerous." She should have known the rocks could have been the origin of the disease. The fact that it hadn't dawned on her before now made her feel even more useless.

Harald leaned forward in his chair. "I don't follow. You tested them for poisons but didn't find anything. So how are they harmful?"

"The same way the glowing cage kept the Viking warriors from entering," Irja answered.

Leif's intense gaze sharpened even more. "Magic."

Irja nodded.

Naya held up a hand. "Wait, what? We're fighting the black arts now?"

"*Jävlar helvetes skit.*" Harald tugged at his beard. "The gods have always been up against the black arts when it comes to that bastard half god, but now Loki's using magic in the human realm. That has to be forbidden by the Norse gods' council." He looked at the king. "Odin and Freya must be able to step in now."

Irja flinched. The Scandinavian people considered magic the dark arts of Loki and therefore inherently evil.

"Hang on a minute," Naya exclaimed. "Am I the only one who thinks it's crazy we're discussing spells and shit?"

As always when he looked at her, Leif's whole face lit up with the love he had for his queen, even when they were discussing serious matters. "The Norse gods can do magic. It's just not allowed in Midgard anymore." He turned toward Harald. "The Norse gods' council is still dealing with infighting and power struggles. They won't think a few human deaths warrant a confrontation with Loki. A human life span is but a blink of an eye to them."

"Fuck." Naya slumped back in the chair. "We're up against abracadabra and indifferent gods." Her gaze moved from Leif to Harald and then to Irja. "So if the gods can do magic, does that mean you can too?"

Harald shook his head. "Not the way the gods can. There are wise men and women among the Vikings who can make potions and tell fortunes, but their magic is not as powerful as the gods." He turned toward Irja. "Our own healer is able to wield some magic when it comes to curing our warriors."

"That is from practice and research, not magic," Irja hastened to say. "Scott has also touched those stones, as have I." She felt bad for reminding her queen of the danger to her brother, but it was an effective way of changing the topic. Pekka knew how strong her magical abilities were...had been, but she'd never shared that with any of the Vikings or Valkyries. There hadn't been a point to doing so since she would never use them again.

"Shit," Naya said. "As if he hasn't suffered enough. Now he'll be back in the sick bed."

"Have faith, *älskling*," Leif said to his queen. "Ulf has touched the rocks as well, and that is why he and Scott are both on their way here. I asked them to bring the fragments. We don't know yet if they'll react to them. I am confident Irja can find out how to reverse the rocks' effect. Scott was able to match up a few of the symbols, and they are most likely from the Elder Futhark rune alphabet."

Harald leaned farther forward to look at Irja. "Can you match up the remaining rocks so we can read whatever curse they spelled out?"

Irja avoided his gaze. "I am not a sorceress. I don't know how to reverse curses." Another lie, although it was actually true now. She had lost her magic ability.

"We're relying on your incredible research abilities rather than hoping you can somehow morph into a spell caster," Leif said. "If we can figure out what message or

curse the stones spell out, maybe you will remember something you've read in one of your ancient books."

Irja relaxed a little. "It will take ages to piece together the
broken fragments in the correct pattern." A wave of nausea
suddenly swept through her body, and she took a deep
breath when her vision wavered.

"Are you okay?" Naya asked. "You put too much pressure on yourself. I am worried for my brother, as I am for
your brother and Kari and Ulf, but none of us will have a
chance if you don't take care of yourself."

Irja waved a hand and swallowed. "I'll be fine," she lied.
If Loki's spell didn't kill her, the half god himself would
when she told him he couldn't use her to funnel power. She
was going to tell him no before she'd lost her magic, but now
he'd actually shot himself in the foot—so to speak—with a
rock. She giggled.

"You don't seem okay," the king said. "When was the last
time you slept?"

"I've had a few minutes here and there."

"The queen is right," Harald said. "We don't know whether
this spell will affect all of us, but you have to take care of yourself or the lack of sleep will make you sick in other ways."

Irja thought about his words. Maybe touching the stone
fragments was why she could no longer tap into magic. She'd
felt the strands of the Arizona magic just fine and almost drew
some of it inside her. That had been before she'd touched the
broken rocks. She shook her head, both to clear her thoughts
and to dismiss Harald's concern. "I will rest when I have
examined Scott and Ulf." Actually, she would rest after Loki
killed her. Magic or no magic, the half god would end her
time in Midgard now that she had no magic to aid his portal.

"Well, I don't know shit about spells," Naya said. "But I do know about pattern recognition and can help with matching up the remaining stones. If we take pictures of the fragments, I can write an algorithm based on this alphabet Scott has identified and let the computer come up with the most likely letter combinations."

"That's brilliant," Harald exclaimed.

Leif just smiled at Naya, his eyes glowing. There must have been some hidden message in his gaze, because the queen blushed. "It's what I do." She shrugged. "We'll most likely get a lot more results than we'd like, but hopefully, a bunch of them will have word combinations that read as nonsense, and we can concentrate on the ones that have some kind of meaning."

Irja perked up a little. With the computer doing the matching, they may have a chance of getting at least a few results before Loki insisted on another meeting. It wasn't much, but at least the Viking tribe could continue to search for a way to break the curse after she was gone. "When will Ulf and Scott get here?" She needed to distract herself with work and think of her friends and her brother as patients. If she allowed personal feelings to cloud her mind, she would get nowhere. She'd always been able to compartmentalize and keep emotions locked down, deep down. Somehow, that was harder now that she knew she would not see any of the people she cared about after this day ended.

The king checked his watch. "They're about an hour out."

Harald stood. "I'll help with the research. I don't know much about the ancient texts, but I do know how to read."

The king stood as well. "Let's get all the warriors ready

to help with research." He turned toward Naya. "*Älskling,* how long will it take you to write the algorithm?"

"I'll get started on it right now. It should be a simple pattern recognition program. I'll have most of it done by the time the guys get here."

"Let's get to it," the king said. "We will defeat Loki yet again."

Irja sure hoped so. They'd been fighting Loki's minions in Midgard for centuries now, and hopefully her death would prevent him from entering Midgard physically.

She went straight from the king's office to the bedroom Kari and Pekka were resting in. Sten, the youngest of the Vikings both in terms of how long he had been in Midgard and how old he was when he first arrived in Valhalla, had been watching the two patients while she'd attended the meeting.

"Any change?" she asked the dark-blond Viking automatically, even though she knew what the answer would be.

Sten sat in the chair she herself had occupied not so long ago. His smoky-gray eyes were sad as he answered her. "No. They are so peaceful, which somehow makes the whole thing much worse."

Irja nodded. "You can go now. I need to prepare for Ulf and Scott's arrival."

Sten's eyebrows shot up. "They are coming home?"

In her sleep-deprived state, she'd forgotten the news might not have reached everyone yet. "They figured out what's causing this sickness." She gestured toward her sleeping brother and Kari. "Unfortunately, both Ulf and Scott may also be"—she paused to find the right word—"infected." She didn't want to use *cursed.* It felt too foul in her mouth.

"Then you might need two more beds," Sten said. "I will arrange for them." He stood, and then bowed to her. That was the second time she'd been honored today. If she wasn't so tired and filled with dread, she would have smiled.

CHAPTER 12

SCOTT HAD WATCHED ULF LIKE A HAWK FOR ANY SIGNS of fever during their entire journey back to Washington State. Leif had sent a helicopter to pick them up at the mansion in Sedona and take them to the local airport. Then they'd taken a private jet to Pine Rapids, where Per and Sten had picked them up in a black Escalade. They were almost back at the fortress, and so far Ulf had not shown any sign of succumbing to the sickness.

"Stop staring at me," the tall blond Viking growled.

"I'm not." They were both sitting in the back seat while Per drove. Scott felt just fine but didn't want to sit in the front seat in case Ulf all of a sudden fainted or started sweating or had convulsions. All those things could possibly happen, judging by how the disease had affected Pekka.

"I can feel you eyeing me," Ulf said without turning. "And that goes for you too." He shot a look forward, presumably meeting Per's eyes in the rearview mirror. "If I start feeling bad, I will tell you."

Sten harrumphed from the front seat. "Like that one time when you got shot in the leg and kept fighting for another thirty minutes until we'd defeated all the wolverines." He briefly turned around and raised his eyebrows at Scott before facing the road again. "We didn't know he was bleeding until we got back to the fortress and Irja chewed us out for not noticing his pant leg was soaked in blood. We couldn't tell since he was wearing black pants. He even hid the limp from us when walking from the car to the front door."

"It was just a scratch," Ulf grumbled.

"Sure," Sten countered. "One that had you on bed rest for two days after Irja dug out the bullet that had embedded in your shin bone."

Ulf shrugged. "I healed."

"Is there ever a time when you guys don't heal?" Scott wasn't being sarcastic. He really wanted to know. The Vikings got hurt like normal people—well, not really like regular humans because they kept fighting after receiving wounds that would slay anyone else, as evident from Sten's story about Ulf's bullet wound. But they did bleed and somehow healed incredibly fast.

Sten kept his eyes on the road as he answered. "We don't actually know for sure. I assume we could bleed out if we didn't get to a healer in time." He shot a look at Ulf, who was still pointedly staring out the side window. "Which is why Irja was upset when Ulf was shot."

Ulf looked at Scott and sighed as if it pained him to have to join the conversation. "Supposedly, we can be killed by beheading, according to some of the old texts Irja has read. Maybe a straight shot or stab into the heart would also do the trick." He smirked. "We just fight too well to let anyone get the chance to find out."

"Why do you ask?" Per wanted to know.

"Yeah, are you planning on executing one of us?" Ulf smiled to take the sting out of his words.

"No, I just wondered because I've always thought of you as immortal, but Irja is very worried about Pekka and Kari. It just hadn't occurred to me that one of you could die."

Ulf nodded. "I guess a curse would do the job. Maybe it's just that we can't be killed by violence because theoretically, that would be an honorable death and therefore send us back to Valhalla. So that half god bastard Loki had to use something as cowardly as a curse."

"I almost died," Per said. "The wolverines were using poison on their claws. The king and I both succumbed. He recovered, but I wasn't strong enough." He looked at Scott through the rearview mirror. "Your sister's blood saved me."

"Do you think Naya's blood could help Pekka and Kari?" he asked.

"I think Irja would have tried that already if she thought there was a chance," Ulf replied.

Crunching gravel under the SUV's tires alerted Scott that they had turned off the main road and were nearing the fortress. The woods around the Viking dwelling were shrouded in spells. It didn't make the place invisible, but regular humans instinctively avoided the area.

"Looks like we have quite the greeting party," Per said.

Leif, Naya, and Irja were all standing on the front stoop. Naya, much shorter than the others, was making up for her slight five-foot-six height by bouncing on the balls of her feet. She rushed down the stairs as the car came into view and had the door on his side of the car open before they came to a complete stop. Grabbing his face with both hands, she stared into his eyes. "Are you okay?" She moved her hands to his neck. "Any fever? Your glands don't feel swollen."

He could barely breathe as she kept probing his throat with her thumbs. "I'm fine." He grabbed her hands and broke her stranglehold. "At least I am now that I can breathe again."

She smiled at him. "I'm just worried. You're finally well again. I don't want to—" She blinked furiously. "I'm glad you're here."

He let go of her for as long as it took to unclip his seat belt and step out of the car to hug her properly. "I've missed you, Neyney," he said, using his childhood nickname for her.

"And I you," she mumbled into his chest before gently pushing away. "How's Ulf?" She tried to peer around to the other side of the car where the Viking had just exited.

Scott focused on his sister's face. "You look a little pale. Is everything okay with you?"

"Not you too." Naya shook her head. "I'm fine, and Leif's on my case about eating right and sleeping enough, so I don't need you to nag me too. Let's get back to how Ulf is doing. He's the one who touched cursed rocks, not me."

Scott let her change the topic but made a mental note to ask Irja about Naya. His sister had never been sick as far as he knew. "He's not showing any signs of sickness."

"Yet," Naya said under her breath and pushed the car door shut. As soon as she did, Per drove away to park the SUV. She took a few steps until she caught up with Ulf. "Are you feeling okay?"

The tall Viking's arms waved in the air like windmills when Naya treated him to the same examination she had given Scott. Scott hid his laugh behind a cough and watched the Norse warrior try to get out of the queen's choke hold. "I'm fine," Ulf said, firmly removing Naya's fingers from his throat. He covered up the action with a bow over her captured hands before releasing them. "Do not worry about me, *min drottning*. I am not yet showing any signs of the disease."

"Good," Naya said. "Then let's get to work. I've finished writing the pattern recognition code, but we need to take pictures of all the stone fragments. Did you bring them?"

Ulf blinked a few times at the fast change in topic but recovered quickly. "I did."

"No time to waste then." Naya grabbed his arm and dragged him up the stairs and into the fortress.

Scott followed behind, his eyes on Irja, who was still standing to the side of the door at the top of the steps. She looked even paler than when he'd last seen her. Her dark eyes stood out starkly against her white skin. A low rumble reverberated deep in his chest and traveled up through his throat.

Irja's eyes widened as she watched him stride toward her.

Shit. I actually growled at her. Ulf and Finn's nonsense about berserkers must have really gotten to him.

Leif, who had stepped down the stairs and was walking toward Scott, stopped midstride. His head swiveled between Scott and Irja. A slow smile crept over his face, and as he shook Scott's hand while clasping his shoulder, there was a glint in his eyes. "Welcome back, brother," the king said. "Naya and I are very glad to have you back. I hope you stay for a long while before dashing out on another out-of-state mission." He looked over his shoulder toward Irja, and his smile widened. "We would like you and your new inner warrior to stay a very long while."

He squeezed Scott's hand for emphasis, and something clicked and then vibrated inside Scott's body. It was as if a cable had been connected, pulled tight, and then flicked like a thick guitar string. For a short moment, he saw a glowing web in his mind's eye with a bright light in the middle. He didn't know how, but somehow he knew that the glow in the center was Leif.

The weird vision disappeared when the king dropped his hand. "I will join Naya and Ulf to watch their computer wizardry." Leif nodded once to Scott, climbed the stairs, and then repeated the gesture to Irja before disappearing into the fortress.

Scott bent to grab his and Ulf's bags, and then walked up the steps to the Valkyrie who occupied his thoughts every minute of every hour of every day. He dropped the bags and moved as if to take her hand but changed his mind midgesture and dropped his arm by his side again. "How are you? You look tired." He cursed himself silently. Yeah, that was the right thing to say to a woman you hoped to impress. Point out how out of sorts she looked. He sure was a winner.

Irja didn't seem to take offense though. Her gaze moved over his face and down his body. "Don't worry about me. It's more important to find out how you are doing. You've been in contact with the rock fragments more than I have."

This time, he did reach for her hand. When their fingers made contact, that same click he felt when the king touched him echoed deep inside him. But then it turned into something close to a purr. Great, now he was a freaking cat. "I do worry about you. I worry about you all the time, even when there are no cursed rocks around to make us sick." He tried for a smile.

Irja stared at their clasped hands. "It can't be," she murmured on a breath.

"What can't be?" Scott asked, but then, in a moment

of clarity, he knew exactly what she meant. "You feel that strange vibration inside you too, don't you?"

She pulled her hand from his grip. Uncertain laughter spilled from her lips. "I'm so tired, I don't know what I feel." She swept a hand over her forehead. "I want to examine both you and Ulf to make sure you are okay." She looked away. "And if you are not, it will give me a baseline from which to measure the progress of the disease."

Scott swallowed a sigh. She was not going to discuss this weird connection they shared. Fine. He'd get her to admit it eventually, but now wasn't the time, when she was so obviously distraught about her brother and Kari. And potentially him and Ulf. "Let me take a shower first," he said. "It will clear the travel dust both from my body and my mind."

Irja nodded and preceded him into the fortress.

Scott's room looked the same as when he'd last left it. Someone had dusted it, but all his books were in the haphazard stacks he'd arranged in the bookshelves that took up a third of one of the walls. He'd always been an avid reader and didn't discriminate between fiction and nonfiction, as evident by the many volumes on astronomy and history that fought for space with science fiction, thrillers, graphic novels, and even a few romance novels on the shelves. He dumped his and Ulf's bags on the floor next to the queen bed that, together with two small nightstands, took up most of the space in the room.

He hadn't used the need to wash up as an excuse to avoid being examined by Irja. True, he had wanted some breathing

room since his reaction whenever she was near both confused and frustrated him. But also, even though their travel
had been done by luxury transports, his constant worrying about Ulf had taken its toll. And he'd secretly second-
guessed every cough or twitch he himself had experienced.
So far he felt fine, and he hoped because he'd been able to
enter the wolverines' glowing cage when the others had not,
Norse magic just didn't work on him. He was well aware this
was false hope; if the immortal Vikings who could withstand
anything—including bullet wounds—fell ill from the curse,
chances were that Scott would succumb to the symptoms
soon. Pekka had fallen ill in less than a day, so the fact that
Scott and Ulf were still standing was a miracle in itself.

Scott shed the rest of his clothes and stepped into the
attached bathroom. The showerhead had several different
settings, and he chose one that offered high-pressure pulses.
In combination with a water temperature close to that of
ice, it wasn't long before Scott felt very much awake and
alert. After the shower, he toweled off quickly and had just
stepped into a pair of clean boxer briefs when there was a
knock on the door. Ulf must have come for his bag.

"Come in," Scott called out and continued drying his
hair. He stopped midrub as Irja entered.

"Oh," she said, blushing. "I thought you said it was okay
to come in."

Scott blinked rapidly, trying to get his brain to engage,
but all he could do was stand there like a fool. "I thought
you were Ulf." He shook his head, and the stupid piece of
terry cloth fell to the floor. "I mean, I did say it was okay to
come in. I just wasn't expecting you. I thought we'd agreed
I'd come to your lab."

"I can wait for you there." Avoiding his eyes, Irja reached for the door handle.

"No. It's okay. I'm ready." He rushed forward to stop her leaving. "I'll have to take at least my shirt off again anyway, so we may as well do the examination here." As soon as his hand touched hers, the same wild feeling he'd had when he first arrived and they'd touched came over him again. His heart raced and his nostrils flared. Everything but Irja faded away. She was his whole world. She meant everything.

Her pupils dilated, and she inhaled quickly. "I don't know. I—" She shook her head as if to clear it.

"You feel this too," Scott insisted, his voice several octaves lower than normal and strangely raspy. He had wanted to give her more time to get used to the idea of the two of them being close. All those good intentions flew out the window now. He couldn't resist their attraction any longer.

Correction.

He didn't *want* to resist their connection any longer. He may slip into a coma any minute because of the cursed stones, and this time he may not wake up. Leaving this earth without having a chance to be with Irja was suddenly not an option.

"It doesn't matter," Irja shot back. "We don't have time for this."

Anger like he'd never felt before rose in his chest. How could she dismiss this? This connection, this spark between them was the most important thing in his world right now.

Mine, something growled deep inside him.

Before, the strange rumblings in his chest had felt like they were from something other than himself, but now he realized the growl was a part of him, a deep presence he suddenly recognized.

He agreed. Irja was his.

Somehow, he needed her to understand that whatever this was between them, it wasn't something she could escape. It wasn't something *they* could escape.

He lifted her hand and twisted his own so their palms met. Entwining his fingers with hers, he pulled her closer and slid his other arm around her back. She was almost as tall as him, the top of her head reaching the bridge of his nose. "We have no choice in this," he said, lowering his voice to a grave whisper. "You're going to have to make time for this. Make time for us."

She dropped the bag she was holding in her free hand, but she didn't resist him. "My patients need me. I have more tests to run."

He released her hand and trailed the knuckles of one hand down the side of her temple and cheek. "I know. Everyone needs you." He looked her straight in her beautiful dark eyes.

She met his gaze, but swallowed loudly.

He spread his fingers and caressed her throat. Slowly drifting his hand lower, he slipped his fingertips under her blouse and massaged her collarbone. "You do so much for all the people in this fortress. And so much for the other tribes. But for once, let me do something for you."

Irja moaned, and the sound turned into a rumble in her chest. Her head fell to the side, allowing him access to her throat.

The wild thing inside him answered with a growl of its own as Scott bent to kiss the skin just below her earlobe.

He continued massaging her collarbone, trailed his fingers lower to caress the skin at the swell of her breast.

Her mouth fell open, and she expelled a deep sigh. "It feels so good, but we shouldn't—"

"Shh," he whispered against her neck, planting a small kiss on her jaw. "You should allow yourself to feel good." He kissed her again. "Let me make you feel wonderful."

She tensed up for a moment, and he loosened his arm around her back, prepared to let her go if she wanted to. He held his breath, waiting to see what her decision would be. The seconds that ticked by seemed like the most important in his entire life.

When she sighed a small whimper and melted against him, a whoosh of relief burst from his lungs. He claimed her mouth with his, their tongues mating in an intricate dance. His cock strained against the boxer briefs that were fast becoming tight and uncomfortable.

Irja slid her arms around his neck, and her fingers caressed the back of his head. She tugged on his hair, and the fabric of his briefs was about to rip open when his erection jumped in response.

Scott deepened the kiss, and Irja's tongue met his thrust for thrust. He'd never been with a partner who was this responsive to his unspoken cues, someone who matched him this perfectly. Being in a coma for years had severely limited his sexual experience. He'd woken up a virgin, but once he'd been strong enough he had made up for lost time with one of his fellow patients and one of the nurses at the convalescence home. And when he joined the tribe, he'd accompanied the Norse warriors on some of their "wenching" excursions.

But this felt different. This felt so good. This felt right.

He'd fantasized about having Irja in his arms from almost the first time he'd met her. But he never could have predicted how perfect this moment would be. It was as if his soul recognized hers, and for the first time in his life, he felt completely content. If he slipped into unconsciousness tomorrow, so be it, but let him properly love this amazing woman first.

She raked her fingers through his hair and shifted so her tight body pressed against his erection. Scott had to concentrate to not come right there and then. He started reciting the planets of the solar system in his head. Why weren't there more of them?

He slid his hands behind Irja's back and lowered his arms so he could feel her perfect ass. When he gripped her and shifted so her groin pressed against his cock, she moaned.

He started listing the named suns in the Milky Way galaxy to keep from exploding.

CHAPTER 13

FLAMES LICKED IRJA'S SKIN, AND SCORCHING LAVA flowed through her veins. The berserker purred like a lion sunning itself and then growled for more. More skin-to-skin contact. More heat.

Scott trailed kisses down her throat and then licked her collarbone. When he pressed his hard member against her heat, Irja knew she'd explode if she didn't get out of her clothes. She needed him inside her. Now.

She released her grip on Scott's neck, barely remembering to be gentle with his shoulder. She tugged her blouse out of the waistband of her jeans. Tearing at the buttons, she tried to also slide off her boots and stumbled when the leather footwear wouldn't cooperate.

Strong arms gripped her elbows and steadied her. "Slow down." Scott chuckled and captured her mouth in a long kiss. "I'll help you," he whispered before trailing his hot lips down her neck again and stopping on the strip of skin bared by the two undone top buttons of her blouse. His breath teased her cleavage, and her nipples tightened into hard buds that scraped against the soft satin of her bra.

Irja groaned, pulling him closer. At first he resisted but then pressed against her and backed her up toward the bed. The mattress hit the backs of her knees, and she sat down automatically.

Like a cold shower, the jolt pulled her out of her feverish trance of desire. She looked up at Scott. "We need to think about this," she said. This was crazy. She couldn't bed her queen's brother no matter how much she wanted him. Or how delicious he looked in nothing but his underwear.

He leaned over her, sliding his arms up to her shoulders, his palms caressing her biceps on their way. "You think too much." A wry smile stretched his lips. "But I'm not going to coerce you. This has to be your decision."

She was mesmerized by his tanned, muscular chest. A small white scar marred an otherwise perfect left pectoral muscle. Irja frowned and traced the mark with her fingertip. "What happened here?"

Scott's abdomen contracted as he hissed at her touch. He captured her hand under his palm. "You can't touch me like that, sweetness. Not if you want me to be able to resist you."

Irja stared at their hands pressed together against his skin. The steady beating of his heart drummed under her fingers. He was so alive and such a perfect specimen of a man. He was kind and honorable and so very sexy. She shouldn't indulge herself in the pleasure of his body. It was absolutely the wrong thing to do. He had been her patient, and he was her queen's brother. The berserker growled its displeasure at her thoughts.

Mine, its voice whispered in Irja's mind. She jumped. Never before had the beast *spoken* to her.

"Did I hurt you?" Scott asked, releasing her hand. He crouched before her, his eyes searching her face. "I'm sorry. That is the last thing I want to do."

"No," Irja whispered, lost in his dark-blue eyes. They were always warm and kind, but right now they blazed with desire as well. That heat matched her own lust, which kept building despite her attempts to curb it. All these feelings were too overwhelming. She needed to do what she always did when her rational side wasn't in control. She needed to close down her emotions.

Mine, the berserker whispered again. It crouched, impatient, ready to leap at any moment.

She closed her eyes and tried to send her inner warrior to slumber, but in her mind's eye the beast shook its head, refusing the command. The warmth of Scott's hand on her knee made her open her eyes again.

"Hey," he said. "Are you okay?"

The concern she saw in his eyes nearly undid her. This man, this wonderful man wanted her physically but was also emotionally tuned in to her. "I'm not good with feelings." The words blurted out before she could stop them.

He smiled. "You're in good company. Neither am I."

Her fingertips itched to touch him. She reached out and stroked one silky black curl above his ear and then moved her hand to cup his cheek. "You're so beautiful," she murmured. Her inner warrior purred.

Scott blushed, but the heat in his eyes flared up. "I think that's my line."

She leaned forward to taste his lips but stopped just shy of making contact, enjoying his breath mingling with hers for a moment. She moved her hand down to the scar she'd touched earlier. The smattering of hairs adorning his chest felt deliciously coarse against her fingers.

His pupils widened and his nostrils flared. A growl rumbled deep inside his chest.

Her berserker answered.

"How is that possible?" she whispered, leaning back slightly. "You're mortal, but there is a beast warrior inside you."

Scott shook his head. "I don't know. It just appeared." He reached up to tuck a stray strand of hair behind her ear. "Ulf and Finn think it has something to do with how much I've trained with the Norse warriors. Or maybe it's a latent effect from Naya bonding with Leif."

"I've never heard of a secondary effect from a *själsfrände* bond, but then Vikings bonding with mortals is new." She touched the scar again. "You didn't tell me how you got this."

"A stray wolverine claw." He captured her hand in his again, an unspoken question in his eyes.

Her inner warrior's response should worry her since only the berserker of a *själsfrände* would normally behave so responsively to another's. But she and Scott were not mated. If they were, the beginning of the Midgard serpent's tail would have showed up on her hand after their first physical intimacy, like a kiss.

She paused and in her mind recited all the reasons why she should not continue to physically explore this wonderful man. This brave, caring, sexy man. Making a decision, she opened her eyes. "Kiss me," she whispered. This would be a onetime thing. She would most likely die within the next twelve hours, and leaving Midgard without knowing what it would be like to bed Scott would be a big regret. For once in her life, she'd let her emotions take over and just follow them wherever they led.

He hesitated, obviously not prepared for her words. She pulled on one of his chest hairs and smiled when he hissed and then frowned at her. "Kiss me," she repeated more firmly.

"Yes, ma'am." He leaned forward and captured her mouth with his.

She set the pace of their kiss and pulled him down with her as she reclined on the bed. She moaned as she felt his body against hers.

His berserker howled its pleasure. Scott let go of her lips and looked down. "Hell, this thing is such a nuisance."

Irja laughed. "Welcome to my world."

His eyes crinkled as he smiled back at her, and she felt a pang somewhere deep in her chest. "I love being in your world," he answered and leaned in to kiss her again. His clever hands made quick work of unbuttoning and opening her blouse.

The coolness of the air against her skin contrasted exquisitely with the hot kisses he trailed along her neck and down to her cleavage. He nuzzled her nipples through the satin fabric of her bra and her hips bucked off the bed.

Scott pushed her back down with a chuckle and threw a leg over hers, anchoring her in place. She whimpered when his mouth returned to pleasure her breasts.

His hands unbuttoned her jeans and lingered on her zipper for an excruciating amount of time. "I've waited a long time for this." He finally pulled down the metal clasp and then leaned back to pull her jeans down her legs. "These first though," he said when the denim got caught on her boots, and then he made short work of freeing her feet from both them and her socks. The jeans followed, and her legs were finally bare and free. To her disappointment he left the bed, but only for a short moment to lock the door. He returned and kneeled at her feet, his hot gaze traveling over her body. She was inordinately happy she'd worn matching lavender satin underwear that day instead of the practical cotton she donned under her fighting leathers.

Still tangled in her shirt, Irja wriggled to get loose. The fabric ripped, but she didn't care. She needed his skin against hers. Reaching out her hand to him, she implored him without words to get closer.

He was still sitting on his knees beside her feet, staring at her. "You're so beautiful," he said. His chest heaved as he took a deep breath. "This is more than I had ever imagined."

The heat in his gaze made her feel powerful and desirable. "You've imagined us together?" she asked.

"You have no idea how often I've wished for this." Pinkness tinted his cheeks as if he'd said more than he meant to.

Emboldened by his words and the hot blaze she saw in his eyes, she leaned up on her elbows, aware of how the position pushed her chest out. "Wished for what exactly?" she challenged, nudging his leg with her foot.

"Irja." He leaned back and caught her foot in his hand. His nostrils flared again and his berserker rumbled. "I want to go slow, but I don't know if I can control this thing inside me. It's trying to take over." The wildness of his berserker glittered in his eyes.

Her inner warrior threw back its head and howled, responding to the hunger she saw in Scott's gaze.

"I don't want you to go slow," Irja said in a hoarse voice.

Scott's eyebrows shot up. "What if I hurt you?"

She sat up, cupped the back of his neck, and claimed his lips in a deep kiss. She stroked the inside of his mouth with her tongue before she captured his lower lip between her teeth and lightly bit down. They were both breathing heavily, and she could feel his neck muscles tense under the strain. She leaned her forehead against his. "You will never hurt me," she whispered, absolutely certain of her words.

He leaned back. His gaze searched her face as if convincing himself of the truth. "I would never forgive myself if—"

She interrupted him. "It will never happen. Your berserker is part of you. It's your wild and primitive warrior spirit. But it is still you, and you would never hurt your lover." She would never be able to explain to someone else why she was so certain of this, but deep in her soul, she knew he was noble and honorable. A true warrior.

He must have believed her, because he nodded slowly.

"Now, can we please continue?" She allowed some of her own berserker to appear in her eyes.

The savage warrior peeking through Scott's eyes focused on her with an intensity that thrilled her, and still the foolish man hesitated. "I don't know if I can hold this beast back."

She wanted to scream out her impatience, and her berserker howled with its own hunger. "Don't hold anything back." She nibbled his collarbone and then kissed it to take the sting out of her bite. "I want all of you, beast and man."

He claimed her so fast, she barely had time to catch a breath before he pushed her back and kissed her. Planting one hand by her head, the other snaked behind her back and unclasped her bra. The silky garment was quickly pulled off, and then his lips sucked one nipple while his hand and fingers matched the caresses of his tongue and the nips of his teeth on the other.

Irja moaned loudly as heat shot from the tips of her breasts straight to her core. Liquid warmth filled her center. She twisted slightly so she could get a hand on his briefs. Massaging his cock through the cotton, she purred when she felt how rigid and wide it was.

He grabbed her wrist and held her hand still. "I won't last long if you continue that."

"I told you I didn't want to go slow."

Scott gave her a heated look before reaching across her to one of the nightstands. He had to lean over her head to open the drawer, and she bit his nipple as it came near her mouth. He pulled back and kissed her lightly. "Careful with those teeth."

"Did you get a condom?" she asked.

"Yes." He held up the foil package.

"Good." She reached down and pulled off his briefs. As his cock sprang free, she smiled. *Finally.* She closed her fingers around its delicious hardness.

Scott groaned, his head falling back.

It didn't take more than a slight push to get him flat on his back on the bed. When she leaned over and put the tip of his cock in her mouth, he bucked and then lightly grabbed her hair, holding her still. "If you do that, I think this will be over too fast even for you."

She laughed, surprised at how much joy there was in that sound. She tilted her head, looking up at his face. "Do you have an alternate suggestion?"

His eyes turned dark and predatory. "Get rid of those panties."

She wriggled out of her now damp undergarment while he made quick work of covering himself with the condom.

He rolled her over, bracing himself above her by placing one hand on each side of her head. Staring down at her, he smiled slowly before leaning down to kiss her.

She gripped his shoulders, trying to pull him closer, but the infuriating man resisted her. As a Valkyrie, she was stronger than him, and she was about to show him who was really in charge when he whispered "You're mine" against her lips and entered her in one swift motion. Delicious friction enhanced the sensation of him filling her to the fullest.

When he pulled out and repeated the motion, the heat that built between them overpowered all her senses. She whimpered in the back of her throat. Waves of pleasure radiated out from her core through her body. The intensity increased as she bucked her hips, meeting Scott thrust for thrust.

He leaned down and sucked one of her nipples into his mouth.

She opened her legs wider, grabbed his ass, and pushed him deeper inside her.

When he captured the other nipple with his lips, she forgot how to breathe. The waves of pleasure flooding her body intensified even more and focused on one important center. Her entire world became this man, here and now in this room, on this bed.

Scott tilted slightly to the side and pulled her leg over his hip.

As he thrust into her, hitting exactly the right spot, a powerful surge of ecstasy swept through her. She screamed out her release as her inner warrior threw back its head and howled.

She felt Scott's chest rumble as his berserker answered, and then the man also cried out as he climaxed.

A second swell of pleasure flowed through Irja, and for one glorious moment she and the berserker were one being, all their senses combined and focused on the man who collapsed beside them on the bed. *Mine*, the berserker growled, and Irja shared the sentiment.

She pushed her hair back, took a deep breath, and then exhaled. Turning her head, she found Scott watching her, his eyes filled with an emotion that scared her with its intensity.

He blinked, and whatever he'd felt was gone. "You okay?" he asked.

"Very." She smiled at him.

"I have to dispose of—" He gestured toward his crotch.

"Sure, thank you." She yawned, suddenly incredibly tired.

He laughed out loud. "No, sweetness. Thank *you*." He caressed her cheek and then left the bed.

The air felt cold against Irja's skin, so she crawled under the covers. She'd just rest for a moment and then do the medical examination she'd come for in the first place. Then again, what they'd done had been so much more enjoyable than a checkup. Her lips stretched in a lazy smile, and she was asleep before Scott returned from the bathroom.

Dripping water woke her what felt like hours later. Scott must have had another shower or hadn't turned off the sink faucet properly. She shivered as cold air swept over her skin, and she reached for the covers, but only cold, wet stone met her probing hand. Her eyes flew open. She was lying naked on damp ground surrounded by stone walls. Flaming torches attached to the walls illuminated tendrils of water sliding down their surface. That was the source of the dripping she'd heard.

She shivered again. The air was humid and chilly. Pushing off from the floor, she stood and wrapped her arms around her to ward off the cold and cover her chest and crotch.

Hard footsteps echoed in the distance, the sound growing louder as they came closer.

Irja suppressed the chill that rippled through her body—it had nothing to do with the frigid air.

She knew who was coming for her.

CHAPTER 14

LOKI ENTERED THE CAVE DRESSED IN FULL ANCIENT battle gear. A double-bladed battle axe hung across his back. He'd grown a beard since their last encounter. Or maybe he just made facial hair appear at will. The dark auburn strands on his jaw were perfectly sculpted. "Ms. Vainio. How nice of you to join me." He smiled, but there was nothing friendly in the expression. "I've been summoning you for some time, but somehow you've found a way to block my invitations." He sounded perfectly pleasant, almost bored, but a tick in his jaw gave away the anger he tried to hide.

Irja forced herself not to take a step back when he focused the full force of his hazel eyes on her. The pupils were still human. "I am afraid I'm at a loss to even hear your invitations, never mind refuse them." She inclined her head slightly. Didn't hurt to be polite in case that would delay him killing her.

He studied her closely for several moments. "I can't tell if you mock me or if you're telling the truth, Ms. Vainio, and it displeases me." He took a step closer and looked her up and down. Irja fought hard to suppress the shiver of unease rippling through her body. The trickster god circled her with small, precise steps that echoed off the cave walls. "There is something different about you. Something lacking."

Irja kept as still as she could and said nothing. He'd probably be able to detect an outright lie, but that didn't mean she would give him information freely. "I'm sorry to displease you so," she said. "Perhaps it is my clothing you find lacking. As you can see, I am slightly underdressed." She lifted her chin, refusing to let her nakedness make her feel vulnerable. She could fight no matter what she wore—or didn't wear.

"I can see that." He stopped in front of her and pushed a stray strand of hair behind her ear. His fingers were dry but cold, and bile rose in her throat when he turned the gesture into a caress. She had to close her eyes to force it back down. When she opened them again, the half god's gaze had turned lewd, and he trailed it down her body, stopping at the arm covering her breasts. "I quite prefer you in this state of undress, but never let it be said that I am a bad host." He gestured in the air, and a thin homespun cotton shift covered her. It reached down to just below her knees.

She slowly lowered her arms.

"Even in clothes, there is much about you that pleases me." Loki still leered at her chest while he let his fingers trail down her upper arm.

She wanted to cross her arms again but stopped herself. She wouldn't give him the satisfaction of knowing he scared her. Instead, she forced her arms to stay by her sides, knowing he could probably see the outlines of her nipples through the thin cotton. She raised her chin higher and stared him down. "I do not allow anyone to touch me without permission."

Loki threw his head back and laughed. "Such spirit in you." He leaned closer. "But you are weaker since I last saw you. What has happened to your strength?" He raised his hand but stopped midair, his fingers hovering by her temple. "May I?" he asked. The tone of his voice and an arched eyebrow mocked her.

She inclined her head, knowing if she said no, he'd touch her anyway.

He put his middle and ring finger against her temple. This time, his skin was warm against hers. She expected some sort of pain to shoot through her head, but there was nothing. Just the slight pressure of his fingers.

The trickster god frowned and took a deep breath before closing his eyes. He pushed a little harder against her temple, and his forehead smoothed out.

Irja held her breath, steeling herself against whatever mental assault he would launch, but there were still no signs he was inside her mind.

Loki's eyes flew open and flashed the elongated pupils of a goat. Rage blazed in them as he stared at her. "What have you done?" he bellowed. His hand moved lightning fast as he gripped her by the throat, lifting her into the air.

Irja grasped his wrist with both hands and struggled to breathe. She couldn't answer his question even if she wanted to.

"You have emptied yourself of magic," Loki screamed. "I sense no power whatsoever in you."

Despite her predicament, Irja wanted to laugh. She had indeed lost her magic, but that was all his fault. Something of her mirth must have shown in her face, because Loki squeezed harder on her throat. She clawed at his hand, raking it with her nails and leaving trails of blood on his skin. Blackness danced at the edge of her vision as she struggled for breath.

She grew weaker by the moment and instinctively reached for the pressure point on his wrist. It was awkward from her current position, but she dug her fingers in the groove where the blood vessels passed by the underside of his wrist, using her thumbs on the top as leverage.

Apparently, a half god in human form shared their physiology, because Loki's grip loosened, and he dropped her hard on the floor. She fell on her hip, and the impact shot deep pain through her bones. She braced herself against the damp ground as she filled her lungs with delicious oxygen-rich air.

"You've marred my perfect skin," Loki bit out through clenched teeth.

She looked up at him but could only cough in reply as she gasped for air. He'd been about to squeeze the life out of her but was somehow miffed she'd defended herself? He may have human anatomy at the moment, but empathy and reason were not part of the form he'd created for himself.

Loki held up his arm, the torchlight revealing the long scratches with which she'd decorated his forearm. She felt a deep satisfaction that she'd caused him if not pain at least discomfort. She may die in this cave, but she'd drawn blood from her enemy, and that would make it an honorable death. She'd wounded a god—well, half god—and she'd done so without using magic, which made the moment even sweeter.

Her satisfaction was short-lived. Loki's wounds quickly knitted themselves together, and perfect, smooth skin once again adorned his arm. Big droplets of his blood glistened in the torchlight illuminating his arm, and he looked around the cave with a peeved look on his face as if he couldn't believe there wasn't something for him to use to wipe it. His gaze stopped at her where she lay on the ground.

She flinched as he reached down, and satisfaction

gleamed in his goat eyes as he grabbed the hem of her shift. She pulled her legs up to kick out, but all he did was wipe blood on the white cotton that was now also stained with mud and goddess knows what. She didn't want to think about all the different creatures that could have left excrement on the floor of the cave.

"You fight well, Irja." He seemed calmer now that she had showed weakness. "I, of course, expected nothing less from a Valkyrie." He shifted his position so his face was right above hers. "But then you're not a true Norse, are you? You're half Finn, so you're only half a Valkyrie."

"And you're only half a god." Irja regretted the words as soon as they left her lips, but it was too late.

The slap Loki delivered snapped her head to the side. Her cheek slammed into the ground so hard her ears rang. He grabbed the front of her shift and pulled her up close to his face. "I am half nothing," he hissed between clenched teeth. "I am as powerful as any god, more powerful than most. You should remember that if you want to live."

Dizziness from the blow made it hard to concentrate on his words, but she focused on the part where it seemed like she had a choice of coming out of this alive. She wanted to see Scott again. The thought of him awoke a deep longing inside her, and her berserker, who had been silent up till this point, snarled quietly.

Loki tilted his head and peered closer at her. "Oh, so there is some spark of power still inside you." He stood and lifted her up to her feet by the grip he still had on her gown. "Let's explore this a bit more." He shook her. "Tell me what happened to your magic," he demanded.

"The stones with the inscribed runes," Irja choked out,

willing to cooperate more now that she knew he hadn't completely made up his mind to kill her.

He frowned. "What stones?"

The grip on her shift loosened, and she stumbled back. She remained bent over with her hands on her knees, trying to find both her center and her breath. "The rocks that the wolverines used to create the portal cage." She looked up at him. "I touched them and lost my magic."

"Those were used in Arizona. Why would you come in contact with them?" A frown marred his perfect brow, and he scratched his handsome beard.

"I was in Sedona trying to cure one of the Valkyries who had succumbed to whatever curse the wolverines invoked with the runes."

"Odin's balls," he bellowed. "Those fucking dimwitted wolverines. They were supposed to collect and destroy the rock fragments after they created the portal."

"They were killed before they could completely destroy them." Irja couldn't keep a smirk off her face. Her warrior tribe was stronger than Loki had thought.

"The cage is impenetrable to any of the Norse warriors. How did they reach my servants?" His focus on her intensified.

Freya's crazy wagon-pulling cats. She'd given away more information than she should. If Loki figured out Scott had breached the cage walls, he would target the queen's brother and maybe Naya herself as well.

Something of her fear must have shown on her face, because Loki tilted his head and took a step toward her with a determined look on his face. "You will tell me," he demanded. He stalked closer, pulling the axe from his back.

Irja scuttled back, her hands bracing for the attack to come. The fight would not last long, but she would die knowing she had protected Scott and her queen the best she could.

Loki raised the axe. A few more steps and he'd be within cleaving distance.

She opened wide the connection with her berserker, willing the beast to take over her body and do as much damage as it could to the half god. Her inner warrior answered the call, but instead of the battle cry she expected, it howled a long and grim cry. The desperate sound escaped through her lips and reverberated between the cave walls, keening on and on.

Somewhere far away from outside the cave, a similar roar answered.

Loki stopped midstep, an astonished look on his face as he stared at her with his axe still held high. "What—"

She didn't hear the rest of his words, because the cave and the half god faded away, and she found herself back in Scott's bedroom. Back on the bed and in the safe embrace of his arms. Her berserker finally stopped howling, and Irja took a deep breath before releasing all the air in her lungs. She collapsed in her lover's arms as the tension abruptly left her body.

Scott held Irja tightly, letting out the breath he'd been holding since he woke up to her flailing and kicking in her sleep. He'd been shouting her name until his voice grew hoarse, but nothing would wake her. As a last resort, he'd grabbed her shoulders and shook her, but she still wouldn't open her eyes.

And then she'd disappeared.

Just flat out vanished into thin air while his hands grasped at nothing.

The beast inside him had been frantic and let out a howl that sounded almost like a shout of pain. It had repeated that screeching horrible noise over and over again while it tried to claw its way out of the mental cage Scott had scrambled to assemble in order to keep the berserker from taking control of his psyche and his body. Ulf and Finn had passed on enough rudimentary information in order for him to get a leash on the inner warrior, but it was obvious he would need some more training. His body was covered in cold sweat not just from his panic over Irja disappearing but also the effort it had taken to control the berserker.

When Irja's inner warrior had finally answered, it sounded as if she was very far away, but then she'd appeared in his bed again as suddenly as she had disappeared. And his berserker had finally calmed down and stopped its screeching.

He wanted to squeeze her as hard as he could so she wouldn't be able to vanish again, but he took a deep breath and forced himself to relax his arms so he wouldn't hurt her. She looked up at him with dark eyes that looked way too big for her pale face.

"Fuck," he exhaled. "You scared the shit out of me."

Irja blinked a few times. "I'm sorry. I—" She looked around the room. "You brought me back."

"I woke you up," Scott corrected her. He still couldn't bend his mind around the whole disappearance thing. He preferred to think that was something he had hallucinated.

And yes, he did recognize how childish and futile that was.

He was deep in a world of inner beasts and magical curses. Someone having a nightmare that made them disappear did not seem like that far of a stretch. But still, there was living with things that were weird and then there was handling outright insane things.

"No," she said. "I wasn't sleeping. I was in a cave with Loki. He was about to kill me, but your berserker called to mine, and that brought me back."

There was a lot to unpack in those sentences, but right now, his brain couldn't handle it. As long as she was safe and sound and where he could touch her, he was okay. He hugged her tighter and then frowned. "What are you wearing?" When he'd slipped into bed with her after disposing of the condom, she'd been asleep and naked. He remembered because he'd enjoyed spooning her, skin to skin.

Irja looked down the length of her body at the muddy homespun gown that reached to her knees. "It's something Loki conjured for me." She rubbed her eyes and studied his face. "How did you bring me back?"

"I don't know." He shifted so he half sat up against the headboard, pulling her up with him. She settled her cheek against his chest. Scott stroked her hair and waited for his heart rate to return to normal.

Well, that of a man with a strange inner beast inside him.

He couldn't remember a time he'd felt as panicked as he'd been just a few moments ago. The beast inside him still paced back and forth, which might explain why his heart was still trying to jump out of his chest, but at least the inner warrior wasn't trying to claw its way out anymore. "My berserker went…well, berserk…and kept howling for you."

She looked at him. "I could hear it." Her hand trailed

down his chest. "In the cave with Loki, I could hear it answer my inner warrior's shout for help."

He peered closer at her face. "Is that a bruise on your cheek?" He bit back a curse and had to clamp down on his mental connection with the inner beast as it roared in anger.

She put a hand up to her cheek. "Loki hit me."

Scott's berserker growled, and he wanted to join in. "He did what?" He sat up straighter. "Tell me all of it. Start from the beginning."

Irja scooted up so she sat next to him against the headboard. "I think we should get everyone else together first so I only have to tell the story once." She looked over at the bag she'd brought. It was still by the door where she'd left it. "I never gave you the exam I came to administer."

He put his arm around her and drew her closer. "I don't really care about that right now. I'm obviously functioning just fine at the moment."

She pulled away and scooted off the bed. "Let me at least take a blood sample so I have a baseline in case you succumb to the curse." Irja walked over to the door and retrieved the bag.

Scott got off the bed too. He'd put on his boxer briefs before getting into bed with Irja, so at least he wasn't completely naked as he faced her. "What's going on?" He could feel her emotionally shutting down. She was all business again, as if they hadn't just had the best sex he'd ever experienced and she disappeared into thin air. "Why are you pulling away?" His berserker whined as if it too could tell she was withdrawing.

She looked at him, and for a brief moment he could see everything she was feeling in those gorgeous eyes of hers, but then a veil came down and she was looking at him the way she had when he was nothing but her patient. "Our brief respite is over. If we're going to defeat Loki and reverse the curse, I need to take samples. I need to know what I'm up against."

She'd turned all cold and logical again. Even though he recognized this was her way of coping with the stress of this impossible situation, his jaw clenched so hard he could hear his teeth grinding against each other. He walked toward her and deliberately stood too close, crowding her. She fiddled with her bag, and he used the tip of one knuckle to lift her chin so she'd look at him again.

"We," he said and waited until she met his gaze properly. "What *we* are up against. You are not fighting this battle alone. Whether you like it or not, you and I are now a team." He shook his head. "No, we are more than that. We are a couple."

Her cheeks turned pink and she looked away. "This was a onetime thing. It can't happen again."

He held out his arm so she could take the damn blood sample. "Oh, it will happen again," he said. "You can count on it. I know it. Our berserkers know it. So you may just as well get used to it too."

He'd finally gotten her to let down her emotional walls. She'd *finally* joined him in bed. No way was he letting her sabotage their relationship now, no matter how much she wanted to protect herself emotionally and hide behind work and duty.

She was his.

The berserker bellowed its agreement.

CHAPTER 15

By the time Scott had managed to gather Leif and Naya in the king's office, dawn's first rays of sun made rainbows on the floor as they shone through the massive stained-glass window that took up most of the wall behind the king's desk. He had resolved nothing with Irja before she left his bedroom. She had taken that sample of blood and paused only long enough to ask him to wake the king and queen and also Astrid and Luke. Before he'd been able to ask her any more questions, she'd scurried out of his room, mumbling something about taking a shower.

The people she'd requested were now waiting for her to appear, as were Ulf and Harald. Scott had also included Ulf because he figured the Viking had a right to know what was going on since he was most likely to succumb to the curse next. And Harald was there because the king didn't hold official meetings without his red-bearded second-in-command. At least that was how Harald preferred it. Apparently, the ginger Viking had the stereotypical temper associated with red hair.

Naya and Harald sprawled in the chairs in front of the big desk but had turned them slightly so they could see the people sitting in the three couches flanking a big coffee table on the other side of the room. Ulf was on one couch by himself, and Astrid and Luke were cuddled up together on another. The mortal man with silver-blond hair and the warrior Valkyrie made a striking couple. Scott was very fond of Astrid ever since she'd saved him from the wolverine kidnapping. However, she tended to act like another big sister—an extremely bossy one—so he avoided conversations with her. Astrid's mouth stretched in a huge yawn that she tried to cover with her hand.

Scott had opted to lean up against the mantel over the fireplace. The adrenaline rush from Irja's nightmare and disappearance still lingered in his muscles, and he was too jumpy to sit. He turned back to study Naya again and frowned as he looked her over. She looked pale and wan, more than what the early hour should have caused.

Naya caught him looking at her. "What's gotten your panties in a twist?" she asked.

"Nothing," he muttered, knowing if he said something about her not looking well in front of the others—especially in front of Leif—she'd just dig her heels in and refuse to discuss it. His sister was not only a magnificent fighter and computer coder, her stubbornness was legendary. He would approach her about it later when it was just the two of them.

His berserker did a goofy leap whenever he looked at Naya, and something must have shown on his face, because her eyebrows shot up as she met his gaze. Before she could say something, Ulf decided to drop one of his usual idiotic statements into the conversation.

"So Irja came to see you in the middle of the night and asked you to wake us all and come here?" The Viking's tone and facial expression were too casual and too innocent. Scott regretted including the bastard in the meeting.

"Yep." Scott crossed his arms over his chest. The gesture was meant to get Ulf—and anyone else with impertinent questions—to shut up. It didn't work.

"Interesting," Astrid interjected, her jade-green eyes glittering with mischief. "Her room is all the way down the hall from you." She dragged out the word *all* longer than necessary. "It seems like she would have knocked on one of the doors closer to hers to get this emergency meeting organized." Luke nudged her with his elbow. "What?" she asked, turning to her *själsfrände* with fake innocence plastered on her face. "I'm just asking."

Luke rolled his eyes and shook his head.

As the only other mortal male in the room, Scott kind of felt a kinship with the dude. The fact that he had Scott's back made him like the guy even more. He met Luke's gunmetal-gray gaze and nodded his thanks.

"There's probably a perfectly innocent explanation for why Irja talked with Scott so early in the morning," Luke said. "Or maybe a not-so-innocent explanation." He grinned at Scott.

Scott mentally put Luke's name on his shit list, just under Astrid's and above Ulf's. The Valkyrie was currently in the number one position, but that might change. The list would probably grow and be rearranged as the meeting progressed.

"Where is Irja?" Leif asked. "Is she okay?" There was no teasing or humor in his voice. He assessed Scott with ice-blue eyes that could have frozen a fjord and covered the nearby mountains in thick glaciers.

"She's fine now," Scott answered and then silently cursed himself for letting that last word sneak out.

"Now?" Leif and Harald echoed while Astrid, Luke, and even Naya were on instant alert, glaring at him.

His berserker grunted a warning at the perceived threat. How could they possibly think he'd ever hurt Irja?

Fuck, even his own sister wanted a piece of him.

He clenched his jaw and held up his hands in the universal sign of surrender. "I think she wants to tell you herself."

Leif put two palms flat on the desk and stood. "You will tell us now. Is Irja hurt?"

Shit, his brother-in-law was big. Scott swallowed and forced his berserker to stand down. "She's fine," he hurried to assure the king. "I promise she is unharmed except for a bruise or two."

Now Astrid stood as well. "Bruised?" she bellowed. "You bruised her?"

The anger he'd tried to keep under control now flooded his senses. His inner warrior went on full alert and howled. "I would never hurt her," he yelled back at Astrid, taking a step toward her. That made Luke instantly jump off the couch, in battle stance next to his mate, ready to back her up.

Astrid took a step toward Scott, and when his berserker growled louder, her eyebrows shot to her hairline. "Fuck," she whispered.

Scott looked around the room. Everyone was staring at him as if he'd just performed the most amazing magic trick. Everyone except for Leif and Ulf. Those bastards looked smug as fuck. "What?" Scott asked. "What did I do?"

"You have a berserker," Harald said.

"He does," Ulf confirmed. "Finn and I noticed it when he fought with us in the Sedona desert."

"Isn't that interesting," the king said, looking at Naya, who was beaming a full-wattage smile at Scott as if he'd just gifted her with a million-dollar winning lottery ticket.

"Wow," his sister said. "This is more than I could ever have hoped for."

Oh shit. This situation had gotten out of hand at the speed of light. Irja would not like the conclusion Naya would draw from this. He was fairly certain his sister had just entered full matchmaking mode and thought Scott had acquired a berserker from a *själsfrände* bond with Irja. Not that he would mind that, but the inner beast had shown up before they'd had sex, and as he understood it, there had to be some sort of intimacy before a couple's berserkers bonded.

Just then, the door opened and Irja entered the room. Everyone's heads immediately swiveled her way. "What?" she asked. "What happened?"

"Scott has acquired a berserker," Naya said. "Just like Luke did when he became Astrid's *själsfrände*."

Yep, there it was. His sister's mind had taken exactly the path he'd predicted. Scott sighed inwardly.

"And like you did when you became Leif's," Ulf pointed out, grinning at Scott. Unhelpful bastard.

"It's not what you think." Irja took a seat on the third and still empty couch. "Scott had his berserker before—" She shot Scott a horrified look.

"Before what?" Astrid asked with a smirk.

"Before I arrived from Sedona, just like Ulf said," Scott said. His eyes were still locked with Irja's, and she sent him a small grateful smile that lit up her face. Even tired and with a bruised cheek, the woman was so beautiful—no, that wasn't the right word. It was too limited and didn't cover the full effect she had on him. She was striking, smart, driven. He couldn't look away from her.

She was perfect.

The berserker purred in agreement, and Scott rubbed

his ribs as the unfamiliar sound spread tingling vibrations through his chest.

Luke's loud laughter startled him, and he turned toward the ex-marine who had sat back down. The dude bellowed out his glee. "Scott, my friend, you are a goner."

Harald and Ulf joined in the laughter, and then Astrid added her cackle. Leif only smiled broadly, but his shoulders shook as if he had trouble containing his mirth. Even Naya giggled loudly but tried to hide it by turning her back to him. His own sister a traitor.

Irja glanced away from him and seemed very fascinated by her hands in her lap. Her cheeks flushed pink.

Scott fisted his hands and was about to yell at the whole collection of assholes when Naya noticed Irja's discomfort. "Hey," his sister said and walked over to sit next to her friend. "It's a good thing. If you're bonded with my brother, we'll be even closer sisters."

Irja held out her left hand. "We're not bonded." Her skin was smooth and clean, not a snake tail tattoo in sight anywhere.

Scott swallowed the disappointment rising in his chest. It didn't matter whether the crazy Norse bond was in place or not. Irja and he belonged together. They didn't need a magical tattoo to mark up her perfect skin to prove it.

Astrid cleared her throat. "Um, remember how it took a while before the Midgard serpent's mark showed up on my hand?"

Luke grabbed her tattooed hand in his, which had a similar mark. "Yeah, but we decided that's because you're so stubborn."

Astrid raised her eyebrows and tilted her head toward Irja.

Luke looked over at the dark-haired medical officer. "Oh, good point," he said, flashing Irja an apologetic smile. "I'm sorry, but you pretty much match my warrior Valkyrie in stubbornness."

Harald and Ulf chuckled but quickly covered the sounds with fake coughs as both Astrid and Irja shot them dark looks.

Leif held up a hand. "Let's remember why we're here so early in the morning. Irja, what happened to your cheek? Who hurt you?" He flashed Scott another fjord-cold stare. "And tell us the full truth. You are among friends, and we will protect you."

The king's ice-blue eyes focused on Irja, and although her cheeks still felt warm from the group's teasing, she met his gaze and prepared to tell her story as calmly as possible. She hated being the center of attention, and the confrontation with Loki had scared her badly. Her nerves still felt tender and raw, although the shower she'd grabbed before the meeting had helped her composure a little. She glanced briefly at Scott. The fact that the queen's brother had been able to bring her back from her nightmare was both comforting and worrisome.

There was no time to analyze the Scott situation now. She sat up straighter. She needed to come clean to her warrior tribe about having magical abilities and tell them what she had learned from Loki. "Somehow, Loki has figured out a way to communicate with me when I sleep."

Harald stood. "For how long? Why haven't you reported this threat?"

Leif moved around the desk and put his hand on Harald's shoulder. He pushed his second-in-command back down in the chair. "Hear Irja out and determine what the actual threat is before you attack," the king said. "She's an experienced warrior and knows how to assess a situation." His gaze turned slightly frosty when he looked at Irja as if he was warning her that she better know whether a threat should be reported or not.

Irja swallowed. She hated to disappoint her king. "It's happened twice, once on the plane here and once last night." Scott made a choking sound, but she ignored him.

Naya grabbed her hand. "Are you okay? Did Loki hurt you?"

"I'm fine." Irja smiled to reassure her queen—and friend. "The first time, he spouted off a bunch of threats. This time, he got angry and hit me." Scott opened his mouth as if to interject, but shut it again when Naya shot him a look.

"Tell us the whole story," the queen requested, then turned to face Scott. "And control yourself. Stop interrupting."

He scowled at his sister but kept quiet.

Irja quickly summarized the dream meeting she'd had with Loki while on the plane from Sedona and then recounted what had happened in the cave. She skipped some details, such as how close she'd come to dying and how much Loki striking her had hurt, but didn't hold back when it came to him targeting her because of the magical abilities. She did, however, leave out how Scott's berserker had called her back. There was no need to share that she'd been in the queen's brother's bed while having the dream.

When she finished, she couldn't look up. She didn't want to see how her battle brothers and sisters would look at her now. How Scott would look at her. Seeing the disgust and fear on their faces would be too much.

Stunned silence filled the room. For once, even Astrid—the resident wiseass—was out of words.

All her life, Irja had been "other." Not Finnish and not Sami but an odd mixture that neither culture could accept. Add to that her weird abilities, and she'd always been viewed with suspicion and fear. With the immortal warriors, she'd finally found her tribe. But even with them, she hadn't been able to share all of herself. Only her brother knew her completely, but now she was going to lose him because she'd been too proud to use her magic. She'd been too scared that one of the Vikings or Valkyries would get hurt. Because that was what happened when she used her abilities. Someone close to her was maimed or died.

If she was honest with herself, she also hadn't wanted to tell them because she knew they would view her differently and she would once again be on the outside looking in. The friendships she had found in this group, especially the bond she had with Astrid and Naya, meant too much to her. She hadn't wanted to risk losing that.

The silence in the room grew heavier.

"Fuck," Harald finally whispered, and Irja looked up. The king shot the redheaded Viking a warning look. "What?" Harald said. "We were all thinking it. Irja's been able to do magic this whole time, and we could have used it as a weapon, but she didn't want to share it with us."

"Shut your trap." Astrid stood. "She's shared it with us every single time she's healed one of us."

"No," Irja protested. "The healing is all training and modern medicine."

"Oh please." Astrid rolled her eyes. "You are an incredibly skilled physician, but do you seriously think all the wonder cures you've handed out over the years had nothing to do with your magical abilities?"

Naya nodded. "She's right. We've always known you have these amazing instincts when it comes to not only how to treat an injury but how to come up with just the right antidote or medicine."

"You all thought I was healing with magic?" Irja looked around the room. "I wasn't. I just applied what I'd learned in medical school or through experience." Her voice sounded shrill.

"Or what you found in ancient texts or through your uncanny skill of knowing the precise severity of a broken bone, before taking the X-ray," Ulf added. "Or how the other Norse tribes ask for your help when their healers can't cure severe illness or injury."

Irja shook her head. "No—"

The king interrupted her before she could get any further. "It doesn't matter, Irja. You have served us well, and I have no doubt you will continue to do so."

She still couldn't believe all this time they'd thought she was a witch. That she was using more than her skills while healing. "But if you suspected magic, why didn't you say anything?"

"Say what?" Astrid shrugged. "If you wanted to share your secrets with us, you would have told us."

"Yes," Ulf agreed. "I just thought there was some kind of physician's creed. Like the first rule of healer club is you do not talk about healer club." He grinned.

Irja had avoided it up till now, but she finally looked at

Scott. He gazed back at her with the same warm eyes he'd had before she'd told her story. "You thought I was using magic too?"

He shook his head. "Ever since I came to live with Naya and her new husband"—he shot his sister a grin—"I've been exposed to exponential levels of weirdness." He scratched his jaw. "I'm just your average guy trying to bend my mind around having a beastly warrior soul inside me while fighting creatures created by a half god. I didn't give magic all that much thought before the glowing cage showed up in the desert." He smiled at her. "I just figured you were super skilled because you were immortal and had a lot of time to study."

Astrid snorted. "He was too busy noticing your other assets"—her gaze traveled up and down Irja's body—"to pay attention to your skills. Also, I think he just called you old."

"Shut up," Scott said to her and then turned back to Irja. "Your brother did tell me you were a witch though. Does that help?"

"No," Irja said weakly. "That doesn't help at all." Her thoughts were jumping all over the place. She wouldn't have risked using her abilities whether the Norse warriors knew about them or not—she'd killed a young girl the last time she'd used them—but it would have been nice not to have had to keep that part of herself hidden. Were they really accepting her for who she truly was?

She darted a look at Harald. He looked perturbed but not judgmental or hostile. It seemed he was only irritated that she hadn't given him a chance to use her abilities against their enemies. The red-haired Viking threw an annoyed look at Scott. "I don't think growing up in a rogue lab that tried to make a genetically modified super soldier out of you is in any way considered 'average.'"

"Enough squabbling," Leif said and returned to his chair behind the desk. "Now that we have more information about what Loki wants, what are we going to do about it?"

Harald stroked his chin. "Maybe we can set a trap for him."

"You're talking about tricking the trickster god," Ulf said. "The key word here being 'god,' as in he's a fucking god."

"Yeah, yeah." Harald waved a hand in the air. "He's a half god and super hard to defeat. But we don't have to kill him. We only have to thwart his plans of setting up a stronghold here in Midgard and physically walking among the mortals." He turned to Leif. "We have proof now that Loki is working against the Norse gods' council's rules. You have to tell Odin and Freya."

The king nodded. "I will try to reach Odin, but I can only do so when I dream, and the Wise One has not answered my last few requests."

Ulf snorted. "Probably because he's busy dealing with whatever chaos Loki's created in Asgard to distract from his little portal-to-Midgard project."

"I can try contacting Freya," Astrid said. When everyone turned toward her in surprise, she shrugged. "She called me to her meadow once in a dream." She rubbed her cheek. "Well, I think it was a dream, but when I woke up, I had a mark on my skin from where she slapped me."

Ulf made a choking sound. "The goddess slapped you?"

Astrid threw him a dirty look. "It was totally unprovoked. She was trying to make a point about something." She looked at Luke, who just smiled back, and Astrid's cheeks turned pale pink.

"So it sounds like you have some kind of plan," Naya said to Harald and then turned to Irja. "But what about Pekka and Kari? We still need to wake them up." She darted a look at Scott and then Ulf. "And it would be good if we could piece together the rune combination of the curse before anyone else gets ill."

Scott pushed away from the mantel he'd been leaning against. "While the computer program keeps coming up with possibilities of characters for the rune curse, I'd like to try something else." He looked around the room. "But I will need all of you to help me, and Per, Sten, and Torvald should join us too."

Irja stood. "We've already tried connecting with Pekka and Kari through our berserkers," she protested.

Scott walked toward her and took her hand in his. "I know, but that was before my berserker brought you back from the clutches of Loki." Naya gasped, but Scott ignored her. He cupped Irja's face in his palm. "And sweetness, I don't care how much you want to deny our relationship or your extraordinary abilities, but the fact that our inner warriors recognize each other on a deeper level is fucking magical." He moved his hand to the back of her neck and pulled her in for a deep kiss.

Right in front of everyone.

CHAPTER 16

SCOTT STOOD ON THE BOTTOM STEP OF THE LARGE staircase in the entry hall of the fortress. Gathered before him were all the warriors of the house, and he tried to collect his thoughts so he could put into words his idea of how to wake up Kari and Pekka. The problem was that the plan was based entirely on instinct and hunches. He had no real proof to back it up. Also, kissing Irja had scrambled his mind, but he didn't regret it one bit. After the initial surprise, she'd reciprocated until the wolf whistles from Ulf and Astrid had made her pull away.

He looked over at Irja where she stood toward the back of the group. A blush still colored her cheeks, but she looked at him with clear and calm dark eyes.

Scott scanned the rest of his audience. It had turned out to be very cramped to fit six large Norse warriors, two Valkyries, and three mortals into the small bedroom where Pekka and Kari rested, so Naya organized said brawny warriors and had them carry the two patients and their beds into the big foyer.

His sister stood on the floor right in front of him, looking up with dark-blue eyes filled with curiosity. "Now what?" she asked Scott.

He swept his gaze over the group of assembled men and women again, all looking expectant, but their level of alertness varied. Sten and Per had been responsible for the night shift watching Pekka and Kari, so they were already awake and in the bedroom when the people who'd been at the meeting barged in. During the hustle of moving the patients and their beds, the two younger Vikings had been filled in on what had happened.

Torvald, on the other hand, was newly woken up and looked as confused as he must feel. His gray hair and grizzled beard stuck out in tufts at odd angles. Ulf was rapidly whispering in Torvald's ear, probably filling him in on everything he'd missed while sleeping.

Scott cleared his throat. "I don't know if this will work for sure, but I think we can connect with Pekka's berserker and then pull him and the inner beast out of their slumber."

Ulf shook his head. "We tried that already. You were with us in Sedona when we called to his berserker. Did you forget that it didn't work?" His shoulders slumped as if Scott had let him down, and he crossed his arms over his chest, a defiant grimace on his face.

"Yeah," Astrid said. "Ulf got his ass kicked, remember?" She shot the short-haired Viking a grin when he scowled at her.

Scott held up his hand. "I know Astrid, Naya, and Irja tried to connect with Pekka's inner warrior. And that King Erik and his men, plus Ulf, battled an unseen force when they tried to connect with Kari's. But I think this time will be different."

"How?" Harald demanded. His light-green eyes were intense as they bore into Scott's. "How do you know you're not just wasting our time with something that has already been tried? If the Norse men and women tried to connect with their battle brother and sister without success, what makes you think you can do better?" He took a step forward, fists clenched at his sides.

Leif put his hand on Harald's shoulder but didn't say anything. The king just nodded at Scott to continue.

His throat was dry all of a sudden, but he didn't want to clear it again. He was very aware he was a mortal facing a crowd of immortal warriors. Very skilled and very quick warriors. Clearing his throat would be seen as a weakness, and right now he wanted to appear anything but weak. With as much confidence as he could muster, he squared his shoulders. "There is no guarantee this will work." He swallowed as unobtrusively as he could and avoided Harald's increasingly frigid gaze. "But I have a gut feeling that we'll be able to connect with Pekka and pull him out this time." He ignored Harald's snort and continued. "If we think of the invisible force that Ulf and the other warriors encountered as a wall of resistance, then I may be able to penetrate it the way I was able to force my way into the glowing cage the wolverines created. I mean, they're both linked to their magic. Right? Magic that somehow didn't work on me, maybe because I am mortal. If we treat them both like barriers made of the same building materials, then if I could get through one, I should be able to get through the other."

Naya nodded at him and smiled encouragingly. "Go on."

Scott sent her a grateful look before switching his gaze to Astrid's *själsfrände*. "And maybe Luke will be able to go through the wall as well since he too is mortal."

"But Naya wasn't able to connect with Pekka's berserker before," Torvald pointed out, "and she too is mortal. If the magic kept our strong queen out, why would it not also block you or Luke?"

"Naya is more linked to us than Scott and Luke are," Irja said. "In a way, she is less mortal than they are. Naya's whole blood chemistry was altered once she became our king's *själsfrände*. Luke's blood has shown some changes after he acquired his berserker but not to the extent of Naya's."

"Hold on," Astrid said, looking at Scott. "When you forced your way through the cage walls, had your inner warrior appeared yet?"

"No," Scott admitted.

"So," the blond Valkyrie continued, "maybe the Norse magic now hinders you just like it blocks everyone else."

"True," Scott said. "But we should still try, because in addition to having two"—he looked at Naya and corrected himself—"three mortals, we also have two *själsfrände* bonded couples. And we have Pekka's sister and my berserker who is completely focused on Irja's inner warrior. There is a connection between them. Not a *själsfrände* connection"—*yet*, he added silently—"but a strong bond nevertheless."

A murmur broke out among the gathered warriors. Scott trained his gaze on Leif. It was ultimately the king who would make the decision. His brother-in-law studied him for a moment before turning to look at Naya. Something unspoken passed between them. Actually, it seemed his sister had the final say.

Naya nodded at her husband as she took his hand in hers. "Let's try it," she said. "We have nothing to lose."

"True," Harald grumbled. "We've already moved Pekka and the slumbering *jänta* out here. Might as well see if we can wake these sleeping beauties."

Leif slapped the redheaded Viking on the back so hard, he had to take a step forward to keep from falling. "That's the spirit," the king said. "Positive thinking. I wish all my warriors had your constant optimism." He winked at Scott.

On Naya's suggestion, they pushed the two beds together and then positioned themselves in two circles around the sleeping warriors. The inner circle alternated man and woman. Luke held Astrid's hand, followed by Leif, Naya, Scott, and Irja, who then held Luke's hand to complete the circle. On the outside, Harald, Torvald, Ulf, Sten, and Per formed another circle, but had to stand too far away from each other to hold hands.

They all closed their eyes and on Leif's command tapped into their inner warriors. Scott wasn't sure what he'd expected, but it definitely wasn't the electric jolt that shook his body as if he'd touched an electric fence. In his mind's eye, the warriors appeared as beacons of light interconnected in a web where Leif glowed stronger and brighter than the others. They were surrounded by a great dark void yet somehow stood on solid ground.

Of the glowing web of warriors, Scott instinctively recognized each individual Viking. Somehow, he just *knew* who was who. He felt as one with his berserker but also part of a collective whole through the others' inner warriors. Leif functioned like a central hub with individual connections to each of the others that were all equally strong, except for his tie to Naya.

His sister's glowing inner warrior funneled energy straight to her husband, but she gave each of the warriors smaller tendrils of power. Her connection to Scott was as wide as to the others but glowed off-white, while Naya's connection to the Norse men and women seemed more blueish.

Scott had to remind himself to breathe. In this amazing nexus of energy, he lost sense of himself as an individual.

Letting go and just melting into the collective was a strong temptation. Never before had he felt so driven, so focused on something bigger and more important than himself.

In his mind's eye, he instinctively turned toward Irja's glowing beacon. Astrid and Luke's *själsfrände* bond appeared as a thin coil of light that glowed faintly red. No such connection appeared between Scott and Irja, and yet he felt a flow of warmth between them as if they somehow shared each other's energy. He studied Irja's glowing form, hoping her connection with her brother was similar to his and Naya's, but saw only one glowing trail that connected her to the king and queen.

From Leif, a tendril of power snaked its way out of the web. It wavered in the space as if searching for something to attach to. Scott realized the king was trying to locate Pekka, and he sent out his own vine of energy to aid Leif's. The other warriors added their lines of light, but instead of sending them out into the empty space outside the web like Scott had done, they shot straight to Leif's and connected with the searching end of his tendril. Scott did the same, and a cone of light strings formed, all connected at the apex. That joined point of light glowed brighter and then shot out across the vastness outside the web. The bright apex pulled Scott's awareness with it, and a moment later he sensed another faint point of light far away ahead of them. Somewhere deep inside him, he understood the dim brightness belonged in the web. It absolutely needed to be part of the warriors' connection or the nexus would not function correctly. His focus narrowed. His whole essence concentrated on how to reconnect the missing light to the others. They had found Pekka.

The joint point of light rushed closer to the slumbering warrior, but before they could reach him, they slammed into an invisible barrier. The apex shattered, and the warriors tumbled along the barrier as shadow figures that looked like faint outlines of their physical forms. Somehow their berserkers were all connected on this metaphysical plane. Without having to think about it, Scott—or his berserker, or both of them together—took up an attack position next to his battle brothers and sisters. Luke and Naya flanked him, and together they pushed against the invisible wall that separated them from Pekka.

The other Norse men and women fanned out behind them. Leif bellowed a war cry that the other warriors answered as one. Scott's berserker yelled in unison with his human voice, and a joyful rage filled his body. This must be the battle fever Finn and Ulf had described to him. It felt glorious, and he wrapped it around himself like a cape.

He charged forward but had to stop when the barrier blocked him again. Luke put his hand on Scott's left shoulder, pressing his own right one into the invisible wall. Scott twisted so he could copy Luke's maneuver. He then put his hand on Naya's left shoulder while she also pressed her right one into the barrier.

The other warriors lined up behind the trio in rows of three that copied Naya, Scott, and Luke's formation. Immediately behind them were Leif, who touched Naya's shoulder, Irja, who placed her hand next to Luke's on Scott's shoulder, and then Astrid lending her support to Luke. Ulf, Harald, and Torvald came next while Per and Sten pushed from the very back. A surge of power flowed through their human battle ram as Per and Sten completed the configuration. As the cusp of that wave reached the front row, the entire formation moved forward as one.

They heaved, pressing their shoulders deep into the barrier, and then rested for a brief moment before heaving again. It was the same motion they would have used with a regular ram when breaking down a door. As it was their own bodies doing the work, it was also their flesh that took the brunt of the impact each time the force of the wall pushed back.

Press forward and ease off, press forward and ease off—over and over again.

Each step forward moved them a fraction of an inch toward Pekka, and it was like fighting their way through a huge elastic resistance that just wouldn't relent.

Sweat drenched Scott's forehead. His rubbery legs shook as if he'd run for hours. Naya's breathing turned more and more labored, her raspy gasps echoing in Scott's ears.

He turned toward his sister. Her shadow outline grew fainter and fainter with every heave. He wanted to tell her to stop, but before he could get the words out, she cried out and collapsed. Leif immediately crouched down by her side, and the warriors behind Scott and Luke adjusted so the formation became three rows of two with Torvald holding up the back position on his own. Scott hesitated, wanting to aid his sister, but Leif looked up at him and shouted, "Go."

The heaving and resting repetition continued. After what felt like hours and hours, they'd left Naya and Leif behind. The king still funneled energy to the battering warriors, but Scott could no longer feel his sister in the web. His berserker whimpered but then threw back its head and screamed out its rage. Scott's throat felt raw, so he must have joined in with the beast's battle cry. The voices of the warriors behind him blended with his, and Luke's cry echoed loudly in Scott's ears.

In unison, the human battle ram heaved forward in one extreme push. Something gave, and Scott propelled forward into a space that had none of the elastic resistance. He took a deep breath and turned as Luke popped through the wall and fell to his knees, retching. On the other side of the wall, he could see Irja and Astrid and the rest of the warriors behind them. Harald's lips moved, but no sound traveled through the wall. Scott threw the king's second-in-command an apologetic glance before leaning down to check on Luke.

He put his hand on Luke's shoulder. "Are you okay?"

"Just give me a moment to catch my breath." He braced himself against the ground and pushed himself up. At first he stood on shaky legs, leaning against Scott, but then found his balance and straightened. He turned to look toward the barrier. "Guess we're the only ones who made it through."

Astrid raised her fist and pounded on the invisible wall, her mouth open in a silent scream.

Irja's hands were fisted by her sides, her eyes dark and stormy as they moved between Scott and something behind him.

He turned and found the faint outline of Pekka's physical body floating in the air as if suspended by invisible strings. The warrior looked as asleep as he had been in real life. "Let's do this." Scott slapped Luke's shoulder.

Luke walked up to Pekka and swept his hand above and below the body to check for restraints. Nothing stopped his motion. Grabbing Pekka's shoulders, he nodded for Scott to grab the feet. Together, they tried to move the sleeping warrior sideways but couldn't shift him even an inch.

Shit, why couldn't anything ever be easy in the Norse world?

Luke's eyes focused on something over Scott's shoulder, so he turned to see what had caught the warrior's attention.

Irja and Astrid held hands while bracing their palms against the barrier. The other warriors stood behind them, their hands clasping the Valkyries' shoulders. All of them bowed their heads as if in prayer.

Scott's skin prickled, and a surge of energy coursed through his body. His berserker purred as it absorbed wave after wave of power.

Turning back to face Luke, Scott braced his feet against the ground—or whatever it was they were standing on. The support beneath his feet was as invisible as the barrier and the force field that was keeping Pekka in locked-down suspension.

Scott counted down, and on three, the two of them pulled and pushed Pekka's body with all their might. It barely moved, but they leaned into their heave, arms bulging and sweat beading their brows.

Luke grimaced as if in extreme pain, and Scott could feel his own face scrunch up in a similar expression. His shoulders strained so hard it felt like his tendons would snap at any moment. Just when it seemed like his body would collapse from the pain, another burst of energy came from the warriors behind the barrier. He forced his aching, shaky muscles to put everything into one last heave.

Finally, Pekka's body popped out of the force field. Scott tried to catch the warrior but ended up in a heap on the ground with the unconscious Viking on top of him.

Luke sat down next to him with an exhausted groan. "I'll help you get out from under there soon," he said. "I just need a moment to figure out how to make my muscles move again."

"Don't wait too long," Scott grunted out. "We still need to get him through the barrier."

"Fuck." Luke sighed, looking toward the wall. He blew a kiss, presumably to his *själsfrände*. It better be to Astrid and not Irja.

At the thought, a wave of rage flooded Scott's senses, and he pushed out from under Pekka's body. He faced the barrier and instantly calmed down when he saw Irja watching them with tears in her eyes. "We got this," he said to Luke.

The other warrior looked around. "Do you see any signs of Kari anywhere?"

Scott did a three-sixty. "No, it's just the same spooky dark void that we've been in for ages. I wish we could search for her, but she'd glow if we were connected to her. And I think we better get out of here before we're completely exhausted." The truth was he'd never been as tired as he was at that moment. But somehow he'd find the energy he needed to get Pekka to Irja. He owed her so much. Wanted to give her so much.

They stood and lifted Pekka to his feet and then slung his arms around their shoulders so he was propped up between them. When they got to the invisible wall, Irja trailed a finger on the other side, tracing her brother's face. Scott tried to give her an encouraging smile, but he hurt so badly it came out more like a grimace. "Ready?" he asked Luke, hunkering down to press through the wall again.

"No, but let's do this anyway."

Gritting his teeth, Scott placed his shoulder against the barrier and prepared for more pain. It was worse than he could have imagined. Astrid and Irja leaned against the other side of the barrier, their faces pale masks of concentration as they funneled all their energy to Scott and Luke. The warriors behind the Valkyries had similar expressions.

As he heaved and eased back in symmetry with Luke, both of them forcing their way through the elastic barrier, Scott lost all sense of time. There was only pain and an incredible drain of energy. His muscles shook with the effort.

The only thing that made him not pass out was keeping his focus on Irja. He stared at her beautiful face, thinking about holding it between his hands and kissing her soft lips. He imagined embracing her. Remembered what it felt like to have her in his arms, how sleeping next to her made everything in the world feel right. How it felt like he had finally found his home.

He needed to be by her side again. Would do anything, push through any exhaustion, endure any pain to make it through the wall so he could be by her side.

He grunted out his misery as he made his body push forward. His inner warrior bellowed out its pain and frustration. Luke's berserker answered with its own howl.

On the other side, Torvald grimaced and collapsed to the ground.

Irja made a move as if she wanted to go and check on the older Viking, but Astrid gripped her shoulder and shook her head. Instead, Sten leaned down and saw to Torvald while the two Valkyries touched the wall again. Scott kept eye contact with Irja, but a motion at the back of the warriors on the other side of the wall made him look up over their heads.

Leif had caught up with the others. He carried Naya in his arms but adjusted her weight so he could lay a hand on Harald's shoulder. Scott winced when he saw his sister's still body. He sent a silent prayer to any god or goddess who would listen, asking them to please protect his sister.

Moisture gathered in his eyes, and he quickly blinked it away. From the concern in Irja's gaze, it was clear that she'd caught his tears. "We need you," she mouthed to him.

Scott looked over at Luke, who met his eyes and nodded. "Let's do this," Luke said. His voice sounded as if it was inside Scott's head, and there was a weird echoing effect.

They made sure they were properly propping up Pekka and clasped hands on each other's shoulders behind his back. A jolt of electricity flowed up Scott's arm when he made contact with Luke. They extended their free arms toward Astrid and Irja.

Luke counted down, and on one, the two heaved Pekka's body as they strained against the wall with all their might.

Astrid's mouth was wide open in a silent scream as she stared at Luke. Scott moved his eyes to meet Irja's again. Her pupils were huge, and her face had lost all its color. His berserker whined with concern. On the other side, Irja's inner warrior answered with a weak snarl. The Valkyrie's head shot up, and a small thread of hope slowly unwound in his chest. This was the first time their berserkers had connected since they'd entered this weird void. Irja grinned at him.

Something must have happened between Luke and Astrid as well because a small smile played on his face as he gazed at the blond Valkyrie. She in turn stared at Luke as if her gaze could burn a hole through the wall. Scott and

Luke kept pushing and straining against the resistance of the invisible wall. Astrid yelled her silent war cry again. This time, Irja joined in.

Scott's berserker blended its own roar with the women's, and as he threw his head back to allow the beast's bellow out through his throat, he heard Luke's howl inside his head.

And then all of a sudden the resistance let go, and he could hear the Valkyries' screams join his and Luke's.

They'd made it to the other side.

Irja rushed forward and embraced both Scott and Pekka in one big hug. Luke let go of Pekka's body to wrap his arms around Astrid.

Leif shouted at Irja to come and take care of Naya and Torvald, but she wouldn't let go of her brother and Scott. The berserker hummed its approval of being near Irja again. Scott didn't want to let her go, but the king kept bellowing her name.

Sten tried to tell the king that Torvald would be okay, but Leif just kept calling for Irja, who shook her head and refused to heed his order.

Everyone joined in on the discussion, and in the chaos it was impossible to tell who was shouting what. A loud whistle pierced the cacophony, and everyone shut up.

"I said," Astrid gritted out between clenched teeth, "grab each other's hands and let's get the fuck out of here. Concentrate on getting us all back to the fortress."

Grumbling, the warriors did as they were told.

When he joined the circle of clasped hands, Scott's eardrums popped so loudly he cried out and closed his eyes. When he opened them again, he found himself back in the foyer of the Viking fortress.

The warriors immediately started their loud bickering again.

Scott kept his arms around Irja, who gasped when she turned toward Pekka's bed. Her brother was sitting up with his head braced in his hands.

"Irja," Leif bellowed. "I need you now." Desperation laced his voice.

She looked between her brother and her king.

Scott framed her face with his hands and gazed into her beautiful dark eyes. "Go," he told her. "Go care for my sister. I will take care of your brother."

Irja hesitated a moment longer, but with one lingering look at Pekka, she nodded and rushed to Leif's side.

The king stood with Naya's limp body in his arms as one tear slowly trailed down his cheek.

CHAPTER 17

CHAOS ERUPTED IN THE FOYER AS THE WARRIORS hollered at each other about how to take care of Torvald and Pekka. The older Viking had come to and was leaning against Kari's bed. She was still quietly sleeping and looked strangely serene amid the pandemonium of the warriors bellowing and stomping around.

Irja fought the powerful draw of wanting to see to her brother and rushed to her king's side. Pekka was sitting up, so he'd probably be okay.

"I'm here," she told her king.

Leif cradled the slight queen in his arms. "She's not responsive. I can't connect with her berserker, and she won't wake up." The queen's weight should be insignificant to the strong, immortal Viking king, but he staggered as if he was about to collapse. He must be as exhausted and drained as Irja felt.

A chill ran down Irja's spine. Last time they thought they'd lost the queen, the king had gone completely bonkers, and she'd had to sedate him. She cupped Naya's cheek. Her skin felt cool and dry against Irja's fingers. "She's not running a fever." She gazed into Leif's worried eyes. "Maybe she just collapsed from exhaustion."

"No," he whispered hoarsely and then cleared his throat. "I can feel that something is wrong. She's not been well for a while but refused to discuss it with me."

Irja glanced to check on Pekka again. Her brother sat

straighter now, only shielding his eyes with one hand. He and Scott seemed to be having an intense conversation. She longed to go to the two men who were the most important in her life. The thought startled her.

Freya's Mercy. She cared enough about Scott to consider him important.

"Irja," Leif bellowed. "Pay attention."

She'd missed what he'd said. "I'm sorry." She rubbed the space between her eyebrows. "My brain is firing on only a few synapses."

"We're all exhausted." Leif's voice lowered a few decibels. "And I know you want to check on your brother, but I need you. Your queen needs you."

Irja shook herself mentally and straightened. "Let's get Naya upstairs so I can examine her."

Leif nodded and headed up the staircase with his *själsfrände* in his arms. Irja surveyed the room again. Scott and Pekka were still talking. Luke had locked his arms around Astrid in a tight embrace. The Valkyrie met Irja's gaze and then turned her head to look toward Pekka and Scott. She turned back to Irja and nodded once. Astrid would watch over Irja's brother and her…whatever Scott had become to her.

She hurried after her king and queen. She dashed to her room to retrieve her medical bag, then rushed to the royal bedroom.

Leif had placed Naya on the king-size bed and sat in a chair, holding her hand. He turned when Irja stormed into the room. "I can sense her inner warrior again," he said. "But it won't communicate with me. It's angry about something or somebody and preparing for attack."

Irja put down the bag and approached the bed. The queen's face was now pale and blotchy. Sweat beaded her forehead. Her eyes moved rapidly behind closed lids, and her body twitched. Reaching for Naya's other hand, Irja tried herself to connect to the queen's berserker. The beast wanted nothing to do with Irja's inner warrior and snarled before shutting off the connection. "It's furious." She frowned. Why was the berserker still in battle mode after they'd returned from rescuing Pekka? Was there a threat present that neither she nor Leif could detect? She connected with her own berserker again; it was agitated over not being able to reach Naya's inner warrior but did not seem alert to anything that was about to attack.

Leif looked at her with desperate eyes. "Do something."

Well, she would if she could figure out what the hell she should do. "Go get a cool, damp washcloth and wipe her forehead," she told the king. It wouldn't necessarily do anything to cure the queen, but it would make her feel better.

And most important, it would keep Leif busy.

He disappeared into the en suite bathroom.

Irja pushed her exhaustion out of the way and opened her medical bag. The only thing she could do was a routine examination and draw more blood.

Leif returned with a washcloth and bathed Naya's face while Irja checked her temperature and pulse. The queen had a slight fever but not high enough to cause concern. Her pulse beat a little more rapidly than Irja would have liked, but it was steady and strong. She sighed.

The king's head shot up. "What's wrong?"

"I don't know," her voice croaked. She cleared her throat. "I'm not seeing anything that would explain why the queen won't wake up. All I can do is draw her blood and run some tests in the lab, but I don't even know what to look for." She bowed her head when the tears threatened to appear. Irja tried hard to always appear capable and confident in front of her king and queen. She couldn't embarrass herself now by losing control.

"We are all very tired." The king's voice was gentle. "But you have never let me down, dear Irja. You are the most accomplished healer any Norse tribe has seen, and I am certain you will figure out what ails my *själsfrände* and make her healthy again."

There was no stopping the tears now. The king's quiet confidence in her made her feel even more of a fraud. Even when some of the other warriors had treated her differently because of her Sami heritage, the king had always made her feel like she was an important member of his tribe. Irja didn't even bother swiping at the tears as they flowed down her cheeks. She instead concentrated on preparing Naya's arm for a blood sample. She still hadn't tested the one she'd collected two days ago.

Was it really only a day since Ulf and Scott had returned to the fortress? It felt like months had passed since she'd fallen asleep in Scott's arms and woken up in Loki's cave. She shuddered.

"You're exhausted," the king said. "I am anxious for you to help my queen, but you must also take care of yourself." The words were uttered with quiet confidence, but his voice broke at the end. It cost him to put his tribe before the needs of his queen and himself. But that was why he was such a good and trusted leader—he would always think of his people first.

"I'm okay," Irja said defiantly. She'd functioned on little to no sleep many times in her life. She could stomach it one more time.

"Of course you are." Leif's voice now dripped with sarcasm. "But you've been assaulted by a half god, battled a Norse curse while rescuing your brother, and found out that you're most likely bonded with the queen's brother. Anyone who'd had to deal with just one of those things would be emotionally and physically exhausted. You've dealt with them all in only twenty-four hours, but sure, let's say you are not affected at all."

Irja shot her king a look while the vial filled with Naya's blood. "I'm not bonded to the queen's brother." She couldn't be. It wasn't safe for Scott to be bonded to her.

"Keep telling yourself that," Leif said and looked away. He stood and went into the bathroom. The faucet came on and off again, and then the king returned with the washcloth. "It's everyday business for you to be able to funnel energy to a mortal without a bond, like your berserker did to Scott's. And it's completely normal for said mortal to develop a berserker, even though we've only seen that twice before, and both of those times it happened through a *själsfrände* bond."

Irja demonstratively held up her hand and turned it so the back faced the king. "There is no serpent's tail on my skin." She didn't know who she was trying to convince the most, herself or the king, but she desperately needed there to not be a bond. If Scott was her *själsfrände*, he would get hurt if she ever turned to magic again. And with Loki as a major threat, it was really only a matter of time before she had to use that ability again. If she could figure out how to refill her powers, that was. She was willing to burn herself out, but anybody bonded to her might also go up in flames when she sacrificed herself, and that she couldn't allow. Naya wouldn't survive it.

At the thought of her queen, she swallowed hard and turned back to the task at hand. The queen needed to survive this before they'd consider other burdens she'd have to deal with.

Leif just shook his head. "Keep lying to yourself if you need to, but you could do worse than being bonded to the queen's brother. He's an honorable and valiant warrior. I am proud to call him my brother-in-law." Irja opened her mouth to reply, but the king held up his hand to stop her. "We can debate this later." His blue eyes softened. "For now, go run your tests, and while you wait for the results, go see your brother. And catch at least an hour or two of sleep."

Irja avoided his gaze as she collected her blood samples and equipment. "*Ja, min kung.*" She slipped from the room.

She would try to see her brother, but only if Scott wasn't also there. She couldn't afford to be sidetracked by emotions. And in her exhausted state, she was too weak to fight her berserker's crazy attraction to the queen's brother—or more correct, its attraction to his inner warrior.

She went to her lab and pulled out Naya's earlier blood sample from the cold storage. She'd run a complete blood count, metabolic panel, and lipid panel on both samples and compare the results. If Naya's changed condition wasn't because of exhaustion, hopefully a change in one of her values would indicate what had caused her to pass out. Then again, the queen's aggressive berserker was more worrying than abnormal blood work. Irja sighed loudly and sat down on a stool.

For a short moment, she bent forward, folded her arms on top of the counter, and rested her forehead against her forearms. She lifted her head and slapped her palms against the counter, pushing herself to standing. Time to suck it up. She couldn't help her patients by indulging in self-pity. There were tests to run, results to compare, and symptoms to list and analyze. She reached for her lab coat and shrugged it on.

Solving medical mysteries was what she did best. It was her duty, her identity. She was a healer who served her king, her queen, and her tribe. She would not let them down.

Scott supported Pekka as they both slowly made it up the stairs. The Finnish warrior's body was extremely weak, but the most worrisome part was that he could no longer see. He'd hidden his blindness from his sister and the other warriors by keeping his hand over his face as if he was exhausted or sensitive to light.

At first, Scott thought he'd hallucinated. When Pekka stood from his bed, Scott had supported him by holding his elbow. But when the Finnish warrior stumbled on the way to the stairs, the hand shielding his eyes had dropped briefly, and Scott had caught a glimpse of Pekka's eyes. It almost looked as if his dark eyes had disappeared. They were covered by a dense white film.

"A few more steps and we're at the top," Scott murmured.

"Thanks," Pekka whispered.

They climbed two more agonizingly slow steps before reaching the landing. Scott felt he had to say something. "Can you see at all?"

Pekka paused for a few heartbeats. "Not a thing," he finally answered. "I can't even make out shapes. It's completely dark in my world right now."

"You're going to have to tell the others, if your vision doesn't return."

"I will," Pekka agreed. "But let's give it a while in case it's just a residual effect from the coma. And I especially do not need to tell my sister while she's obviously stressed out of her mind about the queen."

"So you picked up on Naya being sick?"

A frown marred Pekka's forehead. "It was hard not to, considering Leif's hollering. He only has that desperation in his voice when he's worried about Naya." The corners of his lips hiked up briefly. "Or if he's yelling at Naya, but I didn't hear her shout back, so it must be the former. How is she?"

Scott shook his head as they walked down the hallway, Pekka trailing his fingers along the wall. Then he realized the other warrior couldn't see his head movement. He swallowed the lump of worry for his sister that had lodged in his throat. "She's not been well for the last few days. She collapsed while we were rescuing you."

"What's wrong with her?"

"I'm hoping Irja will find out quickly." He pushed down the guilt rising in his chest. He should have insisted Naya see Irja when he first suspected she wasn't well.

"I didn't know the queen could get ill," Pekka said. "As far as I know, she's only once been in a sick bed, and that was when the wolverines had poisoned her."

"I don't think she was ever sick even before we were captured and used as lab rats," Scott said. Thanks to the injections both he and Naya had received, Naya's immune system was hypervigilant and could defeat just about anything.

They'd arrived at Pekka's room, and Scott opened the door, holding it open as he guided Pekka inside. Scott reached for the light switch, which made a low click as the overhead lamp came on.

Pekka let out a wry chuckle. "I guess I don't really need the lights on." Pekka carefully navigated the threshold and then walked over to his bed, his hand out in front of him, warding for obstacles.

Scott closed the door behind him and sat down in an armchair as Pekka sank down on the bed. The Finn remained sitting for a moment but then lay down on top of the comforter.

"I'm sure Irja will figure out what's going on with your vision." Scott injected as much confidence as he could into his voice. No matter how strong, how would a blind warrior be able to fight? He shook his head to clear it. Before they started worrying about that, Irja needed to examine Pekka. Plus there was still a chance they'd figure out how to break the runes' curse.

"We won't tell my sister about this until we absolutely have to."

"Sure," Scott said. "I'm sure she'll be busy with Naya for at least an hour or so." They both knew Pekka wouldn't be able to keep his blindness secret for long. Even if his sister didn't rush to his side, eventually one of the other warriors would figure it out and tell Irja.

Pekka cursed under his breath. "How did you guys wake me? Why did Naya collapse?"

Scott filled him in on how they'd tried to connect with Pekka's berserker in Sedona unsuccessfully but managed to reach it when the whole tribe tried together. And he explained how the stones with the rune carvings were part of a curse. He left out the part about Irja and his own special connection. This didn't seem the time to tell a guy he was sleeping with his sister. And he decided to let Irja tell her brother about her meetings with Loki herself. She should have the right to decide how much or how little she wanted her brother to worry about. Then again, what she'd told the rest of the tribe in the meeting with the king and the queen would eventually reach Pekka's ears. The Norse warriors were not great at keeping secrets.

"What about Kari? Has anyone checked with King Erik to see if she's woken up?" Pekka said suddenly.

Scott was confused for a moment before he realized Pekka didn't know Kari had traveled with them back to Pine Rapids. "Kari is here. Erik asked us to take her with us when Leif insisted we return to the fortress."

"But I didn't hear her voice in the foyer. Oh—" Pekka's face fell.

"Yeah, I'm sorry. She didn't wake up."

"Did you look for her while you were searching for me?"

"We did, but there wasn't even a glimmer of her or her berserker in the void. And then after Naya collapsed, we needed all our strength to get ourselves and you back here."

Pekka sat up in bed. "We need to go look for her." He swung one leg over the edge of the bed. "Or at least tell Erik how you found me. His tribe can come here, or we'll take Kari to them. They'll be able to connect with her berserker and bring her back." He stood up but tilted heavily to the side and had to sit back down on the bed.

"Whoa." Scott rushed to his side. "You need to lie down."

"We have to get Kari." Pekka rubbed his forehead. "She's been sicker for longer. Who knows what kind of lingering effects she may experience?"

"I'm sorry." Scott pushed the other warrior back down on the bed. "Like I said, Erik and his tribe tried to connect with both you and her in Sedona. It didn't work."

"Maybe if all the warriors of the Taos tribe came together. Maybe it would work then."

"I'll call Erik and suggest it. How about you rest for a while?" Scott didn't think it would work. There were no bonded couples in the Taos tribe. But his words seemed to calm Pekka, who relaxed against the pillow. His breathing evened out as he fell asleep.

Scott contemplated the shitstorm they were currently in. Kari could suffer dire consequences if they didn't figure out how to wake her soon. The best chance of doing so would be to solve and break the curse.

He felt completely useless. There was nothing he could do for his sister and nothing he could do for the woman he loved. A sigh escaped his lips before he could stop it, but this was no time to dwell on his own shortcomings—there were too many and would take days. Instead, he should focus on what he *could* do. Pushing up from the bed, he left the room. Pekka needed nourishment, and even someone as useless as he was could rustle up some grub. And once he'd taken care of that, he'd go and check on his sister. There might not be anything he could do for her, but at least sitting by her side and watching her breathe would make him feel better.

CHAPTER 18

AS SCOTT PUT THE FINISHING TOUCHES TO THE FOOD he'd prepared for Pekka, he blinked against a stray ray of sunlight that had found its way through the kitchen window to lance his eye. The warriors must have spent several hours in the void if a whole day and night had passed since the meeting in Leif's office. Scott hadn't paid attention to what time it was when they'd all made it back to the foyer. There had been too much chaos, too many people, and too many things to worry about.

He looked for a tray on which to place Pekka's meal, if one could call a bowl of broth and some slices of hearty bread a meal. But Pekka's stomach hadn't had anything solid for four days, and he'd wake up hungry if Scott didn't get a move on.

He found a tray in one of the bottom cabinets and loaded up the bland feast. As he turned to head to Pekka's room, he barely avoided colliding with Sten, who came barreling through the kitchen door. The blond Viking's smoky-gray eyes widened as he stepped back to keep from knocking the tray out of Scott's hands.

"There you are," Sten said. "I've been searching the house for you. The king wants you."

Fear froze Scott's blood. "Has something happened to Naya?"

Sten held up a hand. "She is as before, no better, no worse. I don't know why the king has asked for you. I just know he wanted me to find you." Sten noticed the tray and reached for it. "Is that for Pekka? I can take it to him."

Scott hesitated as the desire to see his sister battled with his promise to Pekka. If Pekka was awake when Sten entered the room, they would no longer be able to keep Pekka's blindness a secret.

In the end, saving Irja from one more worry—even if it was only for a little while—won out. "I'll drop it off on my way," he told Sten and hurried out of the kitchen and up the stairs.

Pekka was still asleep when Scott set down the tray by his bedside.

In the king and queen's bedchamber, the lights were dimmed when he entered. He closed the door quietly behind him and walked soundlessly across the thick carpet. The king was asleep in a chair next to the bed. Leif held Naya's hand, and even in rest his face had a pinched look of worry. Deep lines that had not been there twenty-four hours ago trailed down the side of his nose. The dark-blond stubble that graced the king's cheeks made Scott scratch his own day-old beard growth as he studied the slight shape of his sister in the bed.

Naya lay under the covers, and an additional blanket had been draped over her. Her personality took up so much space when she was awake that he always forgot how small she was physically. Even when they were kids, she'd seemed bigger than she actually was. And now that he physically towered over her by several inches, he still felt like she was the big sister both in age and stature. He sat down on the bed next to her and lightly touched her leg under the layers of covers.

Leif startled awake and blinked a few times before he focused on Scott. "You got my message." The king's voice sounded like gravel grinding together.

"Sten found me in the kitchen making some food for Pekka."

"How is Pekka?"

Scott hesitated. How much was he required to tell the king? "He's unchanged from when he woke up," he finally settled on. Normally, Leif would have picked up on the slight pause and probed for answers, but his worry for Naya must be distracting him because he just nodded slightly as he stared at his *själsfrände* in the bed.

"As is my beloved." Pain colored Leif's voice, and Scott's heart ached for his sister and her husband.

"What can I do to help?"

Leif looked up. His ice-blue eyes clouded with pain and worry. "Irja is running all the medical tests, but I can't just sit here and wait. I have to try everything I can think of."

"Tell me what to do."

The king studied him for a beat. "When I try to connect to Naya's berserker, it snarls at me and cuts off the connection. I want you to try to coax it to tell me what's wrong."

Scott rubbed the back of his neck. "I don't know if I'll be able to do that. I'm still new at this."

"It's more about instinct than skill. Your berserker is not a separate entity. It is just another side of you. It's the primitive, aggressive warrior side of you that is often hard to control, but it is still you." He turned to study Naya's face. "Just like you are close to your sister, your inner warrior feels a kinship with hers. The berserker mirrors your feelings. Sometimes that is expressed aggressively, but in a way it's less complicated than what our human side feels and how we act. You can trust what your berserker tells you because it breaks down emotions to their basic components. Is this person a threat or a friend?

"I think in a way that what I feel with my berserker side is purer." He kissed Naya's hand and rested his cheek against it. "My berserker never questioned how I could fall in love with a mortal. It never worried about the consequences of those feelings. It just loved and trusted that I would be loved back."

Scott had to swallow hard to push down the lump of emotions caused by the king's words. He'd always known Leif loved his sister, but hearing the most alpha male he knew speak so eloquently about his feelings threatened to bring tears to his eyes.

He owed his sister so much: his freedom, his life—he owed her everything. And she never asked for anything back other than for him to be happy. Well, and that he share every detail about his life and acknowledge she always knew best, but it all came from love. She deserved to be happy. To be with someone who loved her greatly and unconditionally. And now he knew she had found that with Leif.

His sister deserved this amazing life she had found with the Norse warriors and their king, and he would do any- thing to make that happen. "You may need to coach me," he told the king, "but I will do whatever it takes."

Leif gave a curt nod. "Grab her other hand. Sometimes, it helps to link with someone's inner warrior if you touch them."

Scott scooted closer so he could hold Naya's free hand. He closed his eyes and concentrated on finding his sis- ter's inner warrior. Instead of playfully greeting his sister's warrior spirit, his berserker acted like it was nervous. "My warrior seems skittish," he told the king.

"Center yourself and open your connection wider," Leif coached.

Scott slowed down his breathing and focused on the bond that tied him to the berserker. Imagining it as both stronger and wider, he slowly allowed the inner warrior to take more control over his consciousness. The beast seemed to grow in his mind. It growled in approval but then whimpered. Scott frowned. "It's more afraid than skittish."

"Concentrate on finding a connection with your sister's inner warrior," the king said in a calm voice.

Scott widened his awareness and looked for his sister's berserker. All of a sudden, it was there as a familiar flow of energy unlike any other. His inner warrior yipped with glee, but Naya's snarled and snapped in response. It lashed out and severed the connection. "I found her but she's angry," he told the king. "I mean, I found her warrior but it is angry."

"Can you tell why it's upset?"

Reaching out with his mind and his inner warrior, Scott tried to connect with Naya's beast again. This time, he didn't get as much as a growl before the connection was slashed. "I'm not able to reach her again." He opened his eyes. "I'm sorry." If he was now part of the Viking tribe, then Leif was his king, his leader, and he had let him down.

The other man shook his head. "It was a long shot. I'm not able to connect with her either."

"At least we know her berserker is there. It's not completely missing like Kari's and Pekka's." Scott tried to make himself sound upbeat and hopeful.

The king's eyebrow arched. "We already know this is

unrelated to what ailed Pekka." He obviously wasn't buying Scott's bullshit.

He was saved from answering by a knock on the door.

Irja entered and faltered slightly when she saw him. She quickly recovered, gave him a slight nod, and then focused on Naya as she approached the bed. "How is she? Any change?" She addressed her question to the king, not acknowledging Scott even though she had to lean around him to see her patient.

"She's calmer than she was," Leif answered. "Both Scott and I have tried to connect with her inner warrior to see what has it so riled up, but neither of us was successful."

Irja nodded. "That's good news. That is to say, it's good that she is calmer and that her temperature is down." She glanced at Scott and quickly looked away.

The king watched the two of them, and the corner of his mouth hiked up briefly before he turned somber again. "What news do you have from your laboratory?"

Irja sighed. "None. I never thought I would think of normal values as bad news, but there are no differences from the queen's baseline that I can detect so far." She lifted Naya's hand. "Her pulse is steady and strong. It's as if she's just asleep." She frowned. "I have more tests to run, but I am sorry, *min kung*, I still have no idea what ails our queen." Her voice broke on the last two words.

Scott stood and put his hand on her shoulder. "Have you slept or eaten since we got back?"

She shook off his hand. "There is too much to do."

"Irja," the king said. "You must take care of yourself as well as your patients. My wife is my life, but I would not want to lose both of you because you refused to rest or eat."

"I have made it through plenty of all-nighters before," Irja snapped. She glared at Scott and then the king.

The king stood, still holding Naya's hand. "We talked about this. These are not normal circumstances. You have taxed your energies to the limit already after fighting Loki and pressing through the void to find Pekka. If I have to, I will order you to rest." His eyes softened. "You may see your brother first if you'd like."

"He's fine," Scott hurried to interject. "He is in bed sleeping, and I've made sure he has food waiting next to him when he wakes up." He touched Irja's shoulder again but she shrugged it off. "We will watch over my sister and your brother until you've had some sleep."

Irja muttered something under her breath that he couldn't make out. She leaned over to tuck Naya in and then trailed her fingers across her forehead. "I will be back as soon as I can." It wasn't clear whether she spoke to the queen or the king. She turned abruptly and marched out the door.

"She's upset and worried." The words spilled out before Scott realized he was making excuses for Irja to her king.

"I know," he answered. "I take no offense. Irja has a temper to rival even my Naya's, but she rarely shows it." He suddenly grinned. "Remember what I told you about the berserker feeling more strongly and more purely?"

Scott nodded, wondering where the king was going with his statement.

The king's grin grew wider. "You are in for a wild time, because once you are bonded, her berserker will be a part of you. Everything the beast feels and reacts to will be immediate, including Irja's temper." He turned back to look at Naya, his eyes serious and filled with pain again. "That is why it hurts whenever I cannot connect with my *själsfrände's* inner warrior. It is as if I've lost part of myself, like I am no longer whole."

Still processing the king's words, Scott jerked when the bedroom door flung open with so much force it banged against the wall.

The king immediately placed himself between the entrance and the bed, his right hand clenching as if it needed a sword to grip.

Ulf paused in the doorway when he saw the king in battle stance. "I'm sorry, my king, I did not mean to startle you." He bowed briefly. "I have been in the computer room, working on the algorithms that are processing the runes."

Leif nodded. "What news have you?"

"None about the curse, but there was an alert that could mean wolverine activity."

"In Pine Rapids? Are they building one of their glowing cages?"

Ulf shook his head. "The social media messages that triggered the alert didn't indicate them trying to open another portal, but there seem to be several wolverines. There is chatter about men in Halloween costumes that include hands with claws." He paused. "It's near the college. By one of the women's dorms. Although there is summer school, the school is operating with minimum personnel—including security."

The king cursed in Swedish. Scott didn't know the words but the tone made it clear it was profanity, and he understood why Leif reacted that way. A little more than a year ago, the Viking tribe had found a group of wolverines on a farm on the outskirts of Pine Rapids. They'd also found several women who, after they'd been rescued, explained they'd been kidnapped from their native country of Mexico and sold through an international auction.

"I know you are worried about your *själsfrände*," Ulf said, "but I thought you would want to know immediately."

Leif waved his hand, dismissing the apology. "Of course I did. Any wolverine activity is worth reporting, especially if they seem to be targeting young women." As if the wolverines engaging in human trafficking wasn't enough, the Norse warriors had last year also found a lab set up in such a way that they suspected that the wolverines were starting some sort of breeding program—with mortal women as surrogate mothers. Keeping the wolverines away from young female—and probably fertile—college students was extra important. "We need to act right away." He glanced at Naya. "Our queen would expect nothing less of us. Everyone except Pekka and Irja should gear up immediately."

"*Ja, min kung.*" Ulf bowed again and hastened out the door.

"You have not rested either, have you?" the king asked Scott.

"I am still hyped up on adrenaline from my first experience battling in a strange realm while connected with the other warriors through an internal beast that I did not have just a few days ago." He tried for a smile to better sell the white lie, but his face was too tired.

"Let's make this battle as successful as the last one then," the king said. "We wouldn't want to disappoint your newly found berserker." He thumped Scott on the chest with his fist and must also have made his inner warrior connect with

Scott's, because all of a sudden the beast was battle ready and raring to go.

Down in the foyer, they found the rest of the tribe just as hyped on battle excitement as Scott. Luke handed out power bars and energy gels to the warriors as they strapped on state-of-the-art, super thin, and flexible Kevlar gear and loaded their weapons of choice.

Astrid had at least two handguns attached to her body but also filled every pocket and boot with knives of various shapes and sizes. Sten slung a sniper rifle across his shoulder to rest on his back. The tribe preferred to fight with silent weapons to not alert any local law enforcement, but they always brought guns and rifles as backup.

Scott joined the fray to pick his weapons. He chose three handguns, spare ammunition, and two daggers to strap into the holsters that were specially made inside his boots.

"Listen up," the king hollered, and silence fell instantly. "I know you are all tired and were probably looking forward to some sleep and a good meal. Instead, you are gearing up for another battle and choking down calorie plasma." A chuckle spread through the group. "I wish I could say that after this fight you're guaranteed rest and food, but I can't make that guarantee. But I also know whatever the conditions, you are Odin and Freya's loyal warriors and as such always ready to slay the enemy." His voice rose, and the last three words were more bellow than statement.

A loud cheer went up from the warriors, and Scott felt a click inside him as his inner warrior joined in the holler, thereby engaging Scott's vocal cords. The adrenaline he'd mentioned earlier was truly flooding his body now. Once again, he saw the web of warriors in his mind's eye with Leif as the glowing center, but there was a big piece missing. Naya's place stood out as a gaping void where her calming presence should have been feeding energy to the tribe's members.

"To battle," Harald hollered. "For our king and for our queen."

"To battle," the whole crowd agreed, Scott included, and continued with "For our king and for our queen."

Astrid let out a war cry, and Scott's berserker joined in, which earned him a broad smile from the Valkyrie.

"And for our gods, for Odin and for Freya," Harald shouted.

The group grew frantic. "For Odin and for Freya," Scott found himself shouting in chorus with the rest of the warriors as they all raised their hands in the air. He was swept up in the fervor of the connected berserkers, and his head fell back as his beast roared.

As Leif had described, what he felt through the berserker was pure and uncomplicated.

He wanted to kill the enemy no matter the cost, and he wanted to kill that enemy now.

CHAPTER 19

ONCE AGAIN, IRJA WAS LEFT BEHIND IN THE FORTRESS while everyone else went out to battle. She normally didn't mind, but this time it seemed like bashing in a few wolverine heads was preferable to the fight she was facing here on her own. Except for the calm breathing of the patient, the queen's bedroom was eerily quiet. Irja slumped in the armchair she'd pulled up to the side of the bed. She'd heeded the king's order to rest, but instead of going to her room like he'd probably intended for her to do, she'd catnapped in the chair. It was a very comfortable piece of furniture so she'd fallen asleep quickly, and the proximity to her queen meant she slept much better than she would have in her own room. Even if that sleep had only lasted a little more than an hour, she still felt refreshed. Or so she told herself.

The queen's condition remained unchanged. Irja had triple-checked Naya's test results but still didn't see anything that varied enough from the baseline she had on file for the queen or from the blood sample she'd taken from Naya just days earlier. Sighing, she put down the medical journal she kept for the queen and instead reached for Kari's slimmer file.

The Taos Valkyrie still rested comfortably, but her pulse had weakened. Irja once again reviewed the list of tests she'd run on Kari and looked at the results. Whatever ailed the warrior woman was not physiological, which she of course already knew. She rubbed her eyes. Her medical training was useless when it came to dealing with curses and pissed-off berserkers. All she could rely on was her own instincts and whatever trial and error she dreamed up. Sometimes the ancient books she'd collected through the years gave a clue to what to try next, but this time she was stumped.

She'd even run tests on Ulf to see why he hadn't succumbed to the curse. She'd cornered the Viking before he'd headed out with the other warriors and bullied him into allowing her to collect a vial of his blood. By the way Kari's and Pekka's diseases had progressed, Ulf should be in a coma by now. He was sure he'd touched the stones, but somehow the curse didn't affect him. And they hadn't made Scott sick either.

She worried her lip. Maybe she needed to see what values the queen's brother's blood would give. Thinking about Scott made her feel things she didn't have time for, so she'd tried to put him out of her mind altogether. Seeing him in this bedroom just a few hours earlier had not helped with that. His quiet attempts of comfort had both calmed her and irritated her. When he'd touched her, the berserker had purred in pleasure while Irja the woman wanted to avoid any reminder of how much she liked the feel of his skin against hers.

This line of thought was not getting her closer to an answer for either of her patients. She needed to think outside the box, as the mortals liked to say. She would have to get more creative and reach for something she'd not tried before in order to break this curse.

She looked over at Naya, who slept peacefully. Strange how using the word *sleep* made everyone feel better when the truth was that the queen was in a slumber from which no one knew if she would wake. Irja closed her eyes and opened the bond with her berserker wide. Her inner warrior stood alert, but when she tried to get it to connect with the queen's beast, it refused. She pushed, cajoled, and finally forced her berserker to do her bidding. Beads of sweat popped out on her forehead, but the beast connected with Naya's inner warrior. The queen's berserker at first refused to respond, but Irja kept pushing. She sent as much love and friendship as she could down the bond. She tried sending glimpses of memories that she and Naya had shared.

For a little while, it almost looked like she would succeed, but then the queen's berserker snarled and severed the connection. She might have imagined it, but the snarl sounded like *inkräktare*, intruder. It took her a few moments to catch her breath and feel strong enough to stand up. Naya's slumber remained unchanged.

At least one of Irja's three patients was fully conscious again. It was time to wake up her twin so she could bounce ideas off him about how to cure her patients. Not that she actually had any ideas, but at least the conversation would make her feel better.

A few minutes later, she knocked lightly on Pekka's door before letting herself inside. Only a small lamp illuminated the room, and her brother was sitting up in bed, headphones covering his ears and eyes closed.

She sat down next to him on the bed and touched his leg. His eyes flew open, and she gasped at the blank white orbs. A sob escaped before she could stop it, and she covered her mouth with her hand.

Pekka slowly removed his headphones. "*Sisko*, that must be you creeping around in my room." His sly smile took the sting out of the words.

"What happened to your eyes?"

"Loki's damned curse happened to my whole body," he replied. "The eyes are the only thing that haven't recovered. Perhaps they will in time." It was obvious from his dry tone that he didn't think it very likely.

"What can I do to help?" She needed to go back to the lab or hunt through her library again to see what might have caused this. "We'll figure this out."

Pekka grabbed her hand and brought it to his chest. "Relax, *Sisko*. I am alive, and that is enough for now. You have the queen and Kari to worry about."

"But I need to make you better. I need to—"

"You need to make sure the slumbering Valkyries get better first." His voice was firm. "Talk to me of other things. If you obsess about my eyes, I'll just put the headphones back on and ignore you."

She shook her head and then realized he couldn't see the gesture. "You're too stubborn for your own good."

Pekka smiled. "Many people are of the opinion that *you* are the stubborn twin and I am the easygoing, charming one."

Irja snorted and pulled her hand out of his grip. "That's a lie."

Her brother tilted his head. The eerie white eyes stared out at nothing. "I think Scott would not think it so."

"Since when do you discuss us with the queen's brother?" She looked away.

"Since he has somehow developed a berserker that feels familiar because it carries an essence of you."

"That's rubbish, and you know it. I have nothing to do with Scott's berserker." So what if the only two cases of mortals developing inner warriors happened after they became *själsfrände* with one of the tribe's warriors? She was not bonded to the queen's brother. His beast had nothing to do with her. Besides, it had appeared before they'd slept together.

Pekka stretched his lips in the smile he knew she hated, the one that managed to make him look both smug and condescending at the same time. "Have you never noticed how Luke's inner warrior reminds you of Astrid, and Naya's makes you think of Leif?"

"No." She had, but that was because Luke and Naya were the warriors' *själsfrände*. Of course seeing one of them or connecting with one of their berserkers would remind her of their bonded mate.

"I recognize that tone of voice."

"What tone of voice?"

"The defiant one that means you know I'm right but you prefer to argue because you are too stubborn to give up. See, you are the stubborn twin."

"You're impossible. Be serious, please." He'd succeeded in what he'd set out to do, what he always tried to do, which was to make her feel better, but there were important things to talk about. "If you don't want to talk about your eyes—"

"And you don't want to talk about Scott, what should we discuss?"

"I told the tribe about my magic abilities." She hadn't meant to blurt it out.

Pekka paused for a moment. "That is a really big deal for you." He reached for her hand. "But you know how I feel about your abilities. I don't understand why you refuse to use them."

"You know why." She tried to reclaim her hand, but he held on.

"Because of the ridiculous notion that you think it back-fires." He squeezed her hand.

She bristled. "It's not ridiculous. It's simple physics. You cannot create energy from nothing. It has to come from somewhere. If I take energy to save a life, another life is lost somewhere."

Her twin released her hand and leaned back against the headboard. "You are so frustratingly stubborn about this. You have this amazing ability, a skill that runs all through our family line, and you won't use it because of a ridicu-lous notion that magic has something to do with the law of conservation of energy." She looked up abruptly, and even though he couldn't see her head jerk, Pekka nodded. "Yes, fair sister, I too have taken a few science classes. I know energy cannot be created or destroyed, only changed into different forms." He dropped the mocking tone. "Have you ever stopped to think that maybe magic defies the rules of science?"

"Everything has to obey the rules of science." She needed that to be true. Without the logic and order of biology, phys-ics, and chemistry, her world would be too chaotic.

"Then how do you explain us being reborn as immor-tals?" He sat up straighter, his voice gaining volume. "How do you explain Odin speaking with Leif, and Freya trans-porting Astrid back to the meadow outside Valhalla to speak with her?"

"A warp in the space-time fabric?" She didn't mean for it to come out as a question. Truth be told, she didn't know how to explain those things scientifically. Just like she didn't know how to explain how Loki had managed to invade her dreams or transport her to the cave. But if she thought about it too hard, she'd break her brain, and she needed to keep her mind intact in order to cure Naya and Kari. And to figure out how to give her brother his vision back.

Pekka snorted. "I think Einstein would beg to differ."

"Einstein most certainly did not believe in magic."

"He did believe in imagination and creativity. Why can't magic just be an extension of those wonderful things? Why do you have to wrap it in rules?"

"I don't want to make you angry, but you know why," she cried out. A century ago, he'd raged at her for refusing to use her abilities. He'd then walked out on her and never returned. If it wasn't for Naya discovering Pekka in the black-ops lab she'd broken into to find a cure for her brother, Irja would still wonder what had become of her twin.

"I'm not going to run away again." He cleared his throat. "That was wrong of me. I had no right to ask you for what I did. It was an impossible task. I was distraught and immature, a bad combination when feelings that I didn't know how to handle overwhelmed me."

He'd asked her to resurrect a woman he cared about. She'd been killed in a random mugging. "I would have tried if it wasn't for…" She couldn't continue.

Pekka threw up his hands. "For the last time, you did not kill our father. He was caught under a rockfall."

"But I caused the quake that made the debris slide down the mountain."

"I don't know how to get you to let go of that belief. Our mother was very wrong to tell you that." He squeezed her knee. "You were a little girl, and you saved a fox that would have died had you not intervened. Maybe it was a foolish thing to waste your ability on such an insignificant creature, but it was understandable and it wasn't wrong."

"But I felt the earth rumble as soon as I'd healed the animal."

"A complete coincidence. Besides, you'd need to add energy to cause an earthquake. How would drawing on magical energy from the earth make it move? Wouldn't that be backwards?"

"The flow of energy through the earth to get to me would have caused ripples. That's what triggered the quake." And that was why she'd avoided doing magic. No matter what Pekka thought, giving energy to someone meant taking the life force from someone else. Someone close to her. Someone she cared about.

He shook his head. "I can't make you give up this belief, so I won't try. But you are hindering your natural healing instincts by not using magic."

"It doesn't matter anyway," Irja said. "I have lost all my magical abilities. I touched the stones with the engraved runes and can no longer pull the earth's energies to me." She swallowed. "And that may be why Kari's not waking up and also perhaps why you have lost your vision." She'd not dared say this out loud before. But in the back of her mind, she'd suspected Loki's anger with her was why Pekka and Kari had been kept in their comas. The half god had hinted as much.

"You cannot take all the world's burdens onto your narrow shoulders, *Sisko*. You have to leave some for the rest of us to carry."

"I know you think I have martyr tendencies, but hear me out." Her brother snorted again. "Please," she implored. He nodded once, and she wiggled on the bed to get more comfortable as she prepared to tell her brother about the visits she'd had with Loki.

A wolverine swiped its claws a little too close for comfort, and Scott jumped back to avoid getting skewered. The fight was a disaster, and the fact that none of the warriors had gotten killed yet had more to do with luck than their fighting skills. He knew they were formidable warriors, but somehow they'd all forgotten how to fight as a unit, and instead everyone bumbled around, attacking their opponents randomly and at times getting in one another's way.

"For fuck's sake," he shouted as Torvald bumped into his back and almost caused him to fall. "Watch where you're trampling those giant feet of yours." Maybe it was fitting that they looked like a bunch of bumbling frat guys since they were on a college campus, but he'd rather they fought using the skills they'd been drilling over and over again in training.

The Viking only grunted in response before firing his gun at an attacking wolverine and then turning to chase down another that was retreating, trying to get away by running zigzag between the university buildings. Ordinarily, the warriors avoided using firearms since the noise attracted attention. As well-trained as Pine Rapids PD law enforcement were, they were no match for the wolverines. Having to protect mortals in battle was more of a hassle than even the Vikings and Valkyries wanted to deal with. Especially since the police officers would try to arrest both the Norse warriors and the wolverines, which only added to the chaos.

This battle, though, had turned into a huge mess so quickly that the Vikings and Astrid had not had any choice. Their only chance of defeating Loki's creatures was to fire at them whenever they had a chance.

Scott wiped his grimy, sweaty forehead. This fight was nothing like he'd experienced when fighting with the Norse warriors before. They were extremely lucky not to have attracted attention and killed an innocent bystander by mistake.

Where were the orderly battle formations? Where was the uncanny knowledge of where his battle brothers and sisters were at all times?

He tapped into the connection he had with his berserker. As when he'd tried before during this fight, he was able to reach his own inner warrior, but when he tried to connect with the others, a great swirl of anger and frustration flooded his mind. He quickly shut down the mental bond.

Last time, he'd tried, he'd pushed, but the rage transferring through the bond was so overpowering it short-circuited his mind, and he'd hacked and clawed his way through the fight in a blind rage. He'd not cared who or what he damaged. He was incredibly lucky not to have hurt any of his fellow warriors.

He kept the connection with his own berserker but refused to tap into the web of the other warriors again. There were ten wolverines left to defeat. They'd been attacked by twelve and by some miracle had managed to kill two. With nine of the Norse warriors fighting together, defeating the remaining wolverines shouldn't be a problem, but unless they got their shit together it looked like they might have to retreat.

A wolverine leaped toward him too quickly for him to raise

his gun and discharge it. He instead slashed at it with the knife in his left hand. He didn't make contact, but the threat of the blade was enough that the creature retreated a few paces. The delay allowed him to fire off a shot and kill the fucker.

Ulf appeared on Scott's left flank. "This is a disaster," the short-haired warrior growled. "We need to sort this mess out fast."

"What the fuck is wrong with the berserkers?" Scott asked as Ulf took position behind him so that they stood back-to-back. The Viking hacked at an attacking wolverine with a dagger, sinking it to the hilt into the creature's neck. Scott envied Ulf his reaction time.

"I don't know for sure, but I think it has something to do with the king," Ulf shouted over his shoulder. "His worry for the queen has put him too close to battle fever, and it's somehow affecting the rest of the berserkers."

Astrid came up from behind Scott. She pivoted on one foot and kicked a leaping wolverine in the head. The creature bounced once as it landed on the asphalt but was still conscious enough to crawl away. "We have to get the king to stand down," the Valkyrie shouted.

"How?" Ulf bellowed back.

"Follow me" was Astrid's only response as she turned and made a path through the scrimmage by shoving fighters—wolverine and Norse—out of her way indiscriminately.

Scott turned and looked for guidance from Ulf, but the Viking only shrugged and followed the Valkyrie. Scott held up the tail end of their little procession, grunting as he caught an elbow in the rib from someone or something.

The three of them made their way to where Leif fought with Harald by his side. Instead of the traditional back-to-back battle brothers stance that the king and his *stallare* would normally take, Harald bobbed and weaved around his leader, fighting an uneven battle against the attacking wolverines but also against Leif's flailing arms and knives.

Wide-legged, Astrid planted herself right in front of the king. "*Min kung*," she bellowed up into his face. "With respect, you have to sit this battle out."

Harald stopped, staring at the Valkyrie with an open mouth, but then quickly turned around to side-swipe an attacking wolverine.

"Get the fuck out of my way," Leif snarled at her with a voice that was much deeper than usual and ended on a bellow.

"Your berserker has run haywire for too long," Astrid responded with an equally impressive snarl. She somehow leaned into the king's face, despite Leif being several inches taller than her. "You need to take yourself out of this fight. You're endangering not only your tribe but Odin and Freya's mission."

Leif bared his teeth. "We fight until I say we're done. Standing down is not an option." He moved as if to turn away.

Harald grabbed his elbow, stopping him from turning. "*Min kung*, hear our battle sister."

The king shook off the grip of his *stallare*. "All of you, get the fuck out of my way." He turned back to Astrid. "Especially you. Step aside."

"Have it your way," the Valkyrie replied as she unholstered her gun, twirled it around so her hand gripped it across the stock, and promptly smacked the king on the side of his head. Hard.

Leif immediately crumpled to the ground.

"What the fuck did you just do?" Ulf gasped. The

Vikings stopped fighting momentarily, and miraculously no wolverines were close enough to attack.

"I made the king stand down," Astrid replied as she reholstered the gun.

Harald gaped at her, inhaling sharply and letting out the air in even small puffs as if he tried to say something but couldn't find the words.

Astrid quirked an eyebrow at him, but when no sound came forth, she shrugged. She turned and grabbed Sten and Per, who had fought their way toward the group. "Guard the king," she ordered the two Vikings.

They both nodded. "Is he hurt?" Sten asked.

"Nah," Astrid replied. "He has a thick head."

Per and Sten stared at her for a moment but didn't say anything. "We'll guard him," Per finally said.

Astrid nodded and turned as if to walk away and join in the fight again.

"You struck the king," Harald shouted, apparently finally finding his words.

"I did," Astrid agreed.

"In front of witnesses," Ulf almost whispered.

Astrid nodded.

"Is that allowed?" Scott asked. The events that had just transpired had frozen him in place, and he'd not been able to speak until now.

"No," Harald bellowed. "What the fuck were you thinking? You are in such deep shit." He shook his fist at Astrid.

She grinned at the hand waving in front of her face and then calmly pushed it out of the way. "What else is new?" She turned and sauntered away, waving a jaunty little goodbye over her shoulder. "I'm always in trouble."

CHAPTER 20

THE WARRIORS PILED IN THROUGH THE FORTRESS
entrance with a loud clanging of weapons and bellowing of
voices. Scott now realized this was pretty much how they
always returned from battle, whether their mood was victo-
rious or murderous. Today, the vibe was closer to the latter,
despite having defeated the wolverines. The king's behavior,
however, had everyone tense and frustrated. Leif's unconscious body reclined on a stretcher carried by Per and Sten.

Once Astrid had knocked him out, the chaos that disoriented the rest of the warriors had disappeared and their berserkers had settled down. They had not been able to create
the flawless connections their berserkers usually operated
under in battle. All their training and combat drills had paid
off when the remaining wolverines were swiftly dealt with.
They'd even been able to pack up the creatures' bodies
before sirens announced the Pine Rapids PD's approach.
The dead wolverines had then been dumped where sun-
shine would take care of the bodies completely.

Irja descended the stairs. Her face had a little more color
than when Scott had last seen her. Hopefully, she'd followed
the king's orders and had eaten and rested. "What happened?" she asked, rushing to the king's stretcher.

"He's fine," Astrid answered, her face grim. "He's just
been knocked unconscious."

Harald scraped a hand down his face. "*Jävlar skit, jänta.*
You know what I have to do."

"I do," Astrid answered calmly. She walked toward Harald with her hands raised waist-high in front of her, crossed at the wrists, but the Viking pushed them down. He shook his head, regret evident on his face.

Luke took a step forward. "What the fuck is going on?" Ulf and Torvald stepped up and grabbed him by his arms and shoulders.

"They have to put me in a cell, *älskling*." Astrid sounded as serene and calm as she looked. She stood tall and strong.

"The hell they do." Luke struggled against the two Vikings holding him back. "You saved everyone's life out there today. I'm not letting them treat you as a prisoner."

"They have no choice," Astrid said in that same eerie, calm voice she'd adopted since they got back to the fortress. "I struck the king. I'm lucky Harald didn't execute me on the spot."

"I can't believe you did what you did," Harald said. "But that you did it thinking I would strike you down dead is both foolish and insulting."

"What in all of the Norse gods' names happened out there?" Irja asked.

Scott put his hand on her shoulder. "Leif was out of control, and his berserker's battle fever created chaos in all our minds. We couldn't connect with one another's inner warriors."

Luke glared at Harald, then gazed at each of the Vikings and Scott. "What the hell is wrong with you? You are all alive thanks to her. This is how you thank her? This is how you treat your battle sister?"

Most of the Vikings averted their eyes from Luke, but Ulf shook him and tightened his grip. "You're making this worse. We have to secure her and await the king's verdict. It's the law."

"Fuck your laws," Luke snarled. He turned so his face was close to Ulf's. "And what the fuck do you get out of this? You must be rejoicing that she's in trouble. You've had it in for her ever since she turned you down. And even then you kept hitting on her." He struggled so hard in Torvald and Ulf's grip, he was close to dislocating his shoulder. "Let go of me, and we'll settle this as real men."

Ulf had apologized to Astrid for being infatuated with her and acting like a royal ass, and from what Scott could tell, even though the two weren't exactly friends, at least they tolerated each other and it seemed like there were no hard feelings between them. Apparently, that was not the case between Luke and Ulf.

The blond, short-haired Viking didn't say anything back to defend himself, but he clenched his jaw to the point where Scott could almost hear his teeth grinding.

Astrid took the few steps needed to get in front of Luke, Harald following close behind. She grabbed her *själs-frände*'s face between her palms and turned him toward her. "Beloved, your macho defense is admirable, but they have no choice. I knew the consequences of my action and did it anyway."

"Why?" Luke's eyes turned shiny. "Why do such a thing if you thought they might kill you?"

"So you and the others might live. I would do anything to keep you in this world." She leaned in and gently kissed his lips.

"Fuck this world if you're no longer part of it." Luke's voice broke at the end of his words.

Scott felt his own eyes tear up and had to turn away from the couple in order to clear them. Irja caught his gaze but quickly looked away. When things calmed down a bit, they would have to have a big discussion. She obviously thought they needed to cool things down, but he would set her straight.

Harald cleared his throat. "Let's go."

Astrid nodded and turned away from Luke to follow the red-haired Viking. The two left the foyer, walking toward the basement of the fortress.

"I'm sorry," Ulf said to Luke. "The king should wake up soon, and we'll know his verdict."

"Fuck your verdict," he snarled back. He twisted out of the grip of the two Vikings, who let him go but stood in battle stance on either side of him. Luke looked at the warriors around the room again. "You don't deserve to call yourselves her battle brothers. If she is in any way hurt, I'm coming after each and every one of you." He stomped to the front door and wrenched it open. "Cowards," he threw over his shoulder as he exited. The door slammed closed behind him.

A thick silence fell over the remaining warriors in the foyer until Irja clapped her hands. "Right. Let's get the king to his chamber so I can make sure he's unhurt. And then we'll try to wake him up with some smelling salts."

"I don't want to be in the room when that happens," Torvald muttered.

Per shuffled his feet. "The king is bound to be in an even nastier mood than he was in the fight. Harald says that except for when Naya left him, he hasn't seen Leif this worried since his twins were about to be born."

Irja's head snapped around, her eyes focusing on Per. "What did you just say?"

"The king is in a bad mood," the young Viking stammered.

"Not that," Irja demanded. "The last part."

"Harald says Leif is beside himself because he's worried about Naya." Per shrugged. "I guess he hasn't seen our king this emotional since his wife died."

"Solveig," Irja mumbled, looking into the distance. "And the twins." She sprang into action. "Get the king to his chamber and watch over him until I can get there with some smelling salts. It might be a little while, so you could find some yourself if you'd like." She ran down the hall.

"Where are you going?" Scott shouted after her.

"To the lab" came the reply from down the hallway.

"What just happened?" he asked the room in general but got nothing but shrugs and head shakes in reply.

After confirming her suspicion in the lab, Irja made her way down to the cellar where the holding cells were. Harald had told her since they didn't know whether Leif would be in control of his berserker when he woke up, they'd decided to incapacitate the king in one of the cells. The one other time Leif had succumbed to battle fever, Naya had brought him back. With the queen unconscious, that was not an option this time.

Irja hurried down the steps. The health of the king and queen influenced the whole tribe. If their relationship— their *själsfrände* bond—was in flux or if either of them were unhealthy, the entire tribe was affected.

Astrid's cell door was closed, but there was a small window. Irja pushed the sliding door aside to look in on her friend. The blond Valkyrie looked up and toward the door at the sound of the window opening. She was sitting on the small built-in cot of the cell.

"Hey," she said with a small smile. "Come to join me?"

"No. At least not yet." Irja tried to keep her voice upbeat, but on the inside, she fought despair over how defeated Astrid looked. "Is there anything I can get you?"

"The key to the cell?"

Irja chuckled. "Great try. Do you need water? Food?"

"Do not trouble yourself on my account, my friend. I know you must be beside yourself with worry about Naya and Leif." Astrid paused for a moment. "How is the king? And how is our queen?"

Irja almost blurted out what she'd discovered, but she needed to tell Leif first. "I am going to see to him now."

Astrid nodded. "Keep me posted when you can."

"I will. Take care, my friend." She moved to close the window.

"Wait," Astrid said. "How is Luke?"

Irja hesitated. Should she tell her friend Luke had left the fortress? It would cause Astrid worry, but then not knowing what had happened to her *själsfrände* would make her worry as well. "I don't know," she finally settled for. "He left when you were taken away."

"I figured as much. He's closed himself off from me, and my berserker can't reach him." The blond Valkyrie stood. "Take care of him for me when...if...after I am punished."

Irja swallowed hard. Losing Astrid was not an option—the tribe would never survive killing one of their own. But what the Valkyrie had done was unforgivable and punishable by death. Leif might not have any other choice. "I will," she said, then slid the window closed.

She continued to the cell that contained the king. When she opened the door, he was already conscious. Like Astrid, he was on a small narrow cot, but unlike the Valkyrie, he was not able to move freely. Harald and the others had secured him to the cot with wide leather straps.

"Irja," Leif said as she entered the cell, "what in Odin's name is going on?" He seemed calm if a bit drowsy, but when she connected to his berserker through hers, such overwhelming feelings of rage and despair flooded her senses that she had to clamp down on the bond immediately.

"Your berserker succumbed to battle fever, and you were out of control during the fight with the wolverines. It confused the others' inner warriors to the point where they could no longer fight effectively." She approached him cautiously.

The king closed his eyes and lowered his head. "I remember now. I couldn't control my inner beast. It wanted to kill everything in its path." He opened his eyes and turned his head to look at her. "It's because of Naya, isn't it? I'm endangering everyone because I'm worried about her. Because I'm about to lose her."

She tried to smile, but it felt fake. "The downside of a *själsfrände* bond. And we don't know that we're going to lose her." She refused to even think it. Her friend would live. She had to.

Leif swore. "She makes me so strong but at the same time so weak." He turned to look at her. "We have to find out what's wrong with her."

Irja had to look away because of the despair in the king's

ice-blue eyes. Before she had a chance to share what she'd found, though, he continued.

"If I was going…well…berserk, for lack of a better word, how did the fight go, and how did I end up in here? Is anybody hurt?" He paused for a moment. "Did I hurt anyone?"

Irja shook her head but still couldn't meet his gaze. "No, everyone is okay. The fight was won after Astrid knocked you out." The silence stretched on for so long, she finally looked up at the king. He stared at her, his mouth slightly open.

"Astrid struck me." It was a statement, not a question.

Irja nodded, her eyes still on the king. To her utter surprise, he bent his head back as much as the cot would allow and laughed heartily. The sound stirred Irja's berserker, who became alert as if there were a threat but then seemed confused as to what to do after that.

"Of all the stupid things that warrior has done," the king sputtered. "This must be the worst mess she's ever gotten herself into." He calmed down and paused for a moment. "Where is she now?"

"In a cell a few doors down from this one."

He blinked a few times. "And how's Luke handling that?"

"He's left the fortress."

"That's a wise decision. He's probably not sure whether to lash out at the woman he loves or the people who have imprisoned her right now. I have experienced the same situation." When the king and Naya had first met, she'd snuck out of the fortress to break into the lab that had held her and her brother prisoner to find a cure for Scott. She'd been captured by the security guards. And yet Irja could not hold the queen's rash actions against her, because it was also how Naya had discovered and eventually rescued Pekka.

Irja sank down on the cot next to the king. "You're taking this very well. I must admit I am a bit baffled by your mirth."

The king glared at her. "Oh, don't misunderstand me. There's nothing joyful in my laughter, but that is all I can do at this point." He shook his head as much as his restraints allowed him. "You're in a whole new mess of shit now, Astrid," he bellowed toward the open door.

"I'm pretty much always a hot mess. It's my new normal," came the faint answer from down the hallway.

"*Min kung*," Irja said, touching his hand lightly, "there is something else I must share with you."

Leif sighed deeply. "Who else has gotten themselves into trouble?"

Irja smiled wryly at his choice of words. Technically, she guessed Leif had gotten Naya into trouble. "I finally figured out what ails the queen."

The king jerked. "What?" he demanded.

"She's pregnant."

The king just stared at her for several heartbeats. "That's impossible," he finally said. "There's never been an immortal warrior getting a mortal with child or becoming pregnant by a mortal."

"True," Irja said. "But as we've established several times before, Naya is not an average mortal."

The king tried to lift his hand, but the restraints kept it in place. He sighed. "I can't even rub my face." He turned toward Irja. "I don't mean to criticize, but why did it take you so long to figure this out?"

She squirmed a little. The king had never reprimanded her when she took a long time to find ailments or cures, but she still blamed herself immensely for not catching the queen's condition. "I never thought to test for changing levels of estrogen and progesterone on the warriors. We've never had a pregnant immortal Valkyrie, so it just wasn't on my radar," she said. "I'm so sorry."

"Don't apologize," the king said. "There is no reason for you to think any of us were with child." His lips stretched into a wry smile. "Not even Astrid, although she would be more likely considering Luke is a mortal and his"—he looked embarrassed but then continued—"swimmers are not centuries old. But why is this making Naya sick?"

"I think her berserker is confused by the extra presence inside Naya. I have no way of knowing for sure, of course, but maybe it thinks it's an intruder, so to speak. An enemy."

The king was silent for a moment and then looked up at the ceiling. "If we don't find a way to save her and the baby, I need you to make good on the promise you made me a few years ago." His voice was calm but laced with sadness.

Irja swallowed. "*Min kung*, let's not discuss that now."

He looked at her, his ice-blue eyes deadly serious. "You made a promise, Irja. I need to know you will follow through on it."

Irja nodded. If the king went out of control again, she would sedate him until Odin called him back to Valhalla and put him into the eternal sleep. That was what she had promised years ago when the king had thought he'd lost Naya.

Irja always kept her promises.

Freya help them all.

CHAPTER 21

Scott fidgeted at the edge of the long line of Vikings standing shoulder to shoulder in the meadow behind the fortress. All the warriors attended, even Luke, who had been located via the GPS in his cell phone and picked up by Harald. The *stallare* had described Luke as "slightly unwilling." The truth was he'd been resisting with all his might, but since he'd been completely inebriated and since Harald had super strength, Luke had been hauled back to the Norse dwelling. He was still weaving slightly, but after being hosed down with cold water and filled with strong coffee—plus Harald and Sten were propping him up—Luke looked like he may be able to remain upright for at least a while. The bruises he'd acquired during Harald's manhandling contrasted sharply with his sallow skin.

Pekka was also part of the lineup. Scott had guided him out to the meadow, and when they'd seen his white eyes, the Norse warriors had loudly expressed their dismay. Ulf especially had taken it hard and kept glancing at Pekka. Maybe he was worried the same fate would fall on him since he too had touched the cursed stones but didn't show any symptoms of the disease yet. Scott was fairly certain he did not have to worry about himself slipping into a coma. It seemed his mortality—which was usually a weakness when living among the Vikings—was actually protecting him for once.

At one short end of the meadow, a huge slab of basalt rock with a flat top lay like a raised stage. On top, two stone thrones stood side by side. Normally, the queen and the king sat in those chairs, but today only Leif occupied one. Behind the basalt platform, a large ash stretched its limbs to the sky. The tree symbolized Yggdrasil, the immense mythical ash that the Norse believed connected the nine worlds of their cosmology. Despite there being no wind, the leaves of the tree rustled and the limbs swayed as if it could feel the tension rising among those gathered in the meadow. A chill ran down Scott's spine, and he felt his berserker stir. A murmur broke out among the warriors—their inner warriors had also been alerted by the tree's movement.

Leif held up a hand, and immediately the men quieted and the tree stilled. "We are gathered to witness our battle sister's verdict and punishment." His voice carried beyond the meadow and seemed to grow in volume as it echoed back from several directions.

Luke started to say something but was quickly shut down by Harald. Scott couldn't see exactly what the red-haired Viking had done, but judging from Luke's cutoff groan, it involved something painful.

"Bring out Astrid," Leif shouted, and the same weird echo effect happened again.

The tall blond Valkyrie appeared on the path that led from the fortress, Irja following closely behind like a guard or a jailer despite Astrid not being bound by anything. Even her hands were free, but she walked with her head bowed and her shoulders slumped. She stood before her king, her back toward her battle brothers.

Irja stepped in line and stood next to Scott but stared straight ahead without acknowledging his presence. Her face looked drawn and her mouth grim. He wanted to say something to soothe her worry but didn't find the words. For all he knew, one of her best friends was about to be executed.

Luke snarled but was again abruptly cut off. Astrid's shoulders jerked at the sound, but she didn't turn around. She remained facing the king, her head now raised. A whisper of wind played with her unbound, wavy blond hair, but she made no move to brush it aside when it got in her face.

"Astrid," Leif said. "You are accused of striking your king, a forbidden action among our people." He stood. "How do you answer?" His voice was deep and clear, but this time, it didn't echo back.

"I am guilty." The accused Valkyrie's voice was strong and as clear as the king's.

A murmur broke out again but quieted as Leif held up his hand. "Three of your battle brothers bore witness to your actions. None will tell me why you chose to strike me. What say you as to your reasoning for such a disrespectful crime?"

"I meant no disrespect, *min kung*." Astrid bowed deeply, her hair sweeping the ground in front of her.

"You are aware that striking your king or queen is punishable by death?" Leif asked.

"I am, as I was when I committed the crime."

"And so I ask again, why would you take such an action?" The king widened his stance and clasped his hands in front of him. The motion made Scott notice the sword scabbard strapped to the king's belt. It held Angrim, Leif's sword, named after a berserker from one of the Norse sagas. Scott's mouth went dry when he realized the king had come prepared to strike Astrid down with a blade.

"So that others might live," the Valkyrie answered.

"Explain yourself." This time, the king's voice echoed through the meadow, and the ash's leaves rustled before dying down as the king's words stopped repeating back.

Astrid stood taller, her spine straight and her shoulders squared. "I serve my king, my queen, and my tribe. Had I not done what I did, fellow warriors would have died." She tossed her hair back. "Maybe even my king would have died, which would have killed my queen." She bowed her head slightly. "With respect, *min kung*, I had no other choice."

"Do you claim I was a danger to my people?" Leif's deep voice carried no inflection other than that of a question, but his words caused a stir among the warriors.

Scott's berserker paced, and he had to struggle to keep it calm. The ash tree's limbs swayed back and forth at an alarming rate. A small sizzle of energy arced between his arm and Irja's. Startled, he turned to look at her, and his gaze met her wide eyes, but before he could say something, Astrid spoke again.

"I do," the blond Valkyrie said in a clear and confident voice.

"Do you have any witnesses who can attest to your claim?" The king's voice remained calm, but the ash's limbs swayed in larger arcs, and Scott's berserker paced in tighter circles.

The Valkyrie looked down. "I do not."

The king paused for several heartbeats, watching Astrid, but she didn't raise her head. He held up his hand. "Ulf, Scott, Harald, please step forward."

Scott took a step forward as did the other two.

The king switched his focus, and his gaze landed on

each of the warriors who now stood between Astrid and the others. When the king's eyes landed on Scott, he felt the weight of that look as a heavy physical presence pushing him down. "You were present when your battle sister struck your king?"

"We were," Harald said. Scott decided to let the *stallare* speak for him as well, so he only nodded. Ulf did the same.

"Why did you not intervene and protect your king?" Leif's gaze traveled over them again.

"It happened very fast," Ulf answered. "Our battle sister did not share her intentions, and as you know, she is very quick once she decides to strike."

One side of Leif's mouth quirked almost unnoticeably, but his eyes remained serious. "Do you agree I was a danger to my people?"

Harald cleared his throat, and Ulf looked away. Scott found himself studying his boots. He thought back on the fight with the wolverines and remembered the terrible rage that had entered his mind whenever he tried to connect with the king's berserker through his own inner warrior.

"Do I need to repeat my question?" the king asked, his voice hard.

Ulf swallowed loudly. "With respect, *min kung*, although you may not have directly attacked your people, your berserker was in battle rage, and in that state we could not connect to your inner warrior or to one another's berserkers."

"And your state of mind made us all disoriented and uncoordinated," Harald added. "We had to resort to guns in order to stay unharmed."

The king flinched but recovered quickly. "So you agree your battle sister had no other choice but to strike me?"

"That was not her first choice of action," Ulf said.

"Oh?" One of the king's eyebrows arched.

"No." Ulf cleared his throat before continuing. "Astrid explained to you that your berserker was out of control and asked you to step down from the fight."

"And what was my answer?"

"I believe your words were something like 'get the fuck out of my way.'" Harald coughed.

"So the three of you agree her action was justified?" The king's ice-blue eyes seemed to glow for a fraction of a second.

Scott couldn't find the words to answer the question, but he nodded again. After a while, so did Harald and Ulf. A cold sweat broke out on Scott's forehead and neck. He could feel some of it trail down his back as he wondered if he'd just condemned himself to death by some archaic Norse custom.

"You three step back." Leif's command snapped like a whip.

Harald was the first to rejoin the line of warriors, with Ulf and Scott a close second as they took the necessary backward step at the same time.

"*Tack, min kung*," Harald said, and Ulf inclined his head in a small bow, which Scott copied. He assumed the words of the *stallare* meant something like "Thank you, my king," which, considering his head was still attached to his neck, he could very much support.

"Astrid Idrisdotter, are you prepared to receive your punishment?" Leif asked.

"I am," the Valkyrie said, her voice shaking slightly.

Luke again tried to say something, but Harald was quick to choke his words again.

Leif's gaze quickly flickered to Luke and then back again on Astrid. "Then kneel before your king."

The Valkyrie immediately went down on one knee and bowed her head.

"Battle sister, you are found guilty of the heinous crime of striking your king." Leif's voice did the echo thing again, and the tree behind him swayed in the rhythm of his words being repeated. "As unforgiving as our customs consider this action, I agree that you had no other choice to protect your tribe and your king and queen."

Several of the warriors gasped, Scott included. Astrid raised her head to look at the king.

"You are impatient, impulsive, and impossible, but you are always loyal to our tribe."

The kneeling Valkyrie held out a hand. "My king—"

"Now receive your punishment for your actions," Leif interrupted, and Astrid bowed her head again. "For the action of striking your king, you are not allowed to speak to any of your battle brothers or sisters for thirty days. During this time, you will train but only with Ulf, and it must be done in silence. You will take your meals in solitude in your cell, which is also where you will sleep." Astrid's head shot up, but Leif carried on. "Do you understand your punishment?"

"I do," the Valkyrie said.

"Good, then go and be with your *själsfrände*. You have exactly one hour together before your solitude and silence begins." The ash tree's limbs shook violently for a moment before becoming absolutely still.

A joyful roar from the warriors rose over the meadow. Scott's berserker joined in, and he leaned his head back to let the inner beast's bellow join the others'.

Luke rushed to Astrid's side and embraced her. "Never do anything this stupid again."

"You know I can't promise that," the Valkyrie replied, tears streaming down her face. She leaned back and studied his bruised face. "What happened to you?"

"Let's discuss it in thirty days," Luke replied.

Scott turned to say something to Irja but she had already left. Pekka had also disappeared. He swore as he realized she had once again avoided him successfully.

Before he had a chance to go look for the elusive Valkyrie, Ulf stepped up to him. "I think I may have something on what those runes on the stones spell out."

"What is it?"

"Let me get the king and Irja so I can show you all at the same time."

"Irja has gone somewhere with Pekka." He didn't mean for his voice to sound as surly as it did.

Ulf cocked an eyebrow. "Okay, just the king for now then."

Leif was immediately interested once he heard what Ulf wanted to show him, and in less than ten minutes, the three of them were back in the fortress and gathered in the computer room.

"I feel like we should somehow celebrate Astrid not getting killed," Scott said.

Leif quirked an eyebrow. "Did you really think I would execute her?"

"I wasn't sure," Scott admitted. "Maybe you didn't have a choice according to Norse customs."

Leif turned to Ulf. "But you must have known she'd be okay."

The blond Viking shrugged and then looked away sheepishly.

"Seriously?" the king asked, incredulous. "Everyone thought there was a chance I would kill her?" Scott's berserker stirred as the tension in the room rose and the king's agitation increased, but then Leif shook his head. "Never mind. This is a discussion for a different day."

"So," Ulf said, his relief over changing the subject very obvious in how much fake joy he packed into that small word. "I've run several interpretations of the two runes we've identified for sure. The thurisaz stands for Thor, the god of war and thunder, but can also mean change or cleansing fire. And then we have the ansuz, Odin's symbol. But in addition to the Allfather, the king of the gods, it can also mean revealing message or truth."

"This we already know," Leif sighed. "I thought you said you had something new."

"I do," Ulf hurried to say. "Sorry, I get excited about the process of solving problems as much as finding a solution."

"Something you've no doubt picked up from Naya," Leif said. "She can drone on for hours about algorithms and processes." He smiled, but then sorrow flickered in his eyes, and he turned somber again.

"She taught me everything I know about computers and the Net, so that's probably true." Ulf didn't look up as he tapped a few keys to bring up a screen that showed a string of sentences that each used almost the same words but repeated them in different orders or changed their meanings slightly. "Naya had the idea to not only load the entire Elder Futhark alphabet to piece together the stone fragments but also some other major rune alphabets, alternate meanings of the god's names, and characteristics associated with the different gods."

Scott could feel himself getting as impatient as the king seemed to be. "And what did all that lead to?" Also, mentioning his sister's name made him impatient to break the curse so that Pekka and Kari could recover and Irja could concentrate on curing only Naya.

"Right." Ulf scratched his head and tapped a few keys to bring up yet another screen. "This is the most likely phrase those runes spell out."

Scott leaned forward to better see and almost knocked heads with the king, who'd done the same. On the screen, he read,

A war/fight/skirmish begun, a blind man/warrior/ Viking lost, his love/beloved/wife dying because of the treasure/child/daughter.

"Well, that certainly makes things clear," the king said dryly.

"I know, I know," Ulf said. "I thought the same thing, but then I saw Pekka's eyes and realized this may actually help us."

"You think Pekka is the blind man?" Scott asked.

"He could be," Ulf replied. "But it could also be the king, blinded by his worry for his *själsfrände* or blinded by his berserker being in battle rage." He threw Leif a quick glance. "No offense."

The king just waved the words away. "But what war or fight has started? We have quite a few to choose from."

"That I think alludes to Loki's new offensive with the glowing cages and making direct contact with Irja."

"Then who's dying?" Scott asked and a chill ran down his spine.

Ulf avoided his look. "If Leif is the blind man, then Naya would be the obvious choice. If it's Pekka, I don't know who his beloved is. He's not dating anyone that I know of."

"He cares for Kari," Scott said. "All the signs are there. I just didn't put it together." He thought back on how worried Pekka had been about Kari and how his first thoughts when he woke up had been about her.

Scott had called King Erik and told him about Pekka's suggestion. The king had been as skeptical as Scott about trying again to reach Kari's berserker by bringing all of the Taos tribe to the Valkyrie's bedside, but he was willing to try it. He just needed to sort out a few wolverine issues in Sedona first. Luckily, they had not tried to erect any more glowing cages but they were causing a nuisance nevertheless.

"But there are no treasures or children that fit that last part," Ulf said. "I've searched for an alternate meaning to that rune but have had no luck. It always comes back to those three words: treasure, child, or daughter."

Leif cleared his throat. "This is not how I pictured I would share this news, but here goes." He turned toward Scott. "Your sister is pregnant."

"What do you mean?" he found himself saying stupidly. Of course he knew what pregnant meant, but for some reason he had never thought that was a possibility in Naya and Leif's relationship. Why he hadn't, he didn't know, but he just hadn't.

"I mean"—Leif gave Scott a small smile—"that you are going to be an uncle."

"Congratulations?" Ulf directed the question to the king.

"I hope so," Leif answered.

"How?" Scott rubbed his head, trying to formulate the rest of the question. A small glow of joy burned hot in his chest, and it grew the more he thought about Naya having a child. He'd always thought he and his sister were the end of their family's line, but now there could be a continuation. Someone to carry on their parents' DNA.

"I hope I don't have to explain how babies are made." Leif smiled more broadly.

"No." Scott shook his head. "I know that part. I mean, how do we keep them both alive?" He hadn't met his niece or nephew yet—maybe more likely a niece if the curse could be believed—but already he knew he would love that baby fiercely with all his heart. But why had Irja not shared this news with him? She knew how close he was to his sister. Obviously, he'd imagined there was any intimacy between them beyond the physical. The thought made him both angry and sad.

Leif's face immediately turned somber. "That is the question I've been asking ever since I found out." He grabbed Scott's hand, palm to palm. "I swear to you I will do everything in my power to keep your sister and my child alive."

Scott looked straight into the king's ice-blue eyes. "Whatever you need, I will give it to you. My sister deserves so much, but most of all, she deserves to live—to live happily. If she lost this child, it would destroy her."

The king nodded. "I know. And if I lose her, it would destroy me and the tribe."

Ulf stood and put his hand over the king's and Scott's that were still clasped together. "Whatever the queen needs,

I and the other warriors will do anything we can to provide it."

"Of that I have no doubt," Leif said. "I just don't know what it is that she needs."

"Whatever it is, we will find it," Scott said. He would sacrifice anything and everything to make sure she and her child lived.

CHAPTER 22

IRJA WALKED SLOWLY THROUGH THE FOREST GROVE NEXT to the meadow behind the Viking fortress. Pekka had tucked his hand under her arm and followed but didn't seem to need any guidance as to where to step. He was strangely surefooted for being so new to his blindness.

"Are you remembering these paths from before?" Irja asked him. "You're barely stumbling."

"No. I have no idea where these paths lead, but my berserker is tuned in to yours and is giving me hints on how to steer my body." He squeezed her arm lightly. "I guess that will come in handy if this becomes permanent."

Irja shuddered. "Don't even joke about that. We'll find a way to break the curse." She hoped she sounded a lot more confident than she felt.

"What is it you wanted to talk to me about?" Pekka obviously wanted to change the subject, but so did she, so she followed along.

"The queen is pregnant." She'd thought about how to lead into the startling situation, but in the end there really was no proper introduction.

"That is unexpected but amazing." Her brother smiled.

Irja nodded but then—again—realized he couldn't see her head moving. "It would be if it wasn't for her berserker thinking of the child as an intruder and trying to fight it."

Pekka was silent for a moment. "I guess there has never

been a pregnant immortal warrior before, so a berserker wouldn't know what that looks or feels like."

"I've looked through everything I have in my library about berserkers." Irja rubbed her forehead. Many centuries ago, there had been Norse warriors known as berserkers. They would whip themselves into battle frenzy through rituals that probably involved some sort of drugs. According to legend, there was no way to defeat them since they felt no pain and could fight for hours. They wore wolf or bear skin—the name *berserker* actually meant bear shirt—and the sight of them was said to strike fear in their enemies' hearts.

She'd found a ton of literature about their prowess on the battlefield but nothing about any of them becoming pregnant. Which would have been a small medical miracle, since it seemed all of them had been men. "There's nothing there that helps me figure out how to calm Naya's inner warrior." She told her brother about the king and herself trying to connect with the queen's berserker without success. She'd heard Scott had tried as well with the same result. "I don't know what to do next."

Pekka stopped and pulled his hand from her arm. "*Sisko*, you *do* know what to do next. If you pulled me out into the forest to ask my permission to do the obvious, you know there is no need. I will support you whatever you decide to do, but you also know what I think you should do."

She knew he was talking about using magic, but her mind still couldn't quite accept using her abilities as the next choice. "I can't," she said instead. "I tried pulling on the basalt's power, but after I touched the cursed stones, I'm no longer able to reach the lines of energies."

"Try again." Pekka made it sound so simple.

"The risk is too great."

Her brother grabbed her shoulders. "If you start with the whole conservation of energy thing again, I'm going to have to shake you. Besides, saving a life is not the same as giving a life, so how do you know someone has to die in the process?"

"Because of what happened to Father." Her voice was faint.

"So you base your conclusions on this one event? Where is the science in that? You need a larger sample group. That one case could be a coincidence."

She swallowed the hard lump in her throat. She'd never told him of the other time she'd killed someone while practicing magic. Her mother had made her swear she would never share their secret with anyone else. "I killed someone else besides Father."

Pekka released her shoulders. "Go on."

Irja sighed. "When we were sixteen and you had gone to the market to trade furs, Mother had me help her with a particularly difficult labor. The baby was breech, and we couldn't turn it. The mother had been in labor for thirty hours, and we were losing her."

She could still remember the poor woman's screams as she tried to push her baby out. And how those sounds of agony had grown weaker and weaker as the hours wore on. Modern medicine had taught her the difficulties of that birth most likely had to do with the mother having an unusually shaped uterus. But back then, they'd only known that all their regular methods for turning a breech baby were failing. "Mother told me to funnel all my abilities into keeping both the mom and the baby alive. And I did." Tears trailed down her cheeks now. "But meanwhile, the woman's oldest, a fifteen-year-old daughter, was trampled by one of the horses out in the stable. Everyone thought it was a freak accident, but I know it was one life sacrificed to save two others."

Pekka shook his head. "That is horrible, and I'm so sorry you experienced that, but again, it could have been a complete coincidence."

"You don't understand," Irja whispered. "I felt the older daughter die. I know exactly when it happened, because a burst of power flowed through me as she lost her life. It's what saved the baby and the mother."

Her brother frowned. "But Mother told me she didn't allow you to be the main practitioner while you were still a teenager. She only used you as a conduit."

"What do you mean?"

Pekka sighed. "I loved our mother, but she had many flaws. One of them was her jealousy of you because you had stronger abilities than her. I long suspected training you in magic was just her excuse to use you as a conduit because you amplified her lesser gift." He touched her arm. "You didn't ever practice magic directly after Father died— Mother told me as much. You only funneled power to her."

"But I felt the teenaged girl die," Irja protested weakly. "Mother made me promise never to tell you. She said you would hate me for what I had done."

Her brother pulled her closer and hugged her. "I could never hate you, *Sisko*. You are my other half." He released her but kept holding her by her shoulders, smiling down at her with his empty eyes. "My better half." Pekka turned serious again. "I'm guessing this was the Grimstark family?"

Irja nodded, then caught herself. "Yes."

"A week before her new sister was born, Mother caught Gunhild Grimstark and me making out in the stables. She told me if I didn't leave the girl alone, I'd be sorry." He shook his head. "I was sixteen years old and full of hormones. There was no way I could leave my girlfriend alone. Mother caught me sneaking around in the middle of the night after visiting with Gunhild, and she said I'd regret not doing as she'd told me. A day or two after that, the girl was dead."

Irja gasped. "She couldn't have—"

"Killed her?" Pekka interrupted. "Our mother was at times diabolical, especially when it came to figuring out ways to make you feel bad, so I wouldn't put it past her. But it's more likely that she meant for the girl only to be hurt in the accident and somehow, something went wrong." He shook his head. "I can't believe she made you believe it was your fault. Even for Mother, that is evil."

Irja laughed bitterly. Their mother had never made any secret of the fact that Pekka was her favorite, and she'd been a genius when it came to inventing ways to emotionally hurt Irja. She'd played the two siblings against each other as well as undermined any friendships Irja had tried to forge with peers. "It's brilliant when you think about it. She sent her message to you and made me not only keep quiet about it but had there been any kind of investigation, I'd probably confess just to be rid of the guilt. It's the perfect crime."

Pekka embraced her again. "I had no idea you were carrying this around with you. You should have told me."

Irja buried her face in his shoulder and allowed the tears

to flow freely while she nodded, this time knowing Pekka could feel her head moving.

After a while, she pulled away and dried her tears. "I may never love our mother like you do, but she is our mom, and I choose to believe she didn't mean to kill Gunhild." To think otherwise would be too horrifying.

"Does this mean you are ready to do what is necessary to save Naya?"

"I don't know that I am able to use my abilities, plus the risk of something going wrong is still there."

Pekka shook his head again. "*Sisko*, to live is to take risks. If you never challenge yourself or dare to do something that may have dire consequences, you're not living. You're merely existing."

She thought about his words for several moments. Was that what she had done by avoiding using magic? By avoiding emotions as much as possible? Was she sleepwalking through her own life as a passive observer rather than participating? "If I'm going to try this, I need both you and Leif to be there. I may need to use you as my conduits if I can't properly draw on the basalt's power, and you are the two people my berserker connects closest to."

"And Scott," Pekka said. "He should be there too. Even if you don't believe the two of you share a special bond, his berserker is connected to his sister's. That may help you reach her inner warrior."

"Fine," Irja allowed. "Scott should be there too." She sounded petulant, but she couldn't help it. That spark that arced between them during Astrid's verdict had been startling and worrisome. Her berserker's response to Scott's was already problematic.

She had no idea what kind of tricks the crafty beast would try when it experienced magic powers for the first time.

———————————

The king had been cautiously optimistic when Pekka and Irja suggested that she would try to reach Naya's berserker through magic, but he insisted everyone get a few hours of rest before they made the attempt. Irja must have been more exhausted than she thought, because she had slept through her alarm. So she rushed out the door of her room only to come to a complete stop when she saw who was waiting for her in the hallway.

"Why didn't you tell me my sister was pregnant?" Scott said by way of greeting. His midnight-blue eyes were even darker than usual, and they bore into hers with unrelenting intensity. "You've shared my bed, shared your body with me, but refuse to give me anything else of you." He clenched his jaw and then released it. "That, I can almost come to terms with, but why would you not tell me something as important as my sister being with child?" Anger flashed in his eyes.

"It wasn't my news to share." She'd told the king, but it was up to him to decide who else needed to know.

"It didn't even occur to you to tell me, did it?" He sounded defeated.

She had actually thought about telling him as soon as she'd found out, but she didn't want to worry him further. And again, it wasn't her news to share. "It was up to Leif to inform those who needed to know. I couldn't presume to know my king's mind." Her voice sounded prissy and formal, even to her ears, but that was what happened when she defaulted to professional to keep her emotions at bay.

"She's my sister," he said loudly. "The baby is going to be my niece or nephew. I had a right to know." He shook his head and looked down, taking a deep breath as if trying to control his temper. "I give up." He looked straight at her, his eyes sad but still angry. "You don't want to acknowledge that there is something between us, and perhaps you are right. This attraction is obviously not anything beyond the physical for you, because if it was, you'd have known how much it hurts that you didn't share this news with me."

"It wasn't personal," she tried to explain. But how could she put into words that duty always came before emotions or personal issues? "I didn't treat you any differently than any of the other warriors."

He studied her for several heartbeats, the anger leaving his eyes and only sadness remaining. "Exactly." He turned and walked away.

She didn't understand why the sight of his muscled back disappearing down the hallway would cause her heart to ache or why she had the sudden urge to run after him and tell him he *did* mean more to her than any of the other warriors. Her berserker growled and tried to get her to chase after Scott, but she clamped down on their connection and ordered it to stand down.

It was better this way.

If the queen's brother cut himself off from her, he would run less of a risk of getting hurt should things go wrong when she used magic. Although Pekka's explanations were logical, a small part of her still believed that maybe she'd taken a life the two times she'd tried to save lives.

Besides, there would be plenty of time to sort out whatever the weird connection was that she experienced with Scott once Naya was well again, her brother had his vision back, and Kari woke up.

Duty came first, always. It was what defined her. It was the only way she knew how to keep it together.

But then why did she feel dejected as she headed toward the queen and king's bedroom?

And why were her steps so heavy?

Scott didn't look at her when she entered the room, but Leif nodded at her, and Pekka gave her a little wave. Despite not being able to see, his berserker must have alerted him to her presence.

"What do you need from us?" Leif asked.

She felt nervous all of a sudden, her palms clammy. She wiped them on her pants. "It has been a long time since I practiced magic, and I have not used a conduit before, so don't have too high expectations. This may not work at all." She left out the part that really worried her. That Naya would be in worse shape than she was now after Irja tried to help her.

Leif nodded. "Pekka has told us about your aversion to using your abilities. You don't have to tell us why that is or what made you change your mind. Just know I am grateful that you are making the attempt."

Irja nodded. She looked toward Scott, but he was watching his sister while holding her hand. "It may take me a few tries, so be patient." Her voice shook, betraying how nervous she was.

"Calm yourself, *Sisko*. You know what to do. You've done this before." Her brother's soothing voice centered her and calmed her nerves.

"Alright, here goes." Irja closed her eyes and took a deep breath in through her nose and then exhaled through her mouth. She repeated the pattern while lacing her fingers together and placed her hands palms down on her own abdomen. Her elbows stuck out perpendicularly from her body.

She tapped into the connection with her berserker. The beast was calm but alert, waiting to see what would happen next.

Reaching beyond the connection to her inner warrior, she tapped into that other awareness she had inside her. The one that could see the layers of power that had been interlaced into the ancient rock surrounding the fortress. As when she had tried before, in Pekka's room while he was unconscious, she could sense the energy all around her, but it slipped out of her grasp when she tried to reach for it.

Frustrated, she tried to force the cool blue and green lines of magic to do her bidding, but they wouldn't obey her no matter how hard she tried. She planted her feet more firmly and did the breathing exercises again, pressing her interlaced palms harder against her center.

Once more she reached for the energy in the ancient rock, but it still eluded her, and she cried out in frustration as she tried again, only to fail again.

"Stop trying to do it by yourself," Pekka's calm voice instructed her. "Use your berserker's connection with us."

Of course, that was why they were in the room.

Irja kept her eyes closed but nodded to show she'd understood. "Okay," she then said, because once again she'd forgotten that her brother couldn't see.

She squared her shoulders and dropped the connection

she'd tried to force with the lines of power, instead widening the one she had with her berserker. The beast seemed both curious and alert, as if anticipating a new game it had never played before. She reached beyond their bond and tapped into the web of her fellow warriors, like she would have done if preparing for battle.

The familiar and comforting presence of Pekka showed up immediately. His berserker pranced and jumped, ready to play with hers.

The king's inner warrior wasn't as strong or as much of a central anchor as she was used to, but at least it wasn't raging.

Naya's berserker flashed alert for a short moment, but then snarled and disappeared, leaving a trail of anger. Irja tried to cajole it to come back, but it eluded her.

She then reached for the cool blue and green lines again, this time trying to weave them with the web of connection she had with her fellow warriors, but again they escaped her grasp.

Pekka's berserker moved closer to hers, lending its support, but she couldn't figure out how to use its presence to funnel the magic. Her own energy waned as she tried to use her brother as a conduit, and she could feel her physical body slumping.

And then all of a sudden it was there, an inner warrior beckoning to hers and revealing the path to all that glorious energy woven into the layers of the ancient rock. When she felt the pull of the magic, she didn't know how she could have missed this obvious connection in the first place. The blue and green lines danced in welcome, beckoning for her to come and join them.

The other berserker ran toward hers, the gorgeous bands of power trailing behind it. It invited her inner warrior to dance, and the blue and green lines weaved around them in a glowing double spiral.

Irja reached for them with her awareness, and they immediately jumped to do her bidding, flooding her with magic. She pooled it inside her and bent it to her will, and it took the shape she wanted as if it had been days instead of centuries since she'd last used her ability.

Again, she called on Naya's inner warrior to join the web. The beast snarled and growled, trying to sever the connection she established with it, but this time she had magic on her side.

She weaved blue and green ribbons of power around the beast, partly coaxing and partly forcing it to remain in the web. Extending the lines of energy from her beast that was still dancing with its new best friend, she joined Naya's berserker with the new web of magic and then wove Leif's and Pekka's inner warriors into it as well.

She poured as much love and acceptance as she could down the lines, trying to show Naya's beast that it was one of them, that they were all on its side. Pekka caught on immediately, and his inner warrior flooded the web with feelings of acceptance. After a few moments, the king's did the same.

Irja realized the berserker her beast had been playing and dancing with was Scott's, but she didn't have time to think about what that meant because all of a sudden a new inner warrior joined their web.

It appeared hesitantly on the edge of their connective lines. Much smaller than the other inner warriors, it hesitantly tested their bonds. Leif's berserker howled with joy and ran toward the small shape, which at first seemed taken aback but then leaped onto the back of the king's beast with excited yips.

Naya's inner warrior growled and struggled against the blue and green ribbons Irja had woven around it. As it watched Leif and the small berserker play together, though, it calmed down and instead paced inside its makeshift cage.

Irja loosened the restraints tentatively, and when the beast didn't immediately fly into a rage, she gradually removed all the glowing lines of the cage. The queen's inner warrior cautiously approached the king's berserker and the small beast.

Irja's eyes welled up with tears as she saw the three members of her tribe's royal family making each other's acquaintance for the very first time. And then Scott's inner warrior noticed the three embracing. It broke out of the dance with her beast and rushed to join the royal threesome.

Irja gasped as she felt its absence acutely. Having Scott's berserker close to hers had not only made it possible to bend the lines of magic to her will but it had made her feel complete and more centered.

Without Scott's inner warrior near, she felt abandoned.

Not even Pekka's berserker nudging hers made her feel less alone.

CHAPTER 23

SCOTT MARVELED AT THIS NEW WEB OF CONNECTIONS between the inner warriors. It was as if he'd been caught up in the spectral lines of the aurora borealis, those glowing wonders of nature that appeared at the north pole when energized, charged particles spiraled around the earth's magnetic field lines. He'd once again been pulled toward Irja. This time, it was his inner beast who couldn't resist the attraction, and the blue and green ribbons of light had followed him as he rushed toward her.

Their berserkers had engaged in some strange game, jumping and twirling around each other, and then he'd felt a new presence that pulled even stronger than Irja.

He'd searched for this new beast and discovered a small inner warrior playing with Naya's and Leif's berserkers. Instinctively, he knew this tiny presence was his niece or nephew. It was part of him.

It was blood.

It was family.

He rushed over to greet his new favorite relative, and the little inner warrior launched itself into his arms. He'd never felt so complete, so full of love.

The blue and green lines of Irja's magic bounced and rippled as he poured all the joy and love he experienced into them. He had to use the ribbons of light as an outlet or he'd explode.

For a moment, everything in his world was exactly as it

should be, and he turned toward Irja to include her in this cocoon of contentment. But before he had a chance to reach for her, the lines that connected them all turned sickly neon.

He recognized the colors from the glowing cages of the wolverines and immediately tried to block the energy flowing through him, but it was too late. A foul wind blew through their web, and his niece or nephew was ripped from his arms by an unseen force as the tiny berserker cried out in dismay.

Leif bellowed in rage and tried to chase after the small beast, but he was held back by the strong wind.

Scott turned to see if Irja was okay. She glowed too brightly, as if she was on the verge of burning out, and he tried to run to her, but that same wind held him in place. Then all of a sudden there was no web of glowing lines, no shining berserkers, and they were all pulled back abruptly into the regular world.

His body trembled as a thousand needles pricked his skin, and he found himself back in the queen and king's bedroom.

"What the fuck happened?" Leif hollered. "Bring me back my child."

"Aw, isn't that touching. A father's hankering for his progeny," a mocking voice said from the door. The translucent figure of a tall man with short reddish-blond hair flickered by the door.

"Loki," Leif growled as he struggled against some sort of invisible bond.

Scott was frozen in place, and he looked to see how his sister and Irja fared. Naya slept in the bed as peacefully as she had before Irja invoked the magic, but the Finnish Valkyrie leaned on one knee against the bed, breathing heavily. Neon lines of blue and green connected her with the figure at the door, and she seemed to grow weaker as the man appeared more and more solid. "Release her," he shouted.

The man—Loki—scratched his perfectly groomed beard. "So this is lover boy. Who would have thought a regular mortal could keep up with her?" His smile turned lascivious. "I almost had a go with her myself, you know, but we were interrupted." He turned toward Irja. "Should we have our moment here instead, in front of everyone?"

"Eat shit," Irja growled.

Loki tutted. "Such modern and foul language." He stretched, arms above his head as he turned completely solid. "But such pure and clean magic. Yes, I think I can work wonders with this."

Irja whimpered and seemed to try to pull energy back into herself.

Leif struggled against the invisible force keeping him in place.

Scott realized he hadn't seen Irja's brother. He looked around the room and saw a slumped-over figure in one corner. He tried again to move against the invisible restraints imprisoning him to get to Pekka, but it was no use.

"Now, now," Loki said. "Everyone just remain calm, and we can settle this as civilized people." He threw Leif a glance filled with disdain. "Well, as civilized as you Vikings can manage. And you." He turned to Irja. "My glorious magical portal. Don't exert yourself trying to steal my power back. You know it's no use." He stood taller and pulled hard on the lines connecting him to Irja before severing the connection. The Valkyrie slumped to the floor. "Ah, it is so good to be back in Midgard. It's been centuries since I was here last." He tilted his head. "Actually, close to a millennium, I believe."

"Don't," Irja whispered.

"Don't what, dear?" Loki cocked a hand behind his ear in a mock display of trying to hear better. "Don't take over the world and rule all humankind?" His voice turned harder. "Don't take the power that should have been mine in the first place? Don't take what I deserve? Don't take my birthright back? Well, it's too late for that. I'm finally here, and I'm staying."

"Fuck off," Leif growled. "You deserve nothing and have no birthright, mongrel that you are."

Loki slashed his arm through the air, and the king cried out in pain as he collapsed to the floor. "That's better," the half god said. "I can't stand it when uncivilized brutes try to carry on a conversation with the grown-ups. And he's supposed to be the king destined to defeat me?" He shook his head. "Please."

Pekka groaned and half sat up. "What happened?" His white eyes stared at nothing as he rubbed the back of his neck. "I feel like I've been on the worst mead bender ever."

"And here's her twin," Loki cooed. "Still blind, I see."

"Who the fuck is that?" Pekka asked.

"That's not important right now." The half god turned toward Irja. "Now, my pretty potty mouth, shall we play a game?"

"Leave her alone." Scott pushed with all his might against the invisible force keeping him in place. It did nothing but wear him out.

Loki simply ignored him.

"I'm not having anything to do with you," Irja said through gritted teeth.

"I'm so sad to hear you say that." The half god shook his head in mock disappointment. "I'm feeling very generous at the moment and was going to let you win. Never mind. Instead, I'll leave you with a thank-you gift."

"I want nothing from you." Irja struggled to stand up, but she was frozen in place by Loki's power.

"Oh, I think you'll want this." The half god's hazel eyes glittered dangerously. "I'll even give you a choice as to which gift to receive." He walked over to Irja and leaned down, capturing her chin with his hand. "Now, I can either cure your brother, or I'll let your queen and her child live."

"Fuck off." Irja tried to tear her face from his grip, but he held on.

Loki smiled. "It's a simple choice of who and what you care more about—duty to your queen or love for your only family."

"The whole tribe is my family," Irja replied.

Scott admired how brave she was. He wasn't sure how he would react if a half god had his hands on him. Probably not defiantly.

"Choose," Loki commanded, all play and mockery gone from his voice, which was now hard enough to shatter glass.

"*Sisko*," Pekka said, his tone of voice implying a warning.

The half god waved in his direction, and the Finn slumped down, once again unconscious. "If you don't choose, you will lose both of them. I'll steal the life force from both your brother and the queen's child."

"No," Leif shouted.

Loki lashed out with his hand again, and the king bent

over in pain. "I'll give you to the count of three," the half god said to Irja. "One." He paused for a heartbeat. "Two."

"Fine," Irja cried out. "I'll play your stupid game. Save the queen's child."

Loki straightened and sighed heavily. "I told you this wasn't the game. I wanted to play, but you turned me down on that." Suddenly, he smacked her across the face. "This was a gift. Learn the difference, you ungrateful *jänta*."

"You coward," Scott shouted, hurling himself against the invisible barrier.

Loki turned toward him, a malicious smile on his lips. "You'll regret calling me that." He buffed his nails against his shirt. "But not today. I have other plans to attend to." He turned and walked out the door.

As soon as it closed behind him, the restraints imprisoning Scott disappeared. He rushed to Irja. "Are you okay?"

"Don't worry about me," she said. "Go get the bastard."

As she finished speaking, Leif thundered past them toward the door, and Scott followed. Both rushed out to find the hallway empty. Loki was nowhere to be seen.

"*Jävlar helvetes skit*." Leif stomped his foot.

Scott had no idea what the words meant, but from the king's tone of voice, he knew he agreed.

Harald came running up the stairs. "What in Odin's name is going on? All of a sudden, nobody in the house could move. We were all frozen in place."

"Loki's loose in Midgard," the king said.

"Ah shit." Harald's light-green eyes widened.

"Leif?" Naya's voice sounded weak from inside the bedroom.

The king turned a one-eighty and disappeared back through the door.

Harald watched his retreating back and then turned to Scott. "Do you want to explain what's going on?"

"I don't know that I can." He wanted to see his sister now that she was finally awake and to make sure Irja was okay.

He thought he'd started to get a handle on this weird world the Vikings lived in. He'd almost gotten used to things like wolverine–human hybrids with wicked claws, and the glowing cages were new to everyone, but he thought he'd handled those well too. The berserker thing was still strange, but over time it could possibly become a new normal.

Gods walking the earth though, even half gods, was just not something his mind could bend around.

So he decided to stop trying and instead went to check on the two women in the bedroom, leaving Harald behind.

———————————

Hours later, Irja sat by Naya's bedside. She'd come to check on the queen and the baby, or at least that was what she told herself. The truth was if Astrid wasn't secluded in complete silence, she'd have this conversation with the blond Valkyrie instead.

And anyway, Naya wasn't allowing any more examinations of herself or her child. "You already poked and prodded me after I woke up. Nothing has changed in the last few hours. I'm fine. The baby's fine. Well, at least as fine as we can be with a sinister half god on the loose among unsuspecting mortals." She tapped the back of Irja's hand with her index finger. "But never mind that. I want to talk about this instead."

Irja sighed and pulled her hand out of reach. A snake's tail pointing toward her little finger had appeared while she'd checked and double-checked medical supplies to make sure everything needed to care for wounded warriors was on hand. She'd ignored the tattoo for as long as she could, but there were no more tasks for her to complete, and now here she was.

After Leif had assured himself the queen and her child were okay, he'd organized the tribe into a frenzy of activity. Ulf was to monitor chatter on social media and the Darknet at all hours and look for anything that might lead them to Loki. Scott had volunteered to help.

Harald had divided the rest of the warriors into patrol teams to guard the streets of Pine Rapids around the clock. Leif had called King Erik, and the Taos tribe was sending warriors to help with patrolling the streets. If they managed to track down Loki, the king had promised Leif he'd send everyone he could and come himself in order to help battle the trickster god.

Even Pekka had been put to work. Actually, he'd insisted on helping out. He was in the armory, making sure every weapon was in tip-top shape. Apparently, getting ready for battle as many times as he had, he didn't need sight in order to clean and load firearms.

Irja didn't hold out hope that they'd be able to find, never mind trap Loki. Using her as a conduit, he had siphoned enough power from the basalt rock to be indestructible. Their best chance was to wait for him to grow weak. However, that would only happen if he used his power, and contemplating the destruction he could cause while doing so was too scary for her right now.

"We should prepare for war with a god, if that is even possible, not discussing my—"

"Sex life?" the queen interrupted with a smirk.

"That is not what I meant to say." She could feel her cheeks heat from the blush creeping up her neck and face.

"I wish Astrid could join us for this discussion," Naya said, pushing to sit upright against the headboard.

Irja avoided the queen's gaze. "If she was available, I'd prefer to talk to her about it."

"Because you don't want to discuss Scott's sex life with his sister." Naya made it a statement, not a question, a big grin on her face.

"We're not discussing sex lives. And stop enjoying this so much." She really wished Astrid could have helped her through this instead of the queen.

Naya looked poignantly at Irja's hand. "The only way for this to appear is if you've had hanky-panky with my brother, so we are indeed discussing sex—or love life, if you prefer."

"How do you know it's your brother who has caused this? It could be any of the warriors. Maybe even someone I met in Sedona."

"Please." Naya's eyebrows shot to her hairline so fast, they might have left her face entirely if they weren't attached. "Your berserker and his are so excited to see each other whenever you are in the same room, it's a miracle you don't break down and have sex right on the carpet in front of everyone. Plus the fact that Scott all of a sudden has a berserker was a dead giveaway."

Irja sighed. Had it been so obvious to everyone that there was a bond between her and Scott? Was she the only one who'd not seen it? Or was it just that she was so deep in denial that a neon sign could have announced their connection and she still wouldn't have believed it? "Things are complicated," she told the queen, using the understatement of the year. Things were not complicated; they were shot to hell because she'd managed to drive Scott away, and now she didn't know how to fix it.

"Actually, things are very simple," the queen contradicted. "In order to complete the bond—and avoid being called back to Valhalla and sleep for an eternity—you have to once again do the horizontal tango with my brother."

Irja blinked a few times before she could find her voice. "I can't believe you're being so flippant about this. We're discussing the lives of two people, not what we're ordering for dinner."

Naya just smiled wider. "Remember when I came to you because the serpent's tail had appeared on Leif's hand and somehow I had developed this weird aggressive beast inside me? Remember when Astrid had broken up with Luke and then the snake tattoo turned up on her hand? And she came to you for advice?"

"Yes, of course." Irja frowned. "Those were two incredibly important events for the tribe."

Naya nodded. "So you said at the time. And what else did you tell Astrid and me?"

"I can't remember," Irja said but had to look away so the queen wouldn't see the lie in her eyes.

"Sure you do," Naya countered. "You said that finding one's *själsfrände* was an incredibly rare event and we were both lucky to have it happen to us."

"Well, you were." Even in Irja's ears, that response sounded trite and defensive. "This is a completely different situation." She swallowed. "I've offended Scott, and he doesn't want anything to do with me anymore."

Naya's eyes softened. "Like when I defied Leif's orders and set out on my own to blow up a lab? Or when Astrid thought Luke was only with her to spy on me and then thought he ran a human trafficking ring?" She leaned forward. "Whatever problems you have between you can be solved. I promise."

"It isn't that simple." Irja thought about the anger and hurt she'd seen in Scott's eyes the last time they spoke. How could she overcome that?

"Then make it that simple," Naya insisted. She yawned. "I know I was in a coma for almost two days, but as crazy as it sounds, I'm tired again."

"It's because of the baby." Irja smiled. They would have a child in the tribe. She couldn't quite bend her mind around that yet, but whenever she thought about it, her heart filled with joy.

Naya looked down on her still very flat stomach. "I am very close to freaking out about this." She looked up at Irja, her eyes round and wide. "I have no idea how to take care of a child."

"I'm sure you will have more than a little help from the rest of the warriors."

"Yeah, but I also have no idea how to birth a child. Will any of them help with that?"

Irja grabbed her friend's hand. "I will. I helped my mother deliver several babies."

The queen squeezed her hand. "Thank you. Not only for that but for looking out for all of us and using your ability to help my inner warrior find its way and accept the baby. I know it wasn't easy for you."

"Pekka made me understand that closing off my ability made me weaker, not stronger."

"He's a good brother," Naya said.

"He is," Irja agreed, warmth filling her chest when she thought of her twin.

"Mine is as well. You should go talk to him." The queen yawned again.

"I will." Irja stood and walked toward the door.

"One more thing," Naya called after her.

Irja turned.

"Leif is going to be impossible. He'll insist I stay in bed until this child enters the world. Please tell him pregnant women can function normally and do not need to be in convalescence."

Irja smiled. She had no doubt the king would enter major overprotective mode and try to keep Naya as secluded and still as he could. As usual when Leif tried to impose his will on the queen, fireworks were likely to erupt between them. "We'll see," Irja threw over her shoulder before exiting the room.

"Don't be petty," Naya shouted after her as Irja closed the door.

CHAPTER 24

SCOTT RETURNED TO HIS ROOM FROM MONITORING the computers for signs of wolverines or Loki to find Irja sitting on his bed. She was reading what looked like an old journal. The leather cover looked dry and the spine was cracked.

"Good book?" he asked, not knowing how to handle the conflicting feelings flooding his mind or his body's reaction to being so near her and a bed again. His berserker wasn't conflicted at all. It pranced and carried on as if it had drunk three cups of coffee in quick succession.

Irja jumped as if startled. "Um, yes." She closed the book. "I'm trying to see if there's anything in these old books that would tell me how to locate a god."

"And what do we do once he's been found?"

She shrugged. "I have no idea. Fight to the death and hope we somehow kill him or at least injure him enough to where he can't harm the mortals."

"That seems very defeatist. Are all the warriors so blasé about dying?"

A dry smile lifted her lips. "We've all already died once."

He kept forgetting that. "Couldn't Leif ask Odin for help with capturing Loki and what to do after?"

"He's been trying to contact Odin ever since the first glowing cages showed up, but the Allfather is not answering Leif's requests. It seems something is going on in the Norse gods' council that has both Odin and Freya occupied."

"That's unfortunate." Once again, the bizarreness of talking about gods as if they were regular people struck him. But why was she here? It wasn't to show him her book, of that he was sure. He worked a kink out of his neck and stifled a yawn. The chair in the computer room was comfortable, but after several hours in mostly one position, his muscles were stiff and sore.

Irja jumped up from the bed. "You're exhausted. I should go and let you get some rest." She headed for the door.

He grabbed her hand to stop her. "Irja, why are you here?"

She blinked several times and opened her mouth as if to say something but then closed it again. Finally, she just lowered her gaze and nodded at the hand he was holding. "Because of that."

He frowned, unsure of what she meant, but then he looked at her hand and saw the serpent tail tattoo. Several emotions struggled for dominance. Happiness, because the proof of their *själsfrände* bond meant she would have to admit that there was something special between them. Anticipation, because the next step of completing the bond was for them to have sex again. His berserker howled its approval at the thought. And finally disappointment, because he knew without that stupid tattoo, she never would have sought him out again, would never have entertained the thought of joining him in bed again. "Oh," he said, then grimaced at how unintelligent that small word was. He looked at the hand he held in his and then back up at Irja. Myriad emotions swirled in her eyes, but he couldn't decipher what any of them were. "I don't know what to say."

"I know how you feel," she said with a wry smile.

"But again, why are you here?" He kept his face neutral so she wouldn't suspect how much her next words meant to him. Inside, though, the swirl of emotions battled more intensely.

Irja looked down at their hands. "It's the next step in the *själsfrände* bond."

"So you're only here to complete the bond?" He almost held his breath waiting for her answer.

"Yes." She frowned at him as if he were dense. "I mean, no. But we need to finish our connection. It will make the tribe stronger, because we will be stronger."

His heart sank. Of course, everything for the tribe. "So you're here to screw me because of your duty to the other warriors."

She jerked at the harsh words and pulled her hand away. "This was a mistake," she mumbled, taking a step toward the door. "I told Naya as much, but she wouldn't listen."

"Wait," Scott said, and thankfully, she stopped. "You spoke to my sister about this?"

Irja turned to face him. "Yes, I went to her for advice." She paused. "I'm so bad at this." She took a deep breath and looked him squarely in the eyes. "A *själsfrände* bond is an extremely rare event. Even during the old days, very few people knew someone who had found their soul mate. It was one of those things everyone talked about but almost nobody had seen or experienced." She looked away. "I never expected it to happen to me."

"But there are two couples just in this tribe," Scott said and mentally added that there were actually three now.

"I have no idea why the gods have granted us such a blessing, but it's unheard of. None of the other Norse tribes in Midgard has even one bonded couple. But it makes our group stronger and more cohesive."

Okay, so he could see why this would be a good thing while fighting a half god. "I'm sorry I gave you a hard time. I now understand better why this is important to the tribe."

She swore under her breath. "I am not here to sleep with you because of my duty to the tribe," she said, anger in her voice, and then the words tumbled out of her mouth at lightning speed. "I'm here because since the first moment I met you, I've been attracted to you. I've fantasized about what it would be like to be with you in bed. But you are the queen's brother, and I am not even a Valkyrie. I am half Finn and half Sami, a mongrel of two people, neither of which the Norse think very highly of. But then somehow you still wanted me, and then we made love and it was better than I could ever have imagined." She splayed her arms out. "But then I got scared and screwed it all up, and now I don't know how to fix it."

"You fantasized about me?" His berserker preened.

Her eyebrows rose. "That's the main point you got out of all that?"

"It seemed the most important." He smiled. "Come here." He pulled her toward him and pressed his lips against hers.

Finally, she was in his arms again. It had only been a few days since she'd shared his bed, but that was too long. He needed her there every night and maybe a few times during the day as well.

Their tongues tangled, and he was instantly hard. She moaned into his mouth and pressed more firmly against him, igniting every single one of his nerve endings. This felt so right. If all they did was kiss for the rest of their days, he would be happy.

Irja grabbed the hair on the back of his head and angled his face so she could deepen the kiss. She opened her legs and pushed her center against his thigh.

Scratch that.

Kissing was not enough. He needed more. So much more.

She nibbled along his jaw and then bit down more firmly when she reached his earlobe. His cock pressed so hard against his zipper, it might bust. "Slow down," he panted.

"Don't start with that again," she moaned against his throat, changing position so her heat pressed against his hardness.

He twisted them around so he could back her up toward the bed, but she turned them again before they got there and pushed him down on his back. She leaned over him and pulled off his t-shirt.

He loved her being the aggressor. His berserker howled its approval.

Irja's inner warrior answered with a growl.

She pulled off his boots and made quick work of freeing his legs from his pants while he disposed of the open shirt. He tried to reach for her so he could help her out of her clothes, but she pushed him back down and instead tore off his underwear.

And then the heat of her mouth encircled his cock in the most glorious way. He arched against her as she sucked and licked. "Sweetness, I'll explode if you keep that up." He could barely get the words out.

She released him and stood. "We can't have that," she said and swiftly shed her own clothes.

He got a brief glimpse of her magnificent body before

she straddled him, and he once again bucked against her, his eyes closing because of how amazing and how right she felt against him.

She raised her hips, hovering above him, and grabbed his cock. Teasing the tip of his shaft by circling the opening of her damp heat with it, she slowly sank down until all of him was buried inside her.

He moaned loudly. Or maybe the berserker did.

Her inner warrior answered, and then she rode him faster and faster until he lost sense of time and space.

His balls tightened, and he struggled not to blow his load.

He grabbed her hips, trying to slow her down, but she kept the fast pace and reached behind her, firmly capturing his balls in her hand. When she squeezed, Scott completely lost it and shouted out her name as he came.

Irja wasn't sure where this new assertive version of herself came from, but it turned her on to be the dominant partner. She felt Scott's climax, and it triggered her own.

Wave after wave of pleasure rippled through her body as she peaked and then came again. Suddenly, she felt her soul shoot out of her body into a vast black void. A circle of twirling white lights rushed toward her, and as she passed through it, she was once again whole and standing by a black, glittering pond in the middle of a vast darkness.

On the other side, a woman dressed in a simple white shift waved to her. The woman's silver hair was so long it brushed her hips.

"Freya," Irja whispered as the woman walked toward her.

"Took you long enough to get here," the goddess answered. "I was getting worried there was something wrong with your *själsfrände*. Like maybe he couldn't maintain an erection." She winked.

Irja didn't know what to say, so she just stood there silently. The whole situation was just too surreal.

The goddess's face turned solemn, and she laid her palm against Irja's cheek. "My daughter, we don't have much time."

"Loki is loose in Midgard, and it is my fault," Irja blurted out like a wayward little child.

"It is nobody's fault and least of all yours," Freya countered. "The trickster has planned this for centuries. Starting and fanning flames of political upheaval with a little whispered word here and there until the council was so divided, nobody would notice his little side project of manipulating a way to get to the mortal realm even though it is forbidden to him." She sighed. "I cannot give you direct aid, as we are not allowed to bring our conflicts to Midgard, but I can give you the tool you need to trap the malicious half god and send him back here."

"He's cursed my brother. Pekka is blind, and another Valkyrie lies in a coma because of Loki."

"Yes, I worry about my Kari." Freya lowered her hand. "But sending the traitor back to Asgard will hopefully break the curse." She reached into the pond, her hand disappearing completely into the dense, inky darkness. When she pulled it out, it was as dry as it had been before, but now she held a small scroll. "This is a *seidr* blood spell." Although Freya ruled with the Aesir deities on the Norse gods' council, she was originally from a different tribe of gods and goddesses, the Vanir, who had brought *seidr*—the Norse form of magic—to the gods. "Use this to trap Loki by the ash tree that stands for Yggdrasil, and the power of *seidr* will take care of the rest." She put the scroll in Irja's hand. "Go now, my daughter. I must return. Believe in yourself and your *själsfrände*."

"But how—" Irja started to say, but it was too late. Freya disappeared in the blink of an eye. Ripples appeared on the pond that soon turned into huge waves.

Irja turned to run from the water…darkness…whatever that pond was made out of, but one of the waves rose up and engulfed her. She blacked out and woke up in Scott's bed, her *själsfrände* watching her with worry in his eyes.

"At least your body stayed with me this time, even if your essence disappeared," he said. "Where did you go?"

Irja raised her left arm. The head and partial body tattoo of the Midgard serpent that had been on her bicep since she returned from Valhalla had now completed into a snake's body that spiraled around her arm and ended in the tail on the back of her hand. A series of runes made up the body of the serpent. Freya's blood spell.

She smiled at Scott. "I know how to defeat Loki."

He startled. "How?"

"A goddess told me." She jumped out of the bed and reached for her clothes. "Gather the others. We have a trickster god to trap."

Scott slowly rose from the bed. "I'd sort of hoped for some cuddling and maybe another round before we went into battle fighting gods and Loki's creatures again."

She turned and grabbed his arm where a serpent tattoo

spiraled around it, but instead of runes, his had an intricate pattern of stars and what looked like planets. "You're truly part of the tribe now." She pressed a kiss against his lips. "So you should know that we're pretty much always fighting something."

"So I've noticed," he said, reaching for his pants and his boots. "What do you need me to do?"

"Gather everyone in the meadow behind the fortress. I'll be there shortly."

He nodded. "I can do that. Where are you going?"

"To get some of Loki's blood."

Scott froze. "You're facing him alone?"

She smiled. "No, the idiot wiped off his cheek on the weird homespun shift he had me dressed in when I scratched him. That gown is still in my room."

CHAPTER 25

THE ASH TREE HAD GONE CRAZY. ITS LIMBS SHOOK AND leaves rustled as if the trunk had developed a seizure disorder. Scott had rounded up all the warriors, except Leif had refused to allow Astrid and Naya to participate. The men milled around, grumbling to each other. Each of them was armed to the hilt with swords and knives. Only Scott had opted for a gun. Supposedly, only Viking weapons were effective when battling gods. He was taking his chances with the gun. Even if it didn't work, holding it made him feel better.

Everyone was waiting for Irja.

"I still think we should get Astrid to join us," Ulf muttered.

"Shut up about that," Leif growled. "I've already bent the rules for her punishment. I can't go against my ruling just because we're under threat. We're always under some threat."

"The rules are stupid anyway," Luke said. The king sent him a warning glare, and the mortal man shrugged. "Well, they are," he said but in a much lower voice.

"She could fight in silence and then go back to her cell," Ulf tried again.

Harald walked up to the group and clasped a hand on Scott's shoulder as he turned to Ulf. "Have you ever heard that Valkyrie fight in silence?" he asked. "Her war cry is louder than all of ours together." There was pride in his voice. He faced Scott. "So I see you got a new tattoo. Does Irja have a matching one?" He winked.

Scott forced down the heat rising in his cheeks. "Hers is a little different," he mumbled.

"A third bonded couple in the tribe." Harald rubbed his hands together. "That must be a record." He raised his voice. "We should celebrate the *själsfrände* union between Scott and Irja as soon as we've slain the trickster god."

"Yes," Sten shouted.

"Celebrate," Per echoed, raising his sword in the air.

Leif paced the meadow. "Where is Irja?" He looked around as if she would appear suddenly because he willed it so.

Harald approached the king. "Your berserker is getting a little agitated, my friend." He clasped Leif's bicep. "Perhaps you should calm down."

"I'm calm enough." The king shrugged off the hand of his *stallare*. "Pekka," he shouted across the meadow. "Why in the Allfather's name are you here? Did you forget you're blind?"

"I can see just fine once I tap into the berserker web," Pekka shouted back defiantly. Some of the effect was ruined since he faced the wrong way and basically yelled the words at the forest.

"Then go guard my *själsfrände*," the king shouted back.

Pekka turned around so he now faced Leif. "I'm not needed there. Astrid is guarding the queen. She's sitting outside the door, silent and alone as ordered. Nothing will get past her."

"Thor's balls." Leif glared at Ulf and Luke.

"You didn't say she had to be in the cell during the day,"

Ulf defended himself. "Technically, I'm training her on how to guard a door."

The king just shook his head.

Irja walked down the path leading from the fortress, holding a vial and an intricate small statue that looked like the infinity symbol. She looked magnificent dressed in black pants tucked into motorcycle boots. A leather vest topped the Kevlar on her upper body. All the warriors wore protective gear. Apparently, some modern fight gear was considered appropriate during a battle with a god.

"What took you so long?" the king snarled.

The Valkyrie didn't seem to take offense at his tone. She held up the statue, her new tattoo glistening in the sun. "I had to extract the blood from the cloth of the shift, but what really delayed me was looking for this."

"What is it?" Scott asked, peering closer at the object, which he now saw was two intertwined snakes biting each other's tails and forming what looked like the shape of the number eight.

"It's the symbol most associated with Loki," Irja answered. She climbed up on the slab of basalt. As she'd requested, the thrones had been removed.

The ash tree behind the raised platform bowed its limbs toward Irja as if greeting her.

"Well, I always thought Loki was a snake," Harald said, his eyes on the statue Irja held. "What are you doing now?"

"Tracing the intertwined snakes pattern on top of the rock," she answered as she took out a pouch and poured a white, grainy substance out of it.

"With what?" Ulf asked.

"Ground-up eyes of newts." Irja smiled. "Just kidding. It's salt."

"How does this work?" Leif asked. "How do we get Loki to come here, and how do we trap him?"

Irja stopped in her tracks, her face more solemn. "I have no idea. I'm just following the instructions Freya tattooed into my serpent." She held out her arm.

Harald placed a hand on the king's back. "Let's position the warriors around the perimeter and let the *jänta* get on with her stuff," he said as he firmly led Leif away. As they passed Scott, he heard the red-haired Viking mumble under his breath. It sounded like "Can't wait to slay Loki and for the baby to arrive so this poor bastard can relax."

Irja stood and brushed off her hands. "Alright, I think I'm ready to try this." Her voice shook on the last few words, and Scott realized she was much more nervous than she let on.

He climbed up on the rock and took her hand. "I'll be right here."

She looked surprised, but then nodded. "Yes, this will work better. I need to use you as my conduit, so physical contact is good."

He leaned down and kissed her.

"Not that physical," she said, pushing him away, but there was a smile on her face.

Mission accomplished.

"Okay, Vikings," Harald shouted. "Are you ready for battle?"

"*Ja!*" came the resounding answer. Scott's berserker perked up and bellowed out a war cry. The warriors formed a circle around the large basalt slab, standing equidistant from each other with their backs to Irja and swords out of their scabbards. Scott had trained with the Vikings using the big blades often enough to where the weapon now felt comfortable in his grip.

"We do this for our tribe," Ulf shouted.

"For our tribe," echoed the men.

"For Odin and for Freya," Harald bellowed.

"For Odin and for Freya," the others repeated.

Irja positioned herself and Scott so each stood in one of the loops of the figure eight, their hands clasped above the crossing lines. She closed her eyes and took a deep breath through her nose before exhaling through her mouth.

Following Irja's example, Scott closed his eyes and copied her breathing. Immediately, his awareness was back in the web that was like walking through the glowing lines of the northern lights.

The symbol Irja had traced glowed bright orange, and a circle of bright white points of light surrounded them, each of the warriors standing guard. The lines of power that had previously come from the sides of the web now shot straight up through the figure eight. Irja was pulling them from the big slab of basalt.

She reached down and picked something up with her free hand. It was the vial of Loki's blood she'd prepared. Reaching across to the far point of the loop in which she was standing, she spilled a few drops of blood. She then crossed her arm in front of Scott to do the same on the mirrored spot of his loop. Two more points in each loop were splattered before she poured a more generous portion on the point where the two lines intersected under their clasped hands.

The vial still had a few drops inside, and the berserker web version of Irja shot him a look with glowing eyes before she lifted the small flask to her mouth and drank down the remaining bit. Scott's stomach heaved, and then a rush of power ran through him to Irja.

The blue and green pillars of light swayed from side to side and spiraled around each other in strange mesmerizing patterns. Scott almost lost himself in their dance until Irja gave a little tug on his hand, interrupting the trance.

The orange lines of the figure eight started to glow and rise, and two loop-shaped walls formed and grew taller.

Irja pulled on Scott's hand until they both stood inside one of the loops. The orange light rose like a wall that soon reached above their heads.

Irja tightened the grip on his hand, and her berserker growled a warning.

Instantly, Scott's beast was equally aware.

"Oh, you clever, clever girl," the mocking voice Scott now recognized as Loki's whispered through the web. "You went for help, didn't you?" The outline of the half god showed up inside the other glowing loop. He touched one of the orange walls but pulled back his hand quickly. "Well, I too have some tricks to share." Loki traced a shape in the air with his hand and shouted a word that wasn't in English.

The guardian warriors immediately positioned themselves in battle stance, gripping their broadswords with two hands.

Scott opened his eyes to see what the threat was and wished he hadn't. Hordes of wolverines were running through the meadow toward the raised basalt platform.

"None of these creatures gets through the perimeter," Leif shouted. "Slay all of them. Give Irja enough time to finish trapping that bastard trickster."

Scott took a step toward the edge of the rock to join the warriors, but Irja tugged him back. Her eyes were still closed, and she started tracing strange symbols in the air, using both her free hand and the one holding onto his.

He turned to see if Loki was trapped in the salt version of the figure eight, but the other loop was empty. Closing his eyes, he joined Irja in the glowing web again. The trickster god was definitely present here, and he traced symbols faster than Irja could keep up. Their joined hands seemed to impair her, so Scott moved to stand behind his *själsfrände*, released her hand, and instead wrapped his arms around her waist to keep their physical contact.

Irja nodded, shifted her body slightly, and increased the speed of her symbol tracing.

The wolverines were now noticeable in the glowing berserker web. There were so many Scott couldn't count them. As soon as a Viking struck one down, another took the slain creature's place.

The blue and green lights shooting up from the basalt were still swaying and twirling, but they were slowly changing color into the sickly neon versions, and a few of the lines now connected directly with wolverines, feeding them power.

Scott kept one arm around Irja while he slashed at one of the neon ribbons with his sword.

A twang and a sharp pain that almost made him drop his sword dissuaded him from repeating the action.

Irja's motions slowed as if she were tracing her symbols in molasses while Loki's hands sped up to lightning speed. The crazy half god grinned like a lunatic when the glowing orange walls started lowering. Scott had no idea what to do, so he held on tighter to Irja and whispered encouraging words in her ear.

He told her how much she meant to him. How he looked forward to spending his life with her. That he hoped she would have a baby like Naya, but if not, he couldn't wait for the two of them to spend time with their niece or nephew.

Irja's tracing sped up, but it still was no match for Loki's.

Scott buried his face in Irja's hair. He touched his lips to her neck and reached out with his awareness, willing more lines of power to feed into her and lend her strength.

Before them, an immense shape appeared. He couldn't make out what it was at first but then realized it was an outline of the ash tree. In the berserker web, its limbs appeared silver while each of the leaves twinkled in hues that went from dark copper to the brightest yellow gold.

Loki swore as the walls of the looping figure eight started rising again.

Elated, Scott kept one arm around Irja as he reached through the orange wall and grasped one of the tree's branches.

A surge of energy sizzled through him, burning his nerves.

Flashes of light sparked on the inside of his eyelids, but he held on, funneling the power to Irja.

The tree swayed, and Scott moved with it, anchoring himself with the arm he kept around his *själsfrände*'s waist. The pain along his nerve endings intensified as more and more energy rushed through him, but he held on, both to the holy tree and the magnificent woman.

The sound of the ash's leaves rustling turned into metallic clinks as they brushed up against each other, and then they started falling from the tree. The leaves didn't just look metallic; they were as hard and as sharp as well, cascading to the ground in a beautiful but deadly curtain.

The skin of the arm holding onto the tree was soon shredded. His blood dripped onto the ground, but he didn't care as long as his beloved was safe from the onslaught of metallic leaves. One of them pierced his shoulder, and he cried out in pain, momentarily distracting Irja. When another one stabbed his bicep, he gritted his teeth and kept quiet.

Soon, all the leaves were gone, and only bare silver limbs remained. The tree bowed and touched a limb to the glowing figure eight, and it instantly caught on fire. The flames climbed up the tree, but no heat radiated from the inferno. The branches burned in colors of intense blue and white.

The tree still swayed back and forth. One of the enflamed limbs touched Loki, and he screamed out in pain. A bright white flash shot up from the half god and incinerated him on the spot.

Irja cried out and collapsed in Scott's arms. He sank to the ground while sheltering her in his embrace.

Norse warriors wandered around the meadow. He quickly counted, and it looked like everyone was still standing, even if some of the Vikings had serious wounds and several cradled an arm or a hand against their bodies.

Leif and Harald approached the slab of basalt and climbed up. "You both okay?" the king asked.

Irja looked up at him. "Yes. Loki has been banished from Midgard and is back in the gods' realm."

"Good." Sweat and soot covered Leif's face. "I don't know what you did, but all of a sudden every wolverine, dead and alive, burst into flames and burned to a little pile of ash." He motioned around the meadow.

"Spontaneous combustion," Harald said. "Unfortunately, it happened to the tree as well."

All four of them turned toward where the mighty ash had stood. In its place was only a charred stump.

"A worthy sacrifice if it sent Loki back to Asgard," the king said. He limped over the edge of the rock and hopped down. "I'm going to check on my *själsfrände* and tell Astrid to get back into her cell." He looked over at Scott and Irja. "We'll put on a feast to celebrate your union after we've all caught some sleep." He rubbed his face, making it even grimier. "It may take a day or two before I wake up."

Pekka jumped up on the raised rock platform. "Hey, *Sisko*. I can see your pretty face again." He smiled broadly, his dark eyes twinkling.

Irja started to cry, and Scott cuddled her close. She reached out a hand and grabbed onto her brother's arm.

Naya came running down the path from the fortress. "Kari is awake and totally fine," she yelled, and at her words, Pekka took off running. He barely avoided colliding with Leif, who was rushing toward Naya.

"I told you to stop running," the king bellowed at his wife.

"I want to know what happened out here," she answered.

Scott looked down at the woman in his arms. "Are you okay?"

She snuggled closer. "I am now." She closed her eyes and promptly fell asleep.

Naya looked at the sleeping Valkyrie, a baffled look on her face. She turned to Scott. "Oh, you so owe me a story about all this."

"Patience, Sister. You have to learn patience now that you're almost a parent." He smiled at her and secured his grip around his *själsfrände* as he stood up. "I'll tell you everything later. Right now, I'm taking a really long nap." He stepped down from the rock and onto the path that took him back to the fortress, the place he'd started to think of as home.

But it didn't matter where he lived. As long as the woman he carried in his arms was with him, it would always be where he belonged.

She was his true home.

EPILOGUE

Six months later

IRJA FELT ONLY A LITTLE GUILTY FOR RUNNING OUT ON Naya, whose disposition deteriorated as her circumference increased. It was understandable though; the queen was uncomfortable and therefore irritable. Usually, one of the warriors tried to distract her, mostly herself or Astrid, but today Scott had asked Irja to meet him out in the meadow, so she'd skipped out on her being-a-supportive-friend duty.

Her *själsfrände* paced back and forth in front of the charred remains of the old ash tree that had once majestically spread its branches toward the sky. He looked like he was talking to himself. Whatever monologue he was performing distracted him enough to where he didn't notice her arrival. He startled when he looked up and found her watching him.

"What are you doing?" She tried not to laugh, unsuccessfully.

He cleared his throat and rubbed the back of his neck. "I wanted to show you something. Come here."

She stepped forward to look at where he was pointing. In the middle of the blackened stump, a small green ash sapling had pushed itself through the charred wood. Her breath caught in her throat. "It's coming back," she whispered.

Scott smiled at her. "Either that or a new tree will grow in its place."

She touched the tiny green leaves. "This is wonderful. Who else knows?"

He shrugged. "I discovered it yesterday but don't know if anyone else has seen it."

"Thank you for showing me." A new ash tree would be wonderful. She missed seeing the majestic branches and hearing the rustling of leaves. She turned to look up at Scott and was for a moment confused when she had to bend her head to see him. He'd gone down on one knee.

"Irja." He grabbed her hand and cleared his throat again. "You know you are the love of my life and that our *själsfrände* bond is the best thing that's ever happened to me."

"It's the best thing that's ever happened to me too." The last word came out as a whisper, because her breath caught as it dawned on her what the bent knee meant.

"I would, however, like to make our union more official, and so I ask if you would do me the honor of becoming my wife." He fumbled with something in his pocket and finally pulled out a rectangular box. "I've never seen you wear a ring, so I got you this instead." He mumbled something under his breath several times before handing the box to her. "*Minä rakastan sinua.* Did I say that right?"

Her eyes teared up when she realized that what he must have been practicing over and over was how to say "I love you" in Finnish. His pronunciation could use some work, but she still understood the words. "You said it perfectly. I love you too."

"And what's your answer?" His midnight-blue eyes searched her face. A small drop of sweat ran down his temple.

"I guess that depends on what's in this box," she teased.

She opened the lid and gasped. Inside were two matching leather wristbands, each decorated with narrow silver chains created from tiny loops stacked vertically and then braided in intricate patterns. "You found authentic Sami bracelets," she breathed out. Her hand hovered over the box as she contemplated touching the delicate and beautiful jewelry. "These are the most beautiful pieces I've ever seen."

"Does that mean the answer is—"

"Yes," she interrupted. "The answer is yes."

"Odin's balls, woman," Scott said, sweeping her up in an embrace and twirling her around. "You sure know how to make a man sweat."

She laughed out loud, and as the sound carried across the meadow, she realized she'd laughed more since she met Scott than she'd ever done before in her entire long life.

This man of hers, the queen's brother, the valiant warrior, her lover and her best friend had taught her to feel joy, and she would love him forever for it.

ACKNOWLEDGMENTS

There has been a long gap between the previous Viking Warriors book and this one. It turns out that grief is accumulative and that when you lose both your parents and your father-in-law in less than two years, your creative well can run dry.

I am so grateful for all the people who supported me and reached out during this difficult time, especially my editor, Cat Clyne, who was patience personified as I missed deadline after deadline. Thank you also to so many writing friends who helped me plot and strategize when I was finally able to return to the book: the To Marry a Tiger and the Arctic Thunder sisterhoods, the people at the Smoky and Drake retreats, and as always the amazing Dreamweavers— the 2014 Golden Heart Finalists class.

In addition to my editor, there is a whole team at Sourcebooks that makes the book magic happen and helps me shine. Associate Production Editor Jessica Smith, Copy Editor Sabrina Baskey, Art Director Dawn Adams, and Marketing Specialist Stefani Sloma are fantastic to work with and I am lucky to have them in my corner.

This year I celebrated a twenty-year wedding anniversary with the guy who gave me my real-life HEA. He's my biggest supporter and my most constructive critic, depending on what I need at the time. I couldn't have survived these last two years without him by my side.

Also a big thank you to my Swedish and UK families.

Your love, encouragement, and support always mean the world to me.

And finally, the biggest THANK YOU to my readers. Without you, there would be no Viking Warriors books at all, and you have been very patient waiting for this book. I hope you loved reading it as much as I loved writing it.

ABOUT THE AUTHOR

Asa Maria Bradley grew up in Sweden surrounded by archaeology and history steeped in Norse mythology, which inspired her sexy modern-day Viking Warriors paranormal romance series. She also writes urban fantasy featuring empowered heroines who kick ass while saving the world.

Asa arrived in the United States as a high school exchange student and quickly became addicted to ranch dressing and crime TV shows. *Booklist* attributes her writing with "nonstop action, satisfying romantic encounters, and intriguing world building." Her work has also received the honor of a double nomination for the Romance Writers of America's RITA contest, as well as Holt Medallion and Booksellers' Best Award wins.

She currently lives in the Pacific Northwest with a British husband and a rescue dog of indeterminate breed. When she's not writing or trying to train the dog to obey her commands, she spends way too much time on the internet. You can find links to all her social media and connect with her at AsaMariaBradley.com. While there, sign up for her newsletter to receive exclusive content, news about her books, and qualify for unique giveaways.